MISTY GREY

By LEW ANDERSON

THE LORIAN STONES TRILOGY

Book One: *Tombs of Dross*

Book Two: *Battles Grim*

Book Three: *Pillars and Power*

———————

THE LORIAN CHRONICLES

Horse Boy

———————

Misty Grey

Yodin the Rescuer

The Fire Between Us

LEW ANDERSON

MISTY GREY

TREESTONE BOOKS

TreeStone Books
Northfield, MN

Book cover design by ebooklaunch.com

ISBN 978-1-955486-04-0

Printed in the United States of America

*To master memory,
one must not only learn how to remember
but most importantly,
how to forget.*

PREFACE

Hyperthymesia – the uncommon ability that allows a person to spontaneously recall with great accuracy and detail a vast number of personal events or experiences and their associated dates. —Merriam-Webster

Eidetic – marked by or involving extraordinarily accurate and vivid recall especially of visual images. —Merriam-Webster
– a person able to form or recall eidetic images.

PROLOGUE

"Take the number two bus," a large man said in a frog-like voice, his face concealed by a dark silk scarf. His breath misted in the cold, lingering about his head as if to hide it even more. "Get off at Dale. Walk that block to Weston. He waits there."

A woman of unusual beauty drew her young child close. "The ransom?" she asked, her voice trembling.

The man nodded. "To the ounce." He glanced down at the child clinging to the woman's woolen coat. His gaze met keen eyes that held an eager, inquiring stare. "Exceptional," he said, studying the shivering child. "Exceptional indeed." Then he turned and was gone.

1 LESSONS LEARNED

Did I kill him? Chest heaving, she held her arm back, still poised to strike again. Glancing to the farmhouse, she listened. From the basement window, faint shouts mixed with torturous cries. Her eyes narrowed, now on the lifeless man sprawled over the hood, a pistol glinting beneath his suit coat.

Panting two breaths, she then lowered her arm. Another breath. More cries from the basement. She winced. *Oh, Ganny!* Grabbing the gun, she scrambled into the car.

Fumbling, trembling, she turned the key. Her eyes darted upward, expecting bullets to once more shatter the glass, to scream through like demons of terror.

Slower this time!

But her foot stomped, revving the engine into full roar. And like before, gravel sprayed, the rear fish-tailing as she spun out. Swerving wildly, she cranked the wheel, eyes on the long driveway.

Oh, God! she gasped, the man now sliding off, tumbling over the gravel. But her face tightened, the image of him beating...

Focus!

She clutched the wheel, trying to stop the stupid trembling. This car handled better than the Cadillac, faster with more control. She checked the mirror, surprised to see the driveway empty.

"Oh, Ganny…" she cried, blinking back tears.

Breathing crazy hard, she squealed onto the main road. Tires bounced and caught the tar, lurching her forward. "Better," she breathed out, pleased to have made it first try. "Now keep it under…" She glanced at the dash, searching for the right dial. She winced, hissing through clenched teeth. Three knuckles bled as she clutched the wheel, hot, sharp pain screaming from everywhere.

One week earlier – Wednesday, Oct 21.

"Misty, are you with us?" Mr. Zephyr paused with chalk in hand, his fingers ghostly white from writing geometry formulas.

The teen girl looked up, her kinky hair bobbing. A rusty auburn that never behaved, it bushed out more than usual today. She blinked wide at the blackboard littered with dusty scribblings. Mr. Zephyr gave a curt nod, returning to his beloved scratchings. The lines were sharp, the soulless letters dutifully bearing whatever value he consigned to them.

"Memorize these," he said to the class of glassy-eyed students. "They'll be on the test."

Misty glanced at the board. *Memorize…* Her soft lips mouthed the word. *'To commit to memory, to learn by heart.'* She breathed a subdued sigh, her green eyes drifting back into distant thought. *If only…*

From the back of the classroom, James Longmire watched, his heart burdened. Misty had seemed a bit off today, more off than usual. He'd missed her at lunch, but walking into class he'd asked if things were okay, having noticed her sallow mood.

"I'm fine, James," she had whispered. "See you after class."

James continued to watch, his mind searching. He knew Misty better than anyone.

Over the past nine years, her family, which now consisted of Misty, her mom, and little brother Max, had rented the small, secondary house on his family's hobby farm. Until a few years ago, her father had lived there as well, before his rage finally took him to prison, which brought no little celebration in the Longmire home, though done discreetly, mind you.

On more than one occasion after calling the police, the resulting rebuttal upon both families had left painful scars, literally.

To plot someone's murder had never before entered the robust thought patterns of James Longmire, but in the months preceding the final arrest of Misty's father, James had perfected several genius schemes, and although pricked with shame, of some he was rather proud.

He watched her head sag, her shoulders slumping. *What now?* he wondered. *What's she dwelling on?* He too let go a subtle sigh, his gaze darting to a nerdish boy to his right. The dark blue eyes of James weren't the only ones watching.

Though quiet and reserved, Misty Grey had a strange following. Neither fashionable nor ordinary, she wore a rather unique, trendsetting style… well, maybe in some distant future. She wore no makeup, nor did she need to, having a natural beauty in both form and complexion. Long lashes graced her green eyes, a light green that sometimes looked translucent. Faint freckles dusted her fine cheeks and nose. But it was her lips that always held the final gaze.

Boy or girl, man or woman—their eyes would always come to rest on the full-formed lips, the kind that Hollywood celebrities strive for and boys talk of in smirking tones.

Though pursued by numerous boys, she shunned them all except for James, the only one with whom she could discuss things without feeling she were some weirdo at a freak show. For he knew her like no one else, he knew her secret… like no one else.

"Did you do the assignment, Miss Grey?" asked Mr. Zephyr. "If so, you should have memorized this formula."

Both James and Misty blinked themselves back into the classroom.

Memorize, James thought, glancing from Misty to the blackboard. *If only you knew, Mr. Zephyr, if only you knew…*

It wasn't that Misty couldn't remember things, in fact, that was the problem—remembering things, not the memorizing.

James held his breath, waiting for Misty to answer. He wondered if she had done the assignment. *Memorize,* he mouthed again, his thoughts on Misty.

No, she couldn't memorize… because she couldn't forget. She remembered everything. We're talking… everything!

Ask her what she had for dinner eight years ago on the ninth of July, and she could tell you everything, not that she would, mind you, but she could. She could tell you how it tasted, how it looked, who was there, what needed salt and why dessert tasted different because mom had substituted powdered milk since the regular milk had been thrown out by her father in a rage over their mother spending too much on groceries.

She could tell you the weather report of any given day, of what song was sung by contestant number twelve during the fifth round of whatever popular talent show. She could give you the news report, word by word from any date and time, provided she watched it, of course, which why on earth would she ever do that? She can remember every line written in the sappy love note shoved in her locker by Bucky Farrella, every word spoken to her, against her, behind her back, every slap from her father, his abusive words to her mother and little brother…

No, it wasn't memorizing. Her deepest longing… was to simply forget.

Misty blinked her eyes wide, offering Mr. Zephyr a courteous smile. Being an A-student was not a problem for Misty. Being stuck in public school with no one but James to confide in, was.

"Please give the formula for solving example C," Mr. Zephyr continued, "and if you can, its corresponding answer."

In a monotone voice, void of life and liberty, Misty mumbled out the formula, intentionally pausing to mimic difficulty, although she could have given him every stinking formula, or if he wanted, every single word from every single page of their dreadfully boring geometry textbook.

"That is correct, Miss Grey. And the answer?"

At age seven, while in second grade with Ms. Daneen, she had let her gift show, reciting the Declaration of Independence after reading through it just once. It was to be a class project with each student learning a few lines followed by a group presentation in three weeks.

When Marie Elsa, Misty's real name, stood up at the mention of reciting the Declaration, and taking a deep breath, spewed out the words as fast as she could mutter them, Ms. Daneen did not respond quite as Misty had expected.

Instead of receiving praise for such a feat, Misty was met with a stern rebuke for 'showing off' and 'making pretentious display.'

"Think of your classmates," she said, "all struggling while someone like you recites the entire Declaration." Ms. Daneen paused, looking rather perplexed at little Misty, the girl's kinky hair sprawling out like fluffy red springs, antennae yearning to explore the world beyond.

"How have you come to memorize it?" she asked, as Misty looked longingly at the other children now playing gleefully outside. "Did your father help you? Your mother?"

Misty just continued her longing stare at the jubilant classmates.

"Misty, look at me. Your father, the policeman, he helped you, didn't he? How long did it take?"

Misty looked up into the elderly woman's eyes. "My father?" She looked back outside. "I just… read it."

"No, when did you memorize it?"

Her large eyes now back on Ms. Daneen, little Marie Elsa wondered what she had done wrong. Why was she here instead of out there? "Sorry," she meekly whispered. "Did I...?" What had she done wrong? "Won't do it again, ever. Promise." With tears dripping to her little desk, she asked to go play.

Ms. Daneen sent her out, and taking up pen and paper, wrote a simple note to Mr. Grey, the ramification, which, although swift and painful, left little Misty quite determined to never ever recite, quote, recall, describe, or appear to 'memorize' anything ever again, ever, period!

Except with James.

She knew the answer only because she had seen this example in the textbook. To actually solve it did require some brainpower, which is why she enjoyed James so much.

He was a genius—pure, raw, humble, honest-to-God genius. If anyone on earth could be called such, it was James Longmire. He could solve any mathematical, scientific, IQ test question, philosophical problem, (well maybe not philosophical,) but he sure sounded like he could. Seriously, James was a mathematical mystery. As Misty was with memory, James was with calculating.

Misty shook her head. "Sorry, Mr. Zephyr, but doesn't James have his hand up?"

She flashed a smirking glance to her only friend.

He, like Misty, had learned to keep things quiet, to hide his abilities. Less trouble that way. Brutes don't like to be reminded of their stupidity, especially by guys like James—the good-looking athletic guy whose name comes up every time their girlfriends ask why they aren't 'more like James.'

"Y is eighty-eight degrees, Mr. Zephyr." James dared not smile back at Misty, for that too could result in tiresome confrontation. More than several boys felt Misty was their 'girlfriend,' claimed by some self-initiated rite which had no explanation, but regardless the reasoning, she was their girl, and guys like James better stay clear.

It was never anything serious, just extremely bothersome—test tubes of sulfur and wax left in his locker, turning the whole hall into a rotten egg factory; waxed floor beneath his locker; superglue in the dial of his lock——the kind of annoying stuff that only nerds can generate.

No, it was best to keep their private lives private, as much as that's possible in a small public school with a graduating class of ninety-two.

2 A MOMENT WORTH REMEMBERING

"See you in a bit," James said, offering his artificial goodbye. They would meet up several blocks away, away from peering eyes.

The walk home took forty minutes. The school bus took over an hour, though the ride into school took only ten minutes. But he'd vowed to never let her take the bus home, for unlike the ride in, the afterschool bus was what he described as 'a virtual world of chaotic stupidity personified in human forms being crammed into a yellow prison cell on wheels, pulsing with a voluminous cacophony of cursing, soul-vexing taunts, and crude humor—if the vulgar attempts can be categorized as such.'

No, they had tried it more than once, bouncing along together, distasteful moments both he and Misty truly wished they could forget.

Instead, he'd wait for her to cross the busy intersection, to then follow along a different route until they met up again at Minnick's little store.

Childish, but it helped keep guys like Stanton T. Froulinger off his back—one of the nerds who claimed Misty and was willing to defend his 'right' at any cost.

"Walk with me, James," Misty said, her tone very solemn, eyes looking up like a lost puppy. She then smiled, lowering her voice to sound like a man. "Home, James."

Surprised, James glanced about, seeing not only Stanton T., but also Dreldon Glemor and Buckham Farrella, or Bucky, all drooling over Misty Grey, the girl of their fantastical dreams.

Like wolves, they watched from a distance, too shy to move in close, too smart to know what would happen if they did.

It wasn't James they feared. The three had joined forces once, trying to coax him into a fight. Although stronger and gifted with his hands and limbs, he calmly shook his head, even after Bucky threw a punch, which James simply avoided, Bucky's fist grazing his nose. He didn't push them, threaten them, warn them, or promise any retaliation.

"She's all yours," he had said. "Best of luck, and may the better man win."

No, they didn't fear him—they feared Misty. When Bucky had gotten way too friendly, he learned what 'I said no!' really means coming from a girl who knows how to throw a punch. It took two weeks for his black eye to fade.

Poor Stanton T. almost lost his eager fingers in a paper cutter, and Dreldon just doesn't talk about it to anyone, ever.

For although Misty was slender, she was tough and athletic, rather aggressive and gifted in sports, seasonally sought after by the high school coaches who heard the same response each year. 'You still practice every day?' she'd ask. When they answered the affirmative, Misty would shake her head.

"Why in God's good earth would I want to do that?" she had said to James after one such encounter.

No, the love-sick boys didn't fear James, they feared the girl of their dreams, loving from a distance, claiming and admiring, bragging and dreaming, threatening anyone who approached *their* girl.

"Please," Misty said, seeing the two nerds and Bucky watching like they did every school day at this time. "They'll be fine."

They crossed the street, leaving McKinley High to once again await their dutiful return. Misty sighed.

"Am I really a freak?" she said, her voice wavering. "An *eidetic*?" She spoke the term as if it were some racial slur.

James sighed. The 'freak' declaration had been often spoken

by her dad, and it seemed to bring more pain than any other ill-intended label. Whenever used by someone else, it brought great consternation, which usually slid down into depression of gloomy proportions. Had it not been for James and a little old lady, Mrs. Quinn, Misty would have been in a coffin long ago, assuming they would have found her body.

James weighed his words carefully. The frailty in her voice alarmed him. She was hurting. Fierce anger rose, and so, casting off caution, he said what simply had been on his mind for months.

"You mean 'freak' as in being the most attractive girl in high school, granted your clothes are a bit... unique, which I personally like... and who cultivates zero friendships, except with me, which I also like, very much... who gets straight A's without trying, has more hidden talent than a hundred girls, could excel in any sport, knows more on any given subject than ninety-nine percent of the world's population?" James paused to take a breath. "They're idiots, Misty." He glanced back toward the school. "Stop listening to them."

In silence, Misty shuffled on, head down.

"Who called you a freak?" James asked. "Carla? Hansen? Jaci Jigglebooty? That twerd said something, didn't she?"

Misty huffed a single chuckle. "No, James, it wasn't Jaci. And you shouldn't call her that."

"Well, it does jiggle."

Turning, Misty gave him a quick slap. "Don't *you* be joining the googly-eyed rabble."

The cheeks of James Longmire flushed. He tried to hide it, making it worse. But her gaze had already returned to the pavement. He longed to take her hand but instead spoke softly.

"Something today, or...?"

To Misty, there was no past. She could recall everything as if it were happening in real-time. It didn't matter if someone called her a freak today or ten years ago, it was always fresh. And not just the memory—all the feelings, the smells and sounds, joys and pains, the tastes and tears, all of it as real as the moment it occurred.

"You're not a freak," James said again as they turned to walk Hullett Avenue, a long road that led over the river and ultimately to their adjoining houses. "You are the ideal. The rest of us are defective."

"You're not defective," Misty countered, "you're a genius."

"And so are you," James said adamantly. He had tried this argument before, but to Misty, ingrained with nothing but negative input since childhood, especially concerning her gift, could not believe that smart for her was even remotely possible, let alone, genius.

Misty shook her head. "I'm an idiot who can't even memorize."

James stopped to face her, gently holding her by the shoulders. "I've told you this before, which, of course, you well remember, but I'm going to say it again."

He suddenly found himself just staring into her eyes. She had always been his little sister, his neighbor, the people who rented the house on the farm, whose father was a miserable excuse for paternity.

He slid his hands down her arms to clasp her hands. Never had he touched her this way. Even for him, it was perilous territory.

Misty studied his eyes, her brow tightening.

They stood near an old willow that grew out over the river. Many times they had sat fishing beneath its hanging branches, catching rock bass and sunnies, using nothing but Cheetos for bait. They would bring the fish home, and to the consternation of James' father, throw them in the cow-watering tank.

He led her beneath the sweeping branches to stand beside the tree's large trunk. For a long moment he stood holding her hands, his gaze moving from her eyes down to her intriguing lips. He thought to ask her, to ask permission to kiss her just once, for that was who James was—a nice guy, polite and courteous—and that was why Misty liked him so, letting him in to her secret.

And in that long moment, as they stood together under the old willow, its finger-like leaves falling quietly around them, James whispered in a way he'd never done before.

"I'm sorry," he said, his brow furrowed, "but you're not a freak, Misty. You're…" He swallowed, his cheeks warming. "You are the most…" He swallowed again. "I wish I…" He paused, then releasing her hands, he drew back. "I wish you'd let me beat the slop out of anyone who calls you that again, okay?"

For a moment, Misty only stared up at him, her eyes searching. He had never acted this way, but never had she needed it like she did today. It was something she deeply cherished with James—he seemed to always know what she needed. But this…

Her plush lips lifted in a sweet smile. "No you won't," she said, still looking into the eyes of her lifelong friend. "You won't unless you have to. That's what I like about you, Mr. James."

As they turned to continue home, they walked in silence. But Misty's chest tingled. That had been a special moment, very special, unlike any ever. She glanced down at her hands. *So warm.*

She let it all replay, every word, every sound, every feeling, his hands holding hers, his gaze so intense. For maybe the first time, she felt a sense of joy at having her 'freakish' memory. She smiled, letting go a long sigh.

The hands of James Longmire had a slight tremor as the two teens finished their walk home. What had he been thinking, been *feeling?*

Was I really going to kiss her? He recalled something he'd said recently when asked if he had a thing for Misty Grey. 'Would die for her, if that counts,' he'd answered nonchalantly.

They walked up the long driveway, the autumn air crisping as the sun settled behind the western trees.

"Will you be okay?" he asked, walking her to her door, which was only a few dozen yards from his.

She nodded, dropping her gaze. After a furtive glance up, she wet her lips. "Thank you, James." Her long lashes blinked with hints of moisture. "Thank you for… being you."

From the dining room window at the Longmire home, tight eyes watched as floured hands brushed a lacy apron. "Oh, Lord," came a prayerful whisper, head wagging. "No, James… absolutely no!"

3   THE PI CONTEST

Thursday, October 22

"What do you think?" James asked Misty outside of physics class. "Did you sign up?"

Misty sighed. "I don't know, James. What if…" She sighed again.

"Misty, you could win this. It's two thousand twinkies. But," he hesitated, "it's tomorrow, you know. That's not much time. Have you been, well, is that enough…?" He paused again, searching for the right words. "You'd have to sign up today."

Misty nodded. "Yeah, I know." She looked to the floor. "Mom could really use the money."

James watched her closely. "Job offers too. They're looking for people to work with the memory institute, promote math and memory. The sheet is still on Bane's door."

Mrs. Barns, AKA Captain Bane, was an elderly math teacher who had a hook nose and rather manly face that could pass for a pirate. Posted on her door was the invitation to compete in a national contest for memorizing the randomly infinite numbers of pi.

"But James, it's just numbers. I mean, pi? How boring!"

A tight group of three glamourized girls passed by.

"Surprised you know what that is," spouted Nikki Laurens, head cheerleader who neither brought cheer nor led anyone. She pushed her way between Misty and James, giving him a flirtatious smile. "So, are you coming?" she asked him, sliding a glossy pink fingernail up his sternum to then flick his chin.

He just held her gaze without reply, for this was at least the tenth invite to her Halloween party next Saturday night.

As Nikki moved on, throwing a teasing glance back at James, Misty shook her head, softly muttering, "The numerical value of the ratio of the circumference of a circle to its diameter, approximately 3.141549." She stared off after Nikki. "From the Greek word *periphereia,* which means, circumference."

As if nothing had happened, James asked gently, "So what do you think?" Her family desperately needed the money, but he dared not push that issue too hard. Misty bore the shame of her family's struggles rather deeply, taking on all its degrading connotations. It was a constant battle helping her to separate self-worth from her family's desperation.

He watched her consider the proposal, also concerned of her fear of being in the spotlight, of being exposed, of being labeled a freak.

"You could make it look hard, struggle a bit, a bunch."

Misty knew how to do that all too well. "What's the record?" she asked.

James wondered as her wheels turned. It would already be a lot of unwanted publicity winning a nationwide contest, let alone beat the world record.

"Could you… beat the record?" he asked, wondering out loud. "I mean, it's tomorrow."

"What is it?"

"Over sixty thousand, I think, but that's insane."

"Yuck," Misty said with a sour frown.

"You'd only need to memorize, well, fifteen hundred maybe. Could you do that?" As soon the words left his mouth, he winced.

Misty glared.

"Just think of the money," James said," of your mom." But he too wondered if this were all a very bad idea.

"I don't know, James. What if I mess up or make a fool of

myself?"

"You won't." He swallowed hard. "You can do this. How can I help?"

She straightened, her gaze intense. "It's tomorrow at three?"

James nodded. "If you… I mean… you sure it's enough time though? I don't want you to…"

She sighed heavily, flashing a very cold stare. "Just get me a page or two, doubled-spaced, twelve-point. Bring them to the contest." Then her face lightened. "Please."

Friday, October 23

Misty was third in line, a total of fourteen contestants all vying for a chance to win two thousand dollars. James had given her two full sheets of nothing but numbers.

"Over fifteen hundred per page," he said, wincing a bit. Misty went off to one side and looked the pages over, returning to James in less than five minutes.

"You're not going to do it?" he asked, a bit disappointed.

"Oh, James. How long must I put up with you? Where's the line for slaughter?"

James led her to the backstage waiting area where kids of all ages poured over sheets of numbers, lips moving in nervous, silent recital, all in hopes of getting their name in lights, their hands on the two thousand 'twinkies,' as James called them.

"Just take your time. I'll be in back," James assured her. "Up there in the balcony, okay?"

"If this goes sour…" Her warning glare showed fear, like a little lost girl in a crowd of strangers.

Seeing her fear, James tensed. Her family needed the money, but Misty didn't need this. She had enough junk in her life.

"Maybe…" James looked straight into her eyes. "Maybe this isn't—"

"Line up, my little contestants!" A commanding female voice

ruffled the backstage. "Put all papers and notes aside. Molly Baker, you're first, and then Chancellor darling, you are next, followed by Marie Grey, and then…"

To Misty, the woman's voice drifted into silence as James waved a feeble goodbye, his eyes betraying the worry now pricking his heart.

As he left the backstage to climb the balcony stairs, he scolded himself sharply. "You idiot," he muttered, "what were you thinking?"

Molly Baker got forty-seven numbers correct before falling to pieces. Three judges sat side-by-side verifying the numbers as well as audio recording the contestants for accuracy. When a mistake was verified by all three, the student was given their total and the next victim called in. James felt bad for the girl, knowing she'd probably memorized several hundred.

Chancellor Bickling III, reached seventy-two before faulting. He swore he could have gone much further if given a second chance. Because he literally swore, he was asked to leave with rather stern words.

Misty was the oldest contestant so far, making her feel all the more awkward. For a moment, she stood behind the mic, looking out over the crowd until she found James standing high up in the balcony. She decided to keep her eyes on him the whole time, and soon, the numbers were flowing from her enchanting lips.

At first, she took her time, trying to sound like the previous students, faltering here and there. But then a panic rose. What if she did all this and still lost to some genius in California or New York?

Mom needs that money.

Like rain, the numbers flowed, dozens of them, hundreds of them, dozens of hundreds of endless numbers.

The judges scanned their sheets, soon fumbling and falling

far behind. The audience at first sat stunned with awe and admiration. But then some began to giggle and laugh, believing the odd-dressed girl to be rattling off numbers in jest.

Soon the whole assembly joined in the laughter as Misty, eyes locked on James, spewed out numbers faster and faster.

After what seemed to be far too long, James ran his finger back and forth over his throat, to which Misty nodded, stopping abruptly as if her power plug just got pulled.

Without even glancing toward the judges, she simply turned and walked off stage. The audience applauded, not because of her feat of memory, but for their love of the comedy.

Misty hastened off the backstage with tears welling. Her lips now muttered nasty things about freak shows and James putting her up to something so stupid, the bitter words forced out through clenched teeth.

As the judges could not immediately verify Misty's numbers, the next contestant was called to perform. The audience concluded it was indeed a joke on the part of an odd student who had a rebellious streak simply looking for ways to disrupt good and decent school activities that promote learning and strong character.

For Misty, it was the very thing she had feared. Again, her freakiness had produced nothing but pain. For two days, she didn't answer her phone or the door or the apologies written on cardboard signs outside her window.

James did everything he could to send his message of regret. When he learned the results of the judges, it brought even more apprehension. Although Misty had correctly cited 2,344 numbers in perfect sequence, they collectively concluded that she had cheated. When someone mentioned the boy giving hand signals from the balcony, they knew with certainty of their agreed-upon 'truth.'

"Unanimous belief in a desired reality does not establish it as 'truth,'" James sputtered to his parents in frustration. "Like a bunch of evolutionists," he said, alluding to his pet peeve.

James believed the theory of evolution to be a 'religion masquerading as science,' a view he felt no shame in sharing with any student or teacher at school. Only a few dared enter the ring with James regarding this debate, and very few left with pride intact.

"How do I tell her?" he asked his dad, deeply regretting his role in the whole pi affair.

"Are you sure she didn't cheat?" His father knew Misty was different, but reciting from memory that many numbers was not something he'd expect from Misty. Unable to entertain the idea, he concurred with the judges—she *obviously* had cheated.

4 GANNY'S

Sunday, October 25

Early Sunday evening, Misty made her way through the woods to Mrs. Quinn's, an elderly woman she had adopted as her grandmother. It was Mrs. Valerie Quinn, or Ganny, as Misty called her, that taught the teen girl how to drive—not a car, but life. Ganny helped her learn how to slow down, to take the difficult turns that came up so unexpected, to maneuver through the obstacles that clutter life's road.

She helped her through the potholes and those dark, lonely roads, encouraging her to enjoy the journey, and especially, when Misty was about to crash, how to keep the car on the road, moving forward no matter what unseen dangers loomed ahead.

As Misty neared the small house tucked quaintly among the trees, bird feeders hanging from every willing branch, she smiled at the large goldfish sucking air in the pond beneath the weeping willow under which she and Ganny had sat many, many times. It was a happy place, a place of solitude, of rest, where troubles and worries seemed to lift and float off in the caressing breeze.

Ganny lived alone, tending her gardens and giant goldfish, welcoming any visitors, especially her only 'granddaughter'— Misty. Little carved images of birds and animals sat in windowsills beside candlestick holders of cedar and walnut. Her late husband had turned wood on a lathe, creating more candlestick holders and wooden bowls than one household could ever use, filling the house with a welcoming fragrance of cedar. Ganny carved birds and other things from driftwood and whatever she found on her daily walks, painting them with muted colors, gluing little beads for eyes, and making legs from twisted wire.

"You look more miserable than a coon without its tail," she said, trying to guess what new trouble had attached itself to the gifted young teen.

"Oh, Ganny, wish I'd never been born."

As they sat together, literally, for the two of them scrunched into the old rocker recliner that squeaked with every move, Misty let the tears fall. Ever since she was little, they had sat together in that same worn-out rocker, mulling over life and all its trials. After telling Ganny everything, she muttered some nasty words directed at James.

"He's a good boy," Ganny said. "He cares for you."

The carved birds that lined the windowsill overlooking the backyard with its random bird feeders and suet holders sat silent as if awaiting her reply.

"I shouldn't have listened to him. Shouldn't have done that stupid…" She shook her head.

"God has given you this gift," Ganny said.

"Well, he can have it back."

"No, everyone's been given a gift, not for themselves, but for others, for the world. It's our purpose, our privilege to unwrap the gift, presenting it to the world as best we can. Some use the gift for their own gain. Most leave it unopened. Some let others take it and misuse it, but few, very few learn how to give it to the world, and when they do, lives are forever changed."

"Yeah, but the world doesn't seem to want my freaky gift."

"People don't always want what they need. The world needs your gift."

"Well, then they can have it. I'll give the whole darn curse to whoever wants it." She lay her head back, another round of tears pooling up. "I'm just sick of… remembering everything. My head is packed full, and my heart is…"

"Your heart is heavy, full of too many thoughts and feelings that need to be forgotten. We all struggle with that, just not at your level." Ganny squeezed Misty's hand, rubbing it like she were a small child. "Ever eat something sour?"

Misty nodded, thinking of everything she had eaten that had been sour or bitter, her mind flooding with memories coming at the speed of light.

"The best way to get rid of that taste," Ganny continued, "is to eat something sweet." She paused, letting her words sink in. "James is a good boy, kind and considerate, not like any boy his age, or even older. He cares about you." She finished with a slight chuckle. "Is he not, well, rather sweet?"

Misty sighed, remembering the moment at the river, standing together beneath the willow. James had never taken her hand in that way, ever. Nor had he looked into her eyes like he had that day, glancing at her lips. She was no fool when it came to boys.

But James was different.

She gazed out the window, watching a female cardinal at the feeder, its tufted head with black eyes darting this way and that, so alert, so wary, yet it remained, taking its time to crack and eat the sunflower seeds, skillfully spitting the hulls.

Wary, Misty thought. *Am I too wary, too guarded?*

When Misty had turned fourteen, the Benson boys and their meathead cronies had cornered her a few blocks from school. If an old man with a mean cane and feisty spirit had not happened upon them, she would have gotten some very unpleasant memories to be forever added to the file marked 'delete if ever possible.'

When Ganny had learned of it, they entered into what they called their 'S.P.U.D.' training, or 'Silent Personal Undetectable Defense' training.

For personal reasons, never expounded on, Ganny had acquired a rather extensive knowledge and practice of protecting herself from harm, no matter how imposing the would-be attacker. Misty had witnessed it firsthand when she and Ganny had gone into town one Saturday evening to celebrate Misty's fifteenth birthday.

Coming out of Bizzaro's Pizza, walking down toward the river, they were confronted by three young men who had filled their blood with alcohol levels far beyond the legal limit of sanity. As one grabbed for Ganny's purse, the other two went for Misty.

The riverside lighting was dim, but Misty saw enough to know that Ganny, although well advanced in years, knew her stuff like, well, really knew her stuff. To the sound of knuckles cracking—no, breaking—the man reaching for the purse belted out a cry of sheer agony. As Misty and the two men accosting her glanced at the outcry, Misty heard a crunching sound, like a knee bending in the direction God never intended it to bend. Before that sound had risen over the riverfront, it was followed by a groan of horrific pain as the third and final beast sank to the ground, clutching his groin, eyes bulging.

Whisking Misty away before anyone had seen, they were soon silently on their way back home.

Within a few months of almost daily practicing Ganny's SPUD system of defense, Misty was not only able to keep the two nerds and Bucky at bay but had also learned the meaning of balanced caution. Like the cardinal at the feeder, she knew how to keep alert without living under the nervous apprehension that used to follow her every day.

When a father beats a mother, daughter, and small son, life doesn't seem to hold the same simple joys that others talk about. Trauma lingers, regardless of day or night, uncaring whether the victim is among friends or by themselves. Tormenting fears seem to walk behind, then lurk ahead, shifting with the shadows, ruthlessly waiting to ambush their hapless victim.

Misty had learned how to face those fears, to stop cowering beneath the cloud of trauma and pain, to see trusting as more than vulnerability. Yet, she knew to hold her guard, to watch and observe, detecting the signals that warranted defense, but more importantly, recognizing those that indicated friendly contact, people to trust, and maybe even love.

The balance obtained through Ganny's SPUD training is what kept Misty on the road of life, instead of her story being only a sad depiction in the obituary column of the local paper.

"Thanks, Ganny." Misty munched on some crackers and cheese while the two sat sipping tea sweetened with Ganny's homemade maple syrup. "Thanks for letting me talk."

The old lady smiled, her eyes and mind sharp. "Human steam vents best through the mouth," she said. "Going to school tomorrow?"

"Yeah, SAT testing starts this week. Otherwise…"

Ganny knew the girl may choose to never go back, or maybe in a few weeks or a month, and either way, she would come out with a perfect GPA, if they let her continue her study, that is. Ganny knew of Misty's gift, maybe not to the level that James knew, but she knew Misty to be exceptional, and not just in the areas of memory.

"You do know they're jealous, don't you?" Ganny said, studying the girl's natural beauty. Her auburn hair had learned to flow somewhat in the same direction but still seemed to be reaching out, searching for all that lay within its field of reach.

"Jealous of me? Why?"

"Misty, I know you've heard me say this many times, but you are a great deal more than what you think of yourself. You are more than just your special gift."

Misty gently shook her head. No, she was a freak, an oddball without friends, the latter being of her own choosing. She only did well in school because she couldn't forget. James was smart.

Attractive? Only to nerds and Bucky, well, and those other boys, and that egotistical, but good-looking senior from Rosemount, and yeah, even her English teacher, Mr. Jacobin, but he's a weirdo.

No, they weren't jealous. Nikki and Jaci Jallati were attractive—all the boys fighting to sit near them, employing their obnoxious flirtations, drooling over Jaci's lacy thongs, wondering what she'll wear tomorrow, hoping she'll… whatever.

"It's getting late, Ganny. I better get home."

Ganny didn't respond at first, her thoughts somewhere distant. "Still have that locket I gave you?" she asked in a lowered voice.

"Yes, of course." Misty lifted a small silver locket from beneath her shirt. Ganny had given it to her years ago—a symbol of their friendship. Misty never took it off.

"Oh, looks a little tarnished." Ganny held out her hand. "Let me polish it quick." After a short protest, Misty gave her the locket, knowing it was pointless to argue. The elderly woman took it into a back room and returned shortly, the locket shining like new.

"Thanks, Ganny."

"Greet James for me."

Misty sighed. But as she waved goodbye, she called back from the little wooden gate that opened to the path home. "I will," she called, "for you, I will."

The autumn dew had fallen, the leaves beneath damp and silent. A three-quarter moon had risen, its pale light casting long shadows through the bare trees. She had a small flashlight but felt no need. Walking the well-worn path, she thought over Ganny's words.

"He is sweet," she said under her breath, once again opening the memories from beneath the willow. "And he was just trying to help."

The tingling returned as James held her hands, his fingers soft, yet firm, his eyes earnest and kind.

She smiled as the leaves crunched beneath her feet. "Where would I be without Ganny," she mused, "and James?"

Suddenly, horrible regret rushed in. Heart racing, she ran the rest of the way home, straight for the house of James.

5 BAD NEWS

"He's studying," Mrs. Longmire said. "SATs are tomorrow. Shouldn't you be home preparing?"

"Oh." Misty stood panting, the porch light revealing her dismay. "Please tell him… I said, hi."

Mrs. Longmire forced a polite smile. Although a kind and loving woman, her apprehension had grown. Being a mother, she could see how her son now looked at Misty with more than just neighborly kindness. Although Misty was a nice girl, she was definitely not someone with whom Mrs. Longmire wanted her James to get emotionally involved.

They had rented out the small house to the Greys when money was tight for everyone, and being good Christians, felt it their duty to help a young family in need. It was thought to be only for a year or two, when the Greys got back on their feet financially. They didn't know of, or imagine the issues facing Mr. Grey and the fact that he would never get his family back on their feet, for he couldn't stand on his own. If he wasn't drunk and violently abusive, he was irritable, which meant bullying all who crossed his path, especially those dearest to him, if such a word can be used for someone who beats his own wife and children.

No, Mrs. Longmire had never considered the idea of their two families, so different in so many ways, growing up together, her precious James becoming a big brother to the cute but troubled little Grey girl.

With laden steps, Misty crossed the lawn back to her little house, feet shuffling through dry leaves. Originally a mother-in-law kind of house, it had been remodeled to accommodate a small family with small children, a two-bedroom with a bite-sized bathroom, and an all-in-one living-kitchen-dining room. It was never intended to house a teenage girl and her little brother with two parents fighting whenever they were together.

Misty slept on the sofa in the living-kitchen-dining room, as she wanted to let her brother have his own room. And her mother worked late most nights and needed a dark, quiet place.

Every night Misty rolled out her quilt and pillow, pulling an old worn-out novel from beneath the cushions—a book of faraway adventure, of a girl and a boy stranded on an island, fighting to survive the elements and trials. She liked how necessity demanded they trust and depend on each other. And although she'd read it a dozen times, could recite each page, each paragraph, and each sentence, she read it over and over.

And so, each morning, she'd roll up her quilt and pillow, tucking them beneath the end table, and make her little brother breakfast and a lunch, getting him off to school while making sure they didn't wake their mother who never seemed to get enough rest.

When Misty entered the house, all was quiet. Peeking into her brother's room, she saw him on the floor drawing, something he often did, but as of recent, more than usual with his creations becoming increasingly more detailed.

"Hey, Maxwell. You're up late. What ya drawing?"

Without looking up, he said, "A preliminary schematic of an alien craft with an… electrodynamic-quantum-gravity drive that can hover soundless over water… or desert without making a ripple or stirring a single grain of sand."

"Okaaay." Misty lifted her brows. Along with his drawing

skills, he had also grown in vocabulary, especially for a ten-year-old boy.

"What have you been reading, Max? You sound like a... is that from a comic book?"

"Mom wants you," is all he answered, his eyes never leaving his busy little pencil.

As Misty peered into her mother's room, opening the door just a crack, she heard her mother stir.

"Come in," she said, lying on the worn-out mattress, the room dark and stagnant.

"You work tonight, Mom?"

"At eleven. Be sure and get Max up on time. I'll try to be home before you both leave."

"I will, Mom."

Misty always got her brother up and ready on time, not that she needed to, and always told her mother she would. And like usual, their mother wouldn't make it home before they left, for her shift often had to finish up the leftover materials, and although it gained some much-needed overtime, it made for lonely mornings.

"Max said you... Is everything alright?"

A thick, heavy silence seemed to enter the room as her mother lay quiet in the subtle darkness.

"Your father's... been released..." A sad, defeated kind of chuckle left her mother's throat. "On good behavior..." The grim chuckle became a hopeless whimper.

Goosebumps flushed up Misty's skin, a cold shiver that carried a sudden twitch. They had been told he would serve at least ten years without parole. When called to witness at his trial, they had been assured of their safety, guaranteed witness protection, and all that.

Misty remembered the day in court, her mother's eyes downcast, testifying to her husband's brutal temper and addictive use of anything and everything illegal. She fought to hold back her tears as she told of his treatment of the children, of herself, and even the landlord, Mr. Longmire.

Although in court many times, her father had finally been convicted of killing a man in a barroom brawl, stabbing the victim multiple times in so-called self-defense. Misty had seen him too many times hold a knife to her mother, and several times to her own throat, and even little Max.

When drunk, he became a monster without sense or control. When sober, which had been less and less, he was overbearing and manipulative, his temper always on the verge of exploding. To be around him was an anxious, edgy torment.

"But they said…" Misty's heart surged hard, hot blood filling her neck and face.

Her mother groaned. "He's reformed, they say. A… new man."

"No!" Misty rose from beside her mother's bed. "No! He can't come back here! I will not…!" She didn't know what she would do. Her first thought was to run away, far away. But what of Max and Mom? "No…" she kept muttering, shaking her head, her hands now trembling. "Mom, you can't let him, please don't…"

"I have… no choice. He's my husband."

"No, he's not! He's not… he's not… he's not!"

"He's your father, Misty."

"Darn blast it, Mom! No! Nooo!"

In rash frustration, Misty rushed out of her mother's room, out of the house, and into the cold, dark October night.

Running to stand beneath the window of her life-long friend, Misty stared up at the yellow glow two stories up. A zillion memories poured through her mind, which also meant her heart, and all of them were bad.

"James…" she said weakly, her body trembling.

An oak tree grew near the Longmire house, its branches leaning close to James' window. Within a minute, Misty lay sprawled upon a limb, peering through the glass at James.

Seated at his desk directly beneath the window, the teen boy dutifully studied, a pile of books at each elbow. Behind him, his bed and room were neat and clean with pictures of famous men throughout history—his 'persons of inspiration.'

Misty flung a twig but missed the glass. It struck the siding with barely enough noise to awaken an owl. She flung the next harder, and again missed. Reaching for something larger, she slipped and almost fell. Muttering some angry words, she twisted and pulled till the branch broke free. When it struck the window, poor James bolted backward, nearly falling from his chair.

Standing to lean over his desk, he pressed his face to the glass, squinting into the darkness. Misty waved to him, again nearly falling from the limb.

"Open the window, James! Before I die!" she called in a hushed voice.

Seeing nothing in the darkness, James went back to prepping for the tests that would comprise most of the following week.

Misty's heart sank, her thoughts spirally downward fast as she thought more of her father's release. She glanced up, pondering how high she'd have to climb to make falling… *No, don't go there.*

"James," she moaned, "I need you."

For twenty minutes, Misty lay sprawled on the limb, her eyes following the boy's every move, which wasn't much, for he just sat studying.

"You don't need to study, James. You know it already. Blast it! Open your window! Please…"

When her fingers no longer felt alive, and her toes had long since turned numb, she slowly climbed down. Falling hard the last few feet, her leg scraped the trunk as she tumbled. When she stood, the light from James' window had gone dark.

Unwilling to go home, she thought of returning to Ganny's, but walking the woods now… No, she needed to talk to James.

Lingering beneath the window of James the genius, she stood shivering, her heart so full of misery it felt as though she bled from inside.

How could they release him? How could Mom let him come back?

For a good while, she stood shivering, staring up at the dark window. Turning to walk home, she suddenly scooped up a handful of acorns and with all her might sent them hurling toward the glass. If James didn't answer, she vowed to never speak with him again, ever.

With the room still dark, there came the sound of a window slowly rising. Then the dark silhouette of a head peered out into the cold night.

"Misty? Is that you?"

At first, Misty couldn't answer. She just stood, shivering now more than ever, her heart galloping with fears, worries, memories of James holding her hands, her father beating her mother, her life at school, and now…

"Misty?"

"James, it's me! Can I…?" She didn't know what to ask. She

wanted someone to hold her, to tell her it would be alright, that life was worth living, worth waking up for.

"Misty? What are you doing? It's late."

"James, please… I need to talk."

"But I can't come down, the alarm's on, and Mom and Dad… What's wrong?"

"It's about my… please… can we talk… please?"

Heart thumping, James pulled on a pair of jeans, then rummaged beneath his bed, pulling out boxes of junk in search of the emergency rope ladder he'd made in fifth grade. As Misty stood shivering, he quietly hooked the ladder over his windowsill, and let the crude contraption unroll.

He grabbed a light jacket, planning to climb down. But before he could clear his desk, Misty had crawled up the ladder, shimmied through the window, and was now clamoring over his books and papers.

He helped her stand, her whole body stiff yet shivering. Afraid to turn on his light, they stood facing each other in the darkness, their voices low.

"What's wrong, Misty? If my mom or dad—"

"It's my…" She struggled. "He's been released."

For a moment, the room went silent, for James knew to whom she referred. He recalled one of his elaborate plans for doing away with the beast. A genius plan—it would look like an accident. Never had he actually considered it more than a mental exercise, but now…

His heart thumped even harder, his lips tightening. *Her father released?* He studied the distraught girl before him, his mind racing. *Misty in my room, at night? Using my rope ladder?*

"You're sure?" he asked, to which she nodded. "When?"

She shook her head.

He swallowed, head whirling. *Am I really standing alone with her… in the dark… in my room?* "Misty, I… I can't believe they would… are you sure?"

Misty stepped toward him, her panting breaths brushing his

face. When her hand touched his, he twitched.

"Misty, I'm really sorry. I…" He tried to form a plan, to just think clearly, yet to comfort her, stop her dad's return, do something about her being in his room before…

"Misty, you can't be here. I don't… I can't…"

"Please let me stay. I'll sleep on the floor. Please James, I just need…"

Without warning, she leaned into him, arms limp at her sides. Soft whimpers came in little gasps.

Slowly James put his arms around her, his breath quivering. She sniveled, pressing her cold nose into his neck. Although they had grown up together, had played games, built forts, climbed trees, and a host of other things, never had he held her this way. Not until this summer had he ever thought to hold her this way. But now… *No, James, it's Misty, your best friend.*

But his blood surged all the more. "What can I do?" he softly asked. "How can I help?"

She didn't answer, her arms feebly wrapping about his waist. She pressed him, burying her face further into his neck, hot tears dripping.

For a time they just stood, the window still open, cold October night filling the room as Misty softly wept.

"I don't want him to come back, ever," she whimpered. "I want to stay here, with you."

James fought to sort his thoughts and feelings. Misty's bushy hair tickled his face. She smelled of outside, of autumn air, of… Misty. He gently caressed her back, searching for something to say, to comfort her. Barefoot in t-shirt and jeans, he shivered, the chills coming from more than just the cold.

Misty sniffled loudly. "I wish he would just die," she said, "would leave us alone. God, why would they let him out?"

Suddenly a dim light shone beneath the door, the sound of footsteps coming up the stairs.

"You gotta go! Now!"

Misty clung tighter. She would rather die than go.

"Misty, please!"

With a swish of her head, she wiped her tears across his chest, stepping back, but reluctant to leave.

"You have to go!"

The footsteps stopped outside his door, listening. Then the doorknob slowly turned. As Mrs. Longmire peeked her head into the room, the light from the hall illuminated James shutting his window.

"James, are you alright? I thought I heard something."

"Just getting ready for bed, Mom. Thanks for checking."

"Why's it so cold in here? Was your window open?"

"Yeah, needed to clear my head. Goodnight, Mom. Love you."

Mrs. Longmire stepped into the room. "Misty stopped over," she said.

"Oh, what did she want?"

"Nothing. I told her you were studying."

"You should have called me down, Mom. I would've liked to talk with her."

"Why are those boxes out?" his mother asked. "You might stumble in the morning."

"Oh, yeah." James tried to push the dusty boxes back under the bed. They stopped a good foot short.

"Is everything alright, dear?"

"It's ahh… yeah… actually."

Mrs. Longmire sat on the edge of James' bed. Using her heel, she tried pushing a box further under the bed. It went in a little and then slowly moved back out.

"You can go, Mom. I need to hit the sack."

Mrs. Longmire just sat, silently looking at her son. "I'm concerned," she said slowly, "about your… about the time you spend with the Grey girl."

James stiffened, his eyes glancing to the boxes.

"I just think you shouldn't spend so much time with her, that's all, so you can cultivate other relationships, with other girls, like Nikki Laurens, that pretty cheerleader, or Carla from church. They both seem like really nice girls. You're such a handsome boy, why don't you...?" Her voice trailed off in a controlled frustration. "I mean, she's nice and all, a bit odd, the way she dresses, and her hair going every which way, I mean, don't you think—?"

"That's enough, Mom! I get your point."

For a brief moment she sat silent. "Well," she said, taking a deep breath, mustering strength, "she's not the kind of girl I want to see you get involved with. Think of your future. Is she the one you want to start a family with? I mean, really James?"

"Mom, stop." His heart beat so hard it made his head pulse. He fought to stay calm. "Thanks for your concern." He pulled back the covers so she would rise. "I need to get to sleep. Goodnight." She got up slowly, her eyes watching him. Walking to the doorway, she turned back.

"I just don't think she's the girl for you, James."

"Goodnight, Mom." As she closed the door, a piercing agony ripped through his soul. He fought back anger, as muffled whimpers rose from beneath the bed.

Oh, God... No way could Misty handle this bomb, not now.

And that stupid pi contest. He scolded himself again, shaking his head. "Hey, Mom!" he called out after she closed the door, his heart pounding. He waited till she peeked her head through, his hands trembling.

"Yes?"

"I think she's rather cute, and really smart." His voice faltered a bit. "Honestly, I think she's downright beautiful, very beautiful, could win any modeling contest. No... no contests. I like her, Mom. I like her a lot. She's nothing like those other girls. She's a whole lot more than they could ever be, ever."

Mrs. Longmire stood silent in the doorway, the air thickening with every bated breath.

James swallowed, his lungs working like he'd run a race. "You just need to get to know her, Mom. She's—"

The door shut hard, followed by firm footsteps descending the stairs.

For what seemed a long time, the room felt bound by a heavy, somber silence.

Then James jumped from his bed and pulled the boxes out as quickly and quietly as possible. Without a word, he helped Misty out. Dust balls clung to her hair, but no one cared because no one saw, they were alone again, in the dark.

He reached to take her hands but found her stiff, standing rigid. Tiny quivering sobs rose and fell with each breath. James stood breathing fast through his nose.

He had dropped the ladder out the window as Misty had crawled beneath the bed. The alarm system, installed when Mr. Grey's violent behavior escalated, was rather elaborate. For him to be caught with Misty in his room…

James was not a liar. His parents trusted him for good reason. He hated deception of any kind. Maybe his mom was right. He just put himself in a pile of crud. And to say what he said about Misty…

He took her stiff hands and pulled her close. She didn't respond. With a hand behind her head and the other on her lower back, he held her tight, gently, but tight.

"I meant everything I said," he whispered close to her ear, dusty spirals exploring his face. "Please forget what you heard. My mom, I mean. She…" He sighed, his heart ripping. She'd never forget. Those words will torment her from this day on.

Squeezing her tight to his chest, he pressed his face into her cheek. "I love you, Misty," he whispered. "I will always… love you."

7 HARD CHOICES

As James held Misty tight, her sniffles grew into whimpers, which grew to outright sobs.

"Misty, please, you can't cry now."

The more he tried, the louder it grew.

"Misty, I'll be grounded for life. I'll never get to see you. Please don't cry, not now."

As she gasped and sniveled, he glanced at the door. He thought to put his hand over her mouth, but that was something James could never do.

A subtle flick, and hall light came seeping beneath his door. The steady click, click, click of his mother's wedding ring on the wooden rail. To have Misty in his room alone at night, having already lied about it, and... *I'm dead!*

But to Misty, it only made matters worse. Now her life *was* truly over. Either way, James would never get to see her again. And without him, her only friend, she could never face her father, the twerds at school... the barrage of memories...

Her sniffles broke into stuttering gasps.

James glanced at the light beneath his door, his brain firing hot. Misty went limp in his arms, her whimpers like a little girl. Determined footsteps now came down the hall.

In a burst, James scooped Misty up and into his bed. Climbing in on top of her, he suddenly pressed his lips over Misty's mouth. Yanking the covers back over them with his left hand, he pulled his pillow up over their heads. Though both were breathing hard, he held her tight, literally smothering her cries with his lips.

When the door creaked open just a crack, all was silent, save a weak sniffle or two. The body of James lay quiet beneath the covers, his pillow over his head. He focused, fighting to control his heart and lungs, to breathe a slow steady rhythm, while his mouth still covered the lips of the sniveling girl, the girl with whom his heart was joined.

When the door finally clicked shut, James carefully released his lip hold. Misty inhaled a jagged breath, letting it out slowly.

For some time, James lay atop Misty, both listening, both hearts pounding.

"I'm sorry," he finally whispered. "Did I hurt you?"

Misty didn't move, her lips open as she lay still, her breath unsteady.

James took a deep breath. "I didn't know what else to do. I'm really—"

But Misty had lifted her chin and lightly touched her lips to his.

As if his blood were set on fire, James responded in kind, but his mind contested. Like solving an equation, he instantly knew where this would lead, and knew he would regret it. Mustering his strength, he reluctantly rolled off to lay beside her.

"No," he whispered. "Not like this."

Misty lay silent, her mind and heart so tangled she couldn't move. A warm tear trickled, finding its way into her ear. After a long broken breath, followed by a quick sniffle, she simply whispered, "Want me to go?"

"No, but..." He sighed, his hands quivering.

Her slender fingers found his hand. "You dropped the ladder," she said softly.

He rolled on his side. "Misty, I'm really sorry about all this, about your dad... and my mom... I..."

She squeezed his hand, holding it tight for some time before quietly asking, "Do you have some string and a fishhook?"

In a few minutes, the rope ladder lay hooked on the

windowsill, the cold October night once again filling the room. After a very long, lingering embrace, they stood before his desk.

"I meant what I said, Misty," James whispered. "Everything."

Misty nuzzled her face into his neck, her arms clinging tight. Tears again began to flow as she thought of what lay ahead. "I don't want to go," she said, fighting back the whimpers, her body shivering hard.

James held her close. "I don't want you to go."

After another long embrace, he gently helped her over his desk and out the window. He watched with pounding heart as she ran beneath the trees back to her house.

Blood still surging hot, James crawled into bed, his mind on fire. No way would he be sleeping, at least not for a very long while.

Misty pulled her pillow and quilt from beneath the end table. Her mom had left for work and the house lay quiet, the walls listening to her galloping heart.

Love, James? What do you mean?

Then the words of Mrs. Longmire replayed in perfect tone and pitch, word for word in living sound. 'She's not the kind of girl I want to see you get involved with. Think of your future. Is she the one you want to start a family with? I mean, really James?'

The words cut deep.

She's right, James. You're so smart… so kind…

Wrapping her quilt around her trembling flesh, she went out into the cold autumn night, stocking feet padding over damp leaves. Beneath the streaks of moonlight, she made her way through the quiet woods, the air crisp yet damp, the heart of Misty Grey confused… and hurting.

Monday, October 26

"Misty?" Max called for his sister as he wandered through the empty house. Making himself breakfast, he wondered where she might be. He made his lunch and finished getting ready for school. When the time came to walk down the long sloping driveway, he became concerned. Never had Misty not been there for him. She'd always helped him with breakfast, prepping him for school. Where was she?

"Where's Misty?" James asked Max. He looked back at the little house, expecting her to come out at any moment. They always walked the driveway together, taking the bus to school, for, unlike the long ride home, it was tolerable, a mere ten-minute ride, with far less twerds.

A hundred scenarios billowed through his mind, some very dark and disconcerting. "Did you see her this morning?" he asked with urgency. Max just shook his head. "Did she… is your mom home?" Again, Max shook his head. "So, you haven't seen her?"

James looked about, his heart accelerating. *What've I done? Where could she be?*

"Go meet the bus, Max. I'll look for Misty, okay?" Max nodded, plodding his way down the drive, his backpack swinging from his hand. James went and took a quick look inside Misty's house. Seeing the quilt gone, but Misty's shoes still at the door, he fought to think clearly, his mind and heart like a boiling pot.

"Ganny's," he said, leaving the house. "She must have gone to Ganny's."

Fighting back a zillion dreadful thoughts, he scooped up her shoes and sped off toward the woods that lined their farm. In graceful stride, he leaped the creek that ran between their property and Mrs. Quinn's. As he neared her house, he suddenly stopped.

Within a tangle of brush, just a few feet ahead of him, lay the quilt of Misty Grey. Torn in several places, it seemed securely tangled amid the brambles and brush. He glanced toward Ganny's.

"She's got to be there," he assured himself, his sharp mind trying not to think of the time Misty had tried to make the memories fade. He had been the one to find her sleeping, or rather dying, her blood feeding greedily upon the sleeping pills within her stomach.

As he approached Ganny's door, it suddenly opened. Stretching wide in the morning sun, stood Misty, her eyes puffy and red, a huge yawn covering her face.

"James?" She stopped mid-stretch. "What are you—?" Then she bolted full awake. "School! Max! Oh, God…"

Without another word, she ran down the steps, shouting a haphazard goodbye to Ganny. She raced straight past James, snatching the shoes from his hand.

"Come on, James! We're late!"

"Misty?" He glanced at Ganny who now stood in the doorway, her eyes bright with a cheerful smile. For a second, he just stood there bewildered. Then with a quick wave of hello and goodbye, he ran after Misty, surprised at how fleet-footed she ran, seeing her leap the creek as he had, her stride quick and nimble.

Huffing, they both leaped onto the bus just as the doors were closing. For several minutes, James just sat staring at her, his eyes wide with wonder and relief. Her hair bushed out as usual, needing a brushing, but looking nearly the same. Since she rarely wore makeup, for her to jump up and off to school was not an unusual feat.

James shook his head, heart beating with the memories of last night. When they neared Max's elementary school, they hopped off, for it was faster to walk the remaining two blocks than to stay as the bus lined up behind a dozen others.

"You slept at Ganny's?" he finally asked, their footsteps in sync.

Misty nodded without reply, her eyes forward.

"Are you okay?"

Again she nodded without looking his way.

"I meant what I said last night."

To this she didn't nod but bit her lower lip, her eyes following the cracks along the sidewalk.

"Don't listen to what my mom said. It's not true. I meant what I said about you, every word." His voice broke a little as he spoke. He was not one to say something he didn't mean. In fact, he never said anything that he did not believe was true. Misty knew this well.

"SATs are today," she said softly. "I hope you do well." Then she abruptly stopped to face him. They were near the high school and they both knew the nerds and Bucky would be watching. Misty also knew that word of the pi contest fiasco had probably spread like some infectious disease. She hated school, yet she faced it full-on like a matador staring into the eyes of the charging bull. James marveled at her inner strength—a strange, persistent, even dauntless determination that would not quit.

She reached out and touched his hand, pulling gently on his little finger. "If I pulverize someone today, will you still...?" She sighed, not sure of what it meant to be loved. Never before had she been kissed, and this all from James, her friend. "It's not your fault, the pi thing." She let her eyes rest on his lips, suddenly aware she had licked her own. "We better go. I need to wash up." She smiled a silly smile as they continued on up to the steps and into the chaos called senior high.

Her heart stirred, a twinkle of joy swirling through. Maybe things would be okay. Again, she found herself wetting her lips. She smiled.

If Misty could have known, even an inkling, of what the day held, she would never ever have stepped through the doors of McKinley High.

9 REALIZATIONS

The infectious disease had indeed spread. Degrading variations of 'Cheater, cheater, pumpkin-eater,' came from numerous mouths using expletives of stupidity, thinking they were creative.

"Shouldn't have gone overboard," said Pickery Hall. "They might have fell for it. How'd you guys do it? Judges are miffed. Said you didn't miss a single digit."

When Misty learned the full outcome, she wondered why James had not told her, but then remembered his efforts to talk to her, and with shame and regret, recalled her effective efforts to shun him.

"Testing on Monday mornings should be banned," she muttered as the first sheets were handed out. Although she slept well at Ganny's, it was a short night for they had stayed up quite late talking of all that transpired in the bedroom of James Longmire. Ganny found it humorous, except for the words of Mrs. Longmire.

Misty had never known affection from a man, let alone a passionate kiss with words of love. What did it mean? *Why would James...?* Yet, inside, she knew.

When Misty's quilt had tangled in the briars, it felt like someone pulling at her. An owl had screeched just seconds before and with a pulsing heart, she ran the rest of the way to Ganny's. The fear that had surged felt so strong and real, its tingling still crept over her skin as she sat reading the endless questions, filling in the tiny ovals.

Other memories came with full vibrancy and passion, the memories of James doing what he thought best to keep her quiet. A swirling sensation rose from inside as she felt his weight upon her, his warm lips covering her mouth. Did it really happen, or had she only dreamed it?

"Ten minutes." Mr. Patel's monotone announcement brought Misty back to SAT-land. As quickly as possible she scanned the remaining questions, filling in the obvious answers, forcing her thoughts to stay off James.

When lunchtime came, she had to buy lunch, something rare for her. Sliding through the line, she found herself the talk of the cafeteria. 'How did you do it? Tell us your system? Did you have an earpiece with James reading off the numbers?'

As some asked with admiration, others jeered with extremely unkind remarks. Misty neither replied nor denied. Her mind was on other things.

The nerds and Bucky sat where they always sat, as close to Misty as they could get without incurring her wrath. It was like a lioness taunted by jackals, as long as they kept distance, they wouldn't get swiped. She sighed, pondering their devotion.

At random, she recalled the time when the school's main computer had gotten hacked and held for ransom, the hackers demanding money or they'd do major harm, dispersing all info to the dark web. It was Bucky and the nerds that traced the hackers and retrieved the files, setting up a firewall 'stronger than the federal government's,' Stanton T. had said, sounding as if he had personal knowledge of such firewalls.

Was amazing, Misty thought, glancing their way. *You boys do have skills.*

When James finally showed up and sat beside her, the inquirers seemed to dissipate, except for the nerds and Bucky who stayed, watching every move. Though quiet and reserved, an air of respect followed James. Students looked to him, often asking him advice or offering kind gestures to endear his friendship. He treated everyone as his equal, respecting all who crossed his path, except the few that he considered unworthy of even the simplest of common courtesy.

"How you holding up?" he asked Misty quietly, nodding to a younger student who waved sheepishly to him.

"Why do they test us?" Misty asked cynically. "Are we rats?"

"It's for our own good, to help us know our strengths and weaknesses."

"I know yours, and you know mine, so let's go home." Misty smiled, but pain showed through.

She took a chocolate pudding cup off her tray and slid it over to James.

"Thanks," he said, surprised to see it on her tray.

"For you," she said, gently smiling, then bit her lower lip, breathing hard through her nose.

It was one of the foods she never ate, for though she enjoyed chocolate, the pudding always brought instant trauma. She'd tried telling him the story once—it wasn't good.

Without saying more, James tucked it away, something he'd have to eat later. "Are you sure about your father?" he then asked quietly.

Misty shrugged, deeply regretting she had run out on her mother. "Math is next," she said, mustering another smile.

As memory was to Misty, math came so naturally to James, it was scary. He could multiply numbers faster than someone with a calculator—big numbers—two-digit, even three-digit—like 247 x 82. He loved to square numbers like 74 x 74, or 329 x 329. He said it was easier having less random numbers to work with and just focus on the multiplication.

When they were bored, Misty would pull out her calculator and spew out three numbers to which James would race to have it squared before Misty and her calculator. More often than not, he would beat her or they would tie.

But he rarely let it show, especially in math class. Misty once told him that he belonged in public school like a horse belonged in a zoo. "You should be in college, in Yale or Harvard, or someplace haughty like that, where you can let your genius run."

James would only shake his head.

"Do your best, James. Don't hold back this time."

Under the table he took her hand, his eyes locked on hers. He stared, watching her long lashes, her eyes drawing him into her soul. Soon he was staring at her lips. "I will, if you will."

"Do my best?"

James nodded. "Do your absolute best, hold nothing back."

For Misty, math was weird. In her head, numbers sometimes took on colors or images. Only when she focused did they look like the actual numbers she saw on paper. If she didn't try and solve the equations, they sometimes came like a whiff of inspiration, the answer just presenting itself like someone showing up unexpectedly at your door on Saturday morning. When totally relaxed, she had sometimes beaten James to the answer of his two- and three-digit multiplications. She consigned it to lucky guessing. James called it gifted.

He watched her now, nibbling on her knuckles, something she did when deep in thought. He knew her fears, fears of being 'exceptionalized.' The pi contest was a huge step for her, unfortunately, a huge step backward. He wondered at his own suggestion. Maybe it was better to be considered normal. Misty had said it was 'like being the nail that sticks up above the rest, you'll just get hammered down.'

He wondered about her challenge to him. Caldone Academy was only thirty minutes away, a private school for students like James. He had thought about talking to his parents, revealing his abilities, and changing schools, but money was so tight, and…

He watched Misty still nibbling her knuckles. Without realizing, he softly spoke his thoughts out loud. "I'm sorry about last night," he whispered. "I shouldn't have… I mean, not like that. Was inappropriate, and I… apologize. It won't happen again, I mean, not like that."

Misty just sat stock still, her eyes on her tray.

James wrestled for the right words. "I meant everything," he whispered, leaning in close. "But it was wrong to kiss you... like that."

She looked over at him, her eyes questioning.

He squeezed her hand beneath the table. "I..." His gaze went to her lips. "I want to, believe me." He swallowed. "But I also think, well, I promise to never do that again, not until we're mar..." He paused, as if suddenly aware of his own words. Then his face lightened, smiling wide. He squeezed her hand once more. "I love you, Misty. I've always loved you."

Lost in thought, Misty followed James into math class. Mrs. Barns, or Captain Bane as she was not so affectionately called, greeted the students in her usual sour tone, her voice way too deep and gruff for a woman's, sounding way too much like a sea captain.

Having taught math for a thousand years or more, Mrs. Barns really needed a life outside of the stale, sterile, and stuffy classroom of numbers, equations, and complex calculations, for she had become like a piece of the furniture, a wooden desk, stiff and cold, its varnish yellowing with age.

Misty took her seat beside James, her eyes somewhere distant. So much had happened since that Friday pi contest. Do her best? Her fragile world felt wobblier than usual, like someone evil were shaking the table on which stood her feeble house of cards.

And now James… what were these words from his mouth? What did it mean to love someone? To be loved by someone? She loved Maxwell and her mother. She loved Ganny and…

"Number two pencils only!" barked Captain Bane. "Remain at your desk until everyone is finished." This was met with such moaning and groaning that Mrs. Barns slammed her wooden stick so hard upon her desk it actually hurt the ears of those seated towards the back. "If you had the wherewithal to leave quietly, I would offer such gratuity, but never, in all my years, have I seen a single student, save maybe five, who have shown the wits being capable of exiting without the usual adolescent ruckus. You shall remain seated and silent." Forming a scowl that could frighten the fiercest of jungle beasts, she panned from one side of the room to the other. "You have ninety minutes. Begin!"

Misty glanced at James. As much as she did not wish to 'do her best,' she longed to see him do his. "I will," she whispered.

"Ms. Grey!" Captain Bane bellowed. "I heard of your shenanigans! If you and Mr. Longmire try and scheme something within my classroom, you'll be dealing with more than the ridicule of the riffraff." She glared at Misty, and then to a lonely seat at the back. "Why don't you take yourself to that desk in the back. Let Mr. Longmire do his own work and you do yours."

Multiple snickers rose among the students, with Nikki whispering something nasty to Carla. As Misty sheepishly stood, James jumped to his feet. Face set stern, he addressed Mrs. Barns rather frankly. "I have never helped anyone cheat, especially Misty. She's fully capable without my help."

The teacher's eyes became slits, her lips drawing so tight they disappeared. "Were you not in the balcony during the contest?" Before James could answer she growled out a second question, or rather accusation. "And were you not seen giving hand signals to Ms. Grey? And did not the judges conclusively rule foul play? How dare you say you've never helped her cheat?"

James Longmire flushed bright red, his nostrils flaring with each rising breath. "You don't have a clue, Mrs. Barns. The so-called judges have no proof of foul play, and they won't find any, cause there was none. Misty memorized those numbers, every one of them. She…" He took several deep breaths, glancing her way. "I didn't help Misty at the contest. She memorized them all in—"

Suddenly the door swung open with Principal Jolene P. Pinrick leading three men in dark suits. A tall slender woman, she stood scanning the room, her gaunt cheeks in tighter than usual, her long bony fingers drumming her hips. She craned her neck, eyes squinting at the pondering students, the tendons in her neck sticking out like guide wires holding up her head.

"Marie Elsa Grey?" Her shrill voice cut through the startled classroom. "Is Marie in this class?" Every finger, except James and Mrs. Barns, swung to aim directly at the wide-eyed, cowering girl with twirly auburn hair.

"Oh, no," Misty muttered, "my mom." She shot a terrified glance at James, the same look she got when her dad would come swerving up the driveway late at night.

"Excuse me, Ms. Barns, but we need to see Marie for a moment. Sorry for the interruption." Principal Pinrick beckoned for Misty to come and follow. The men in black suits just stood watching the teen girl make her way through the desks.

"Busssted," said Nikki, snickering to Carla and Jaci.

James, still standing, just stood in silence, his heart pounding with fervor. Two men behind a smaller man, wore dark sunglasses, the kind FBI types wear in the movies.

'They don't want you watching them while they watch you,' Misty had once said while they enjoyed a spy thriller together. Misty's home didn't have a TV and it was rare that she watched anything since everything that passed through her eyes stayed.

With great reluctance, she left with Principal Pinrick, giving one last glance back at James. The smaller man in the middle had taken Misty by the arm as soon as they left the room. Something about it gave James the willies.

His heart hammered as he slowly dropped down into his seat, his mind racing, legs yearning to run out after her.

Captain Bane strode toward his desk, her wooden stick over her shoulder. Stopping to put her other hand on her hip, she glared down at the teen. "Have you any more rabble you'd wish to spew?" She snarled as she stood over him.

The response he considered would not only get him in trouble with the school but also one his parents would never tolerate coming from his lips no matter what the circumstance, especially to someone in authority.

Shaking his head, he folded his hands on his desk, his gaze

on the door. His thoughts were stuck on the forlorn look in Misty's eyes.

As Mrs. Barns stood hovering, someone pointed toward the window, calling out something about Misty. Like a flock of birds, the classroom rose to crowd about the second-floor window. On the street below, outside a long black sedan, a man with sunglasses and, of course, a dark suit, opened the car door as Marie Grey walked hesitantly between the two others. They all followed the little man who strode quickly, a small red folder tucked under his arm.

As the little man entered the front seat, Misty glanced back toward the classroom window. When her eyes found James, her look of fear spoke volumes. Something wasn't right. This was not about her dad. This was something else, something bigger… something dark.

11 ASSOCIATION

"Is this about my dad?" Misty asked, her voice quavering, hands trembling on her knees. She sat pressed between the two men still wearing their sunglasses. The car smelled of cheap aftershave and cigar.

The little man up front turned to eye the girl for a moment, and then without a sound turned to once again face the windshield. The driver, also wearing sunglasses, seemingly purchased or maybe issued by the same department as the other two, drove with silent calm, his large hands in tight leather gloves on the wheel at ten and two.

"Is my mom alright?" Misty tried again. More silence. Her stomach tightened, a sickening woe twisting her gut. After being abruptly escorted from the high school, the little man clutching her arm had told her it was of vital importance that she cooperate without questions, that it was best for her safety and her family's, and that no harm would come to her, although she'd be a little inconvenienced.

Now within the black sedan, scrunched between two large men, fear squeezed her chest, not panic, at least not yet.

SPUD—Ganny's Silent Personal Undetectable Defense. 'Remaining calm is your first weapon.' Misty could hear the words as if Ganny were there in the car with her. 'Take an inventory—what's at your disposal—disregard nothing—a weapon can be as small as a paperclip, a pen, even a pair of sunglasses.'

Misty glanced at the driver who watched her occasionally through his mirror. She looked about the car, trying to keep her nerves in check, which was virtually impossible, but it gave her something to focus on.

When they entered the freeway, heading south, her heart skipped. The nearest city of significance in this direction was over thirty minutes away.

"Where are you taking me?" she asked this time in a direct tone. Again the reply was silence. "Please tell me where we're going."

The little man up front glanced back. "Not far," he said, sounding annoyed as if he'd rather be doing something else. Misty heard a slight accent, Eastern Europe, Russian maybe. Before, in her school, he had spoken with perfect English, his tone pleasant, direct, but kind.

"You haven't told me what this is about." She marveled at her own strength.

"That's not my job," the man said, this time with more of the accent.

Misty had left her backpack at her desk. In her mind, she rummaged through it, longing for all the potential weapons it contained.

Undetectable Defense— 'Don't give your intentions away. If you plan to fight, pretend to cooperate. If you plan to run, pretend to surrender.'

"If you could please tell me something, I would appreciate it. I'm sure you understand."

The little man shook his head. "Not my job." This time his accent shone through completely, but she still couldn't place it.

Seeing no way to obtain information, and with no possible escape at seventy miles an hour, she closed her eyes, picturing their faces, even though behind dark glasses.

But the face that kept coming into her thoughts was not of those with whom she sat, but rather of the one with whom she wished she sat. She thought of James taking her hand beneath the table, his words of love.

Tears pooled as she yearned to cry, to run to Ganny's, for James to hold her again, to squeeze her like he had last night.

To her dismay, they drove on, traveling south with still no explanation. Panic tried to take over more than a few times, but Misty focused on her breathing, counting four beats as she inhaled through her nose, then four beats as she exhaled.

She pulled up several maps within her mind, searching her memory for any possible destinations.

After an hour or more, they exited where no visible towns could be seen. Within minutes they were traveling south again, passing open fields and scattered farms, the sun making its way toward the western sky. She knew on a map where they were, but it still revealed nothing.

Again a rush of fear, a strong urge to panic, but she set her jaw, fingers digging into her knees. Horrid scenes presented themselves, thoughts of gruesome death flashing.

With sinking heart, she resigned herself to face death, grieving that her mother and James would never know what happened. But she wouldn't go quietly. Whatever their intentions, they would meet with fierce opposition. *I'll make you proud, Ganny.*

Her eyes moistened, her unpainted nails digging deeper.

Turning fast, they pulled onto a long dirt driveway running straight toward an old farmhouse set amid a growth of mature trees. Several silos and metal sheds framed the little two-story house, a quaint farm established probably in the early 1900s.

Confused and scared, Misty climbed out and walked with the men toward the house. To try and escape here in the middle of cornfields seemed impossible. Maybe with Ganny's help, it could be managed. She slumped. No, not even with Ganny.

The front door creaked, like the front step, like the wooden floor. A bare house with clean-swept rooms met her troubled eyes. A single chair sat alone in what would have been the living room. Without delay, the little man led Misty to the chair.

"I need to use the toilet," Misty said, sheepishly, but also thinking to explore and take inventory.

Groaning, the man nodded to a dark suit who led her up the stairs to a small bathroom, empty, but clean. Taking her time to scan the landscape, she watched the sun nestle into the horizon of fields beyond.

"Hherrdy up!" The man pounded on the bathroom door, his accent so thick, she barely understood.

Without a word she opened the door, having first checked every cupboard and cabinet, finding nothing but an old brittle comb.

Upon entering the living room, she jolted to a stop. A woman in dark blue clothes, adorned with only simple jewelry, stood as if she'd been waiting for an hour.

"Are you Marie Grey?" the woman asked, her tone direct.

Misty nodded, her heart surging blood way too fast, way too hard. It felt so unreal, so like a movie set for some dark thriller. She swayed, head woozy.

"Please sit, Miss Grey. I just have some questions."

Moving with reluctance, Misty sat on the edge of the chair. The woman snapped her fingers, the sound echoing. A dark suit brought a second chair.

The woman studied Misty for a moment, looking her up and down. "You walk out of some guy's dream?" she asked, taking her time to sit close to Misty. "Those lashes real?" The woman leaned close to examine Misty's eyes.

A small scar marred the woman's forehead, just above her right eye. Her skin shone unusually white and clean. Thin lips formed a fake smile, revealing perfect teeth.

Her dark, short hair hung straight, with clean bangs that curved toward one side as if making way for the scar. She then eyed Misty's full-formed lips, her own pursing as an ornery stare overtook her face.

"How long have you known Veronica Tallon?"

"Who?"

The woman studied Misty's eyes. "How about Mrs. Valerie Quinn?"

"Ganny?" A sudden surge of coldness swept up her back.

The woman nodded. "Her real name, maybe, is Veronica Sage Tallon. Either way, you've known her for some time, correct?"

Misty nodded, her mind swirling.

"Has she given you anything as of lately, anything at all?" The woman paused, searching for the right words. "Anything which she may have told you to hide, or keep close. A gift maybe, something small, one of her carved birds, or a necklace, that sort of thing?"

Misty flushed, her neck and face reddening. *My locket?* She thought of the tiny locket with her picture inside. But she'd lost it.

"You can tell me, Miss Grey. It's rather important, a matter of national security."

"National security?" Misty tried to ask, but her throat had tightened. *Ganny?* She struggled to make sense of it, fear clouding everything. *Am I dreaming?* She swallowed, trying to revive her voice. "Um, why would Ganny give me something of national security?"

"What has she given you? Tell me everything she has given you over the past three months."

Misty shook her head. She hated lying. She had acquired that virtue from James, having pledged to never lie to people dear to her, and those she didn't care about were not worth the trouble anyway, as they would believe what they wanted.

But she did care what this woman thought, for it all seemed rather important—extremely unreal—but life and death important. SPUD. 'It's not a lie,' Ganny's voice came loud and clear, 'if it's self-defense. It's a weapon against your enemy. Believe in it, like it's a knife or a gun. Wield it carefully.'

"Why do you want to know?" Misty squeezed the outside of her thighs, trying to control the trembling. The woman briefly smiled, then her face went flat.

"Miss Grey, I represent the U.S. government. I apologize for these extreme measures. But if you could simply answer my questions, we can move on to more comfortable conditions. Now, can you recall anything agent Tallon may have given you, anything at all?"

"Agent?" Misty's face scrunched. "Who are you?"

"I am agent Larkin. Your friend, Ganny, is retired CIA. We believe she has gone rogue, working for…" The woman sighed as if stressed and tired, facing yet another long day. "I need your cooperation."

"I'd like to go home," Misty said slowly, probing to learn just what these people really wanted, and what they intended for her.

"As soon as you cooperate. This is very important, and rather urgent. Now tell me everything agent Tallon has given you."

"Tea… cookies," Misty said, her long lashes blinking back the tears trying to pool.

The woman sighed several times, glancing at a man standing behind Misty. Her face darkened as she brushed her bangs aside, exposing the single scar. "You cannot tell me anything?" Her eyes grew cold, her face like stone.

Misty shook her head.

The floor creaked and in walked the little man with his red folder under his arm. He handed it to the woman who snapped it open, sending several papers to the floor. Misty caught a glimpse of two of them as the woman huffed and leaned over to gather them. She glanced up and Misty looked away.

After studying the folder, she nodded, handing it back to the little man. A tense silence followed as she sat staring at the teen trembling before her.

"Your mother is well?" she asked in a cold monotone. "And your little brother, Maxwell?" She paused to study Misty. "And I see your father has just been released. I'm sure you're happy about that, hmm?"

Misty's eyes went wide. *Already?*

The woman leaned in close, very close, her nose just inches away. "I believe, Miss Grey, that you have not been all together truthful with me, is that correct?"

Misty just stared, struggling to keep her gaze locked on the woman's dark brown eyes. 'Never drop your head or eyes when lying,' Ganny had told her. It was hard, holding the woman's stare, her hands trembling, her face still flushed.

"You've told me everything?"

Misty nodded.

The woman glanced at the dark suit standing behind the teen girl. Without warning, the cold steel of a gun barrel pressed hard into Misty's right temple. She leaned to escape its painful point, but the barrel kept pressing until she lay almost sideways. For a moment, sheer terror filled her soul. She stared up, wide eyes pleading to the woman.

After a nod, the gun pressure eased and Misty slowly sat upright. Unable to breathe, her lungs felt stuck. Then she gulped, tears wetting her terrified eyes.

The woman looked her over one last time, finally shaking her head. "Outside," she said to the dark suit. "Behind the shed."

"What?" Misty's voice creaked, her mouth gaping. The man clutched her upper arm, his iron-like fingers digging deep into her muscle.

"But… what have I done?" She winced, his grip burning.

With a flick of her bangs, the woman left the room as the dark suit hustled Misty out the back door.

As James returned to his seat, he quickly jotted down three letters and three numbers. Whether rattled by love or by fear—probably both—the billowing dread grew into a persistent hammering. He fought hard to focus, to put his mind back on math.

Finishing the test in under fourteen minutes, he quietly approached Mrs. Barns. Assuming he had a question regarding the test, her old haggard head was already shaking with a frown.

"I wish to apologize," he said quietly, handing her his test. She looked incredulously at the handsome boy, his features like any model young man of intelligence and promise.

"You're finished?" she asked, her upper lip curling. She could have run a Nazi prison camp with only her looks and the dreaded wooden stick.

"Yes," James nodded. His heart thumped, still seeing Misty's face as she entered the car. "Misty didn't cheat," he said very quietly. "I didn't help her. She has… incredible memory, but doesn't want anyone to know." He glanced back toward the window. "I think she's…" He suddenly realized he was confiding in Captain Bane of math class #202.

"She's what?"

"Could I have permission to leave?"

"If I let you leave, I must let others, so, no." She studied his face for a moment. "Why did those men come for Marie?"

James shook his head, brain buzzing. Mrs. Barns looked down at his test. Pulling out an answer sheet, she quickly ran through his test. James waited. When she discovered it to be not only a perfect score but done in one-sixth of the given time allotment, she narrowed her aged eyes once more.

James sighed, rolling his eyes. "I didn't cheat."

She looked down at his test, and then at his hands. He turned them to reveal his sweaty, but empty palms, pulling up his sleeves to show his wrists contained no hidden answers.

"Can we talk outside?" James motioned with his head toward the hallway.

She shook her head, looking past him at the students with heads down, pencils scribbling out equations on scratch paper. After a stern look, she rose and brought a chair up to her desk motioning for James to sit. Her dark eyes narrowed with suspicion as she handed him a test sheet, the questions ranging from simple multiplication to complex fractions, ending with algebraic and calculus questions.

As she watched, James performed, using nothing but his head to solve the equations. With eyes wide, she leaned back, her mouth dangling open. After ten questions, he spun the paper for her to check his answers.

Captain Bane sat dazed. Never, in all her infinitesimal years of teaching math to students without desire or wit, had she encountered one such as James.

Finally, her lips formed a word. "Why?" she asked almost pleading. "Why have you not...?" She couldn't finish, her mouth returning to its gaping position.

"Reasons," James said, his mind on Misty. "I didn't help her, Mrs. Barns. She memorized all those numbers in..." He sighed, having already said too much. "May I go? I really think Misty's in trouble."

Shock still shrouding her face, Mrs. Barns gave a single nod. James gathered his things and slipped out, a nod of thanks as he quietly closed the door, the eye of every student watching him with wonder. A male student opened his mouth to complain, but before he could form any words, the stick of Captain Bane rose with silent finality.

Running the empty halls, James made his way to Principal Pinrick's office.

"Go right in," said her secretary, Yasmeen Amar, her smile bright.

As James entered, he stopped, perplexed at the gaunt woman, her eyes looking distant and troubled. For a moment, he stood awaiting her acknowledgment, her thoughts obviously elsewhere. Only when James took a seat, did she blink back into the present reality.

"Can I help you? You're James, the Longmire boy."

James nodded. "I… I'm concerned for Misty… Marie Grey. Is everything alright? Is it about her dad?"

Ms. Pinrick tilted her head. "What would the National Security Agency want with Marie? 'Urgent,' they said. 'Nothing terribly important,' they said. 'Just a few questions, but urgent.'" She looked extremely puzzled. "Why would they take her from school? I thought they meant here." She brushed her hand over her face. "What will I tell her parents?"

"The NSA?" James now bore the same puzzled expression, his mind scanning the pathways of logic. "Must be a mistake," he muttered. "A typo somewhere."

Together, the two sat in silence, trying to solve the riddle of Misty's disappearance. "What would they want with Misty?" he asked Ms. Pinrick, who just numbly shook her head. "What would she have that they—"

Suddenly pathways opened, streaming bits of thought down a whole new set of channels. "The pi contest?" He shook his head. "No, not the NSA."

"I heard she cheated."

James shook his head. "No, she didn't cheat. She memorized those numbers." He winced. "Could the NSA want Misty for…?" He put his hands together atop his head. "…for her memory?"

Principal Pinrick just stared at him. He stood, asking her for any information about the three men, to which she shook her head, her eyes wimpy like a little girl caught stealing bubblegum.

"Any names?" James asked.

"Yes, a Mr. Smith." She gave a single chuckle, suddenly realizing her mistake. As if pleading, she looked up at James. "Is she in trouble? Did I, did I let her go into some kind of trouble? Oh, God, should I call the police?"

James remembered the license plate number. Handing it to her, he stood while she called the local police. After about ten minutes, which seemed like an hour of nonsense, she finally hung up, saying they would send someone over to investigate.

"May I wait here?"

"Please."

Never had James seen Principal Pinrick so distraught. She had recently watched a rather gruesome documentary on human trafficking among high school girls, and so now her mind grew more and more paralyzed by the possible ramifications of her actions. This could end her career, her reputation within the community. And what of Marie Grey, the poor girl, where has she been taken?

When the police arrived, it was nothing short of a fiasco. Without James being present, nothing worthwhile would have been accomplished.

They promised to check out the plates and report back to Ms. Pinrick, thanking James for his diligent observation, but warning him to stay clear of police business. They would be contacting the parents or guardians, and so he needn't worry. The case of Marie Elsa Grey was in good hands.

When nothing more could be done, James proceeded to his next class. But his mind was elsewhere, his heart and soul wandering the streets for the only girl he would ever love.

13   TO FACE A CHARGING BULL

Misty struggled hard as the dark-suited man dragged her out the back door toward the tool shed, the sun nearing the horizon of empty fields. The air had turned chilly with pockets of warmth still lingering. Struggling over the gravel and dirt, she pleaded for mercy, for an explanation.

"What are you going to do?" she asked, his powerful grip bruising her arm. "Are you going to… shoot me?" Her words sounded strange, bizarre even.

The large man gave no reply.

"You can't shoot me, I'm just a girl. I… I…" She grappled to find a reason. "I matter to someone," she finally blurted. "A boy will miss me. Last night he said he…"

She couldn't finish, for now, a flood of tears filled her eyes, her throat closing shut. "Please, no…" she begged, tugging at his iron grip. Glancing back, Misty saw the woman watching from the window.

As they rounded the shed, Misty suddenly composed herself. In part, it was to bravely face whatever death awaited. But there was more. When the ugly times would come, when her so-called father would beat her mother, and then turn his rage on Misty, she would meet him with a face of dauntless resolve, a will of unbending iron.

The dark-suited man pushed Misty up against the shed's foundation wall. Built of old crumbling limestone, it stood just a bit higher than Misty's head. The ground behind the man slopped away into a ditch full of rusted junk and discarded machinery. Broken jars, rusted cans, and old tires lay buried amid the briars and small trees growing up through the machinery that once worked the fields.

Misty pictured the rusted machinery as if new, its metal glistening and painted, parts oiled and tuned, the owners enjoying another sunset on the farm. But like all things, it too, eventually became useless, destined for the ditch behind the tool shed, the place for garbage, for unwanted things… like teen girls who don't cooperate.

"Wait!" Misty held up both hands, her back against the stone wall. The man flicked the safety off his pistol, lowering it straight at Misty's chest. "There must be a mistake. You have the wrong girl." She stepped toward the man as if to reason with him.

Using his thumb, he cocked the hammer back.

Misty shook her head, again pleading with him.

As the man straightened his arm, the gun three feet from her chest, the girl took one more step.

Perplexed, the man hesitated.

It was all Misty needed.

With her open left hand, she swung hard, driving the man's forearm across his body as she turned aside. The barrel seemed to explode in her face, bursting her ears. A cloud of pale dust erupted from the limestone wall. But her right hand had also struck.

Grasping the barrel, Misty cranked it backward toward the man. Then with a jerk downward, she broke it free of his stocky fingers. Still grasping the barrel, she stood equally surprised as her assailant. Though she and Ganny had rehearsed this maneuver several dozen times, Misty never thought she'd be forced to actually use it.

For half a heartbeat, she just held the gun by its barrel, her ears ringing. She had shot a handgun several times, the most memorable being with James. They had snuck out with his father's 9mm and took a few shots at an old stump. She knew to hold it tight and keep her thumb clear of the recoil.

The startled man stepped toward her, but Misty now had the gun in both hands, aiming straight at his chest. Being a semiautomatic, the gun was ready to fire. The man stared wide-eyed at the girl and the barrel aimed at his beating heart.

"Careful, girlie," he said in a thick Slavic accent. "Trigger veeery touchy."

"Lay down!" Misty ordered. "On your face!" Her heart pounded like drummers going wild in her head. With both ears ringing, she stood panting, her mouth dusty dry. After a few more stern commands, the man slowly got to all fours.

"Lay flat!" Misty ordered, to which he very slowly complied. She tried to think, wishing her heart would slow down, her ears stop ringing. "Who are you people? What do you want with me?"

"I just bodyguard. Please don't shoot, little girlie."

"Who is that woman in there? Who does she work for?"

"Let me up. Then I talk, okay?"

"No! I count to five. Then I shoot." She took a deep breath. "One… two… three…"

"Wait, wait. Maybe I help you escape, huh?" He started to push himself up.

"No! Four…"

"Stop! Listen me. Shoot me, you how escape? Think you strike my face, use gun, huh? Stay here I behind shed. You go to car, drive escape. Idea good, huh? Tell woman you trick me, you run. Plan good, ya?"

Before Misty could think, the man had turned on his side. In a second he would be on his knees. Their eyes met for just a moment. This man had been ready to shoot an innocent girl. That brief look told Misty all she needed.

Holding the gun tight, she squeezed the trigger.

The pistol bucked, the sound thundering, but Misty stood firm. A cry of anguish cut the air as the man rolled to his side, hands clutching his thigh. "Dura!" he growled as Slavic curses gushed from his lips. Misty turned to run. She knew the second shot would raise concern.

Nimble feet slipping over gravel, she rounded the shed and bolted straight for the black sedan, praying the keys were by chance still inside.

Only with Ganny had she driven, and that was inside a parking lot. James had his license but no car. Misty had taken driver's ed, but only classroom. This would be her first real driving experience.

The woman and the little man had been sitting at a table, but as the second shot reached the farmhouse, Larkin rose, looking toward the tool shed. Victor, the man now rolling in misery, was supposed to take the girl's body out into the fields after dark. What was he doing?

Then her eyes widened as a young girl sprinted from the tool shed toward the black sedan.

As the two came running and cursing from the farmhouse, Misty fumbled to start the car. When lights lit up and the engine revved, she pressed the gas pedal to the floor. It sent the car into a spin, swirling rocks and gravel in all directions. When she finally faced the long driveway, she stomped the brakes with both feet, her whole body trembling.

The little man came running toward her, while agent Larkin raised a pistol and fired two shots. Glass shattered into the car, shards pelting her face. For a brief second, Misty sat stunned, clutching the wheel tight.

As a third bullet hummed through the car, Misty punched the pedal. Swerving first to the left, she knocked down a fence post of old wood. Oversteering to the right, she mowed down a row of low bushes. On her third attempt to straighten the car, she put her left side wheels into the driveway's ditch.

As another shot echoed, the black sedan barreled down the driveway, a cloud of dust billowing into the twilight sky.

When she reached the tar road, she again stomped the brake with both feet. The car squealed out onto the road, stopping a foot from the opposite edge.

"Blast it! Reverse! Reverse!"

As she reversed back onto the gravel driveway, she glanced back to see a small white sports car speeding down the driveway, followed by a gray van.

Spinning tires and spitting gravel, Misty came back up onto the road. The car lunged with loud screeching as she caught the tar and sped off, driving at speeds unsafe for any driver, let alone a newbie with terror-filled veins.

For a moment, things seemed okay. Eighty miles an hour wasn't too bad. The car bounced and floated sometimes, but the road was empty and straight.

A yellow sign with a big arrow suddenly appeared and Misty again did her double-foot stomp. With more screeching, she slid almost perfectly sideways for several hundred feet. As she let off the brakes, the car straightened out just in time to make the corner designated at thirty miles an hour.

"I can do this," Misty said in panting breath. She glanced in her mirror to the sports car speeding closer. Pressing the gas pedal once more to the floor, Misty sped out of the corner and shot due west, straight for the glowing horizon.

Nearing one hundred, the car felt at times to be flying. Misty held the wheel tight, her heart speeding at a thousand beats per minute. No matter how fast she drove, the white car seemed to be only seconds behind. The gray van had disappeared, and Misty knew the freeway would be only minutes away. If she could make it to the freeway, there'd be a good chance of getting pulled over, and thereby rescued.

An approaching car flashed its lights, signally Misty to turn hers on. But glancing at the dash while going a hundred miles an hour proved to be risky business, *very* risky business.

"Stuff that!" she shouted, seeing faint lights from the freeway two miles ahead. She glanced in the mirror, the small car now right behind.

A distant whistle blew, its long, low drone spreading over the fields. Some red lights blinked somewhere up ahead.

As she sped toward the freeway, a train loaded with coal sped south. Again the whistle blew, louder this time. The red lights shone brighter—a crossing.

Screaming in rage, Misty stomped the gas pedal, eking out anything the car had left. "Nooo!" she wailed, seeing the red and white gates begin to drop.

She glanced at the train. Then at the road. No other cars had come. Both lanes were clear. The train roared, its blast thundering. She set her jaw, panting fast and shallow.

The whistle screamed.

"Ohhh, God…"

A sudden flash of red and white shattered over the windshield. A blaring wall of black iron filled her right window.

In darkness, the world shrieked, spinning and punching and cutting. Steel screeched, the endless wail drifting into night, howling its way into deepest dark, howling with pain, so much… pain.

"What would the NSA want with Marie?" Mr. Longmire asked, his face turned toward the rental house. James had told them everything during dinner, well not everything.

"Something's not right," James kept saying.

"Mr. Grey being back is certainly not right," said Mrs. Longmire. "I don't know how they can let people like that roam the streets, and now he's back here." She shook her head. "They must go, Willaford. I won't stand for anymore—"

Even as she spoke, a din of violent yelling drifted over from the Greys' house. Mr. Grey had indeed moved back home. His 'good behavior' appeared to already be losing its façade. The shrill voice of Mrs. Grey came loud and clear. She was outside.

James rose to peer out the dining room window. His mother scolded him, saying he was to neither spy nor pry. When Willaford Longmire rose to look, the house grew silent. "Turn out the lights," he whispered, his nose to the cold glass.

Outside, Mrs. Grey stood a few feet from the rental house door. She held something in both hands, her feet shuffling backward. A loud male voice shouted something obscene, and then the shadowy form of Mr. Grey came out into the porch light.

Mrs. Grey took another step back, half crying, half shouting. A moment of silence. Then, without warning, a sudden flash of bright light burst from her hands. The window shook, as a loud thunderclap rippled far into the night.

"Oh… my… word!" exclaimed Mrs. Longmire, stumbling

backward.

A dark form fell to the rental house porch. The shadowy form of Mrs. Grey staggered back, stumbled, then dropped to her rump.

"I think… you should call the police, dear." Mrs. Longmire stood tall and stiff like a statue, her eyes staring wide without a single blink.

James couldn't move. *It's all a wild, crazy dream. It has to be.* He thought of last night, holding Misty close, of the black sedan and all the dark sunglasses. *Now this?*

He reached up and felt the locket under his shirt. He'd found it under the bed, saw it as he tucked the rope ladder back in. He pressed it, as if testing its realness.

"Misty," he whispered, still pressing the locket, "where are you? What is happening?"

15 A DIGITAL BOMB

Wednesday, October 28

As Misty opened her eyes, the white room spun, first one way, then the other. Thudding pain pumped itself into her head with every feeble heartbeat. A dull, aching pain radiated up her right leg into her hip. Bandaging wrapped her left arm and shoulder.

"Where am I?" she muttered, her lips parched and dry.

"You're awake!" A short female nurse bubbling with life walked gently into the room. "How do you feel? I'm Ellie, your nurse." She approached the bed with genuine concern. "Feel dizzy? You're in Mayfield Hospital. And you're looking good, I must say. Makes my day." She glanced at the monitor. "So how we feeling?"

A doctor soon followed, and Misty learned that she'd been brought in by a man and wife who'd seen the whole thing. The man happened to be a paramedic and so wasted no time, using his own vehicle instead of waiting for an ambulance.

"He most likely saved your life," the doctor said solemnly.

Nurse Ellie agreed. "An angel in disguise. You were lucky."

Without ID, they had first given her the pseudonym of 'Sally Jones,' hoping the police would soon learn her true identity.

"Then your mom came in," Ellie said, her smile wide. "She'll be glad to know you're awake."

"My mother?" Misty's shock was obvious.

The doctor undid the wrap from her left arm, examining the

upper arm and shoulder. "Severely bruised," he said, "but nothing broken." It looked terrible—dark blue and swollen. "Surprising really," he added, saying she would need only a sling if she promised to be careful. Her right leg and hip were badly bruised and swollen as well, with a long, thin laceration on her thigh that needed numerous stitches.

"How do you feel?" he asked, looking closely at a gash wound above her right eye.

Alone and afraid, hurting everywhere, wishing… wishing… oh, God. "Okay, I guess," is all she said.

"Twelve stitches in this one," he said, nodding to the gash wound. "Sixty-two in your thigh, if you're one to brag." He studied her with a look of pity, then nodded toward her thigh. "You lost a good deal of blood. You were lucky."

"How long have I been here?" Misty asked.

"It's Wednesday afternoon. You arrived Monday evening." He smiled briefly. "Sorry, no Tuesday for you."

"My… mother is here?"

"They just called her," nurse Ellie said, her smile jubilant. "She's on her way."

As they left the room, Misty tried to eat, her mind full of questions, her heart full of yearnings, yearning for the arms of James to hold her tight and tell her everything would be alright.

It all felt so strange. Him doing what he did. Then the next day, him coming to Ganny's, searching for her. She didn't know what to think, let alone how to act. Then his words at lunch.

For what seemed a long time she sat waiting, wondering. It would be good to see her mother, but… *Was he back? Was he really out? Oh God, will he come here?*

"Marie!" A sharp voice broke the stillness. "My goodness, you're awake!" Misty turned to look, her lungs sucking in a sharp gasp. In the doorway, a slender woman with straight black hair and thin lips, stood dressed in everyday clothes, a small scar marring her forehead.

"Nooo," Misty tried to slink beneath the covers, but agent Larkin raced in, expressing her joy as rambunctiously as possible.

"We've been worried sick over you. How do you feel? Ready to go home?" A large thug in plain clothes went to the end of her bed, his face stern, one hand inside his jacket.

Misty couldn't breathe, her mouth and limbs useless. Only her head moved side-to-side, her eyes staring in dread.

Agent Larkin quickly took the seat next to the bed. "They said we could take you home any time. Isn't that wonderful?" Leaning in close, she whispered, "Say you're ready to leave, or you die, right here, right now." She opened her hand to reveal a small syringe. "Few drops on those lovely lips and you suddenly have organ failure, internal damage previously undetected. Understand?" Her tone darkened, her eyes glaring.

Misty forced a nod, then glanced toward the door.

"Don't even think of it. I thoroughly informed them of your... *condition*." Larkin smiled a sickening grin. "You know, your delusional tendencies, imaginary enemies, schizo-paranoia." She softly chuckled. "So, you ready to go *home*?"

A wave of nausea came hard and fast. She winced, suppressing a heave. Slinking down she pulled the covers toward her mouth. Her desperate eyes watched the thug withdraw his hand, revealing a pistol with a suppressor. Larkin gave him a quick scowl.

"Why don't you tell them you're ready to leave, okay, my little sweetie. I brought you some clothes." She looked at the bandaged wound above Misty's right eye. "Trying to best me?" she asked, her voice strange, as if she were serious. Then she flashed a scornful grin. "Shall we?"

Before Misty knew what was happening, a car door opened, and in she went, with Larkin quickly scooting in beside. Misty fought to stay strong, her leg and hip screaming. Both the doctor and nurse Ellie watched with deep concern, things feeling off, but what could they do? She's a troubled girl with mental issues, best not interfere.

For a few blocks, they rode in silence, then the woman, sitting to Misty's right, burst into a tirade of foul cursing and irate screams, mostly over wrecking the Cadillac. Then came stern warnings of trying any more 'lame-brain stunts' or she would 'suffer something worse than death,' all of it spewing out like toxic waste from an industrial plant.

To Misty, it was nothing new, for it was like having her... having Mr. Grey back. So she just sat, thankful it was only verbal, her worried thoughts on her mom and Max.

She testified against him. Misty winced as she thought of what could be happening. *Is he beating her, hitting Max? Why would they let him out?*

"Do you hear me?" shouted agent Larkin. "No games this time, kiddo."

"No games," Misty muttered, her stare blank.

The thug, Carloff, took a turn rather sharply and agent Larkin lashed out as Misty fell over into the woman.

"You are trash to me, girl. You understand? I don't have time for this." She let loose a string of vulgarity uncommon for even the crudest of women. "If this comes back to me..." She shook her head at Misty. "I'll do more than just kill you, understand?"

For a time they rode in silence, but then the woman began to mutter with frustration. "You've cost me valuable time," she said sternly. "We are so close."

"Close... to what?" Misty asked, surprised at herself.

Larkin scowled, then huffed. "We've hacked them all," she said, her tone cocky. "Utilities—hydro, oil, even nuclear. Banks, corporations, manufacturing, all of them. Every stupid little peon's credit card." She chuckled. "And when the big heads in Washington see us waltzing through their systems..." She burst into laughter. "My god, it gives me tingles."

Under the assumption that Misty would be dead within the

hour, she spoke somewhat freely, or rather boasted, telling the girl snippets of what they had planned.

She was CIA, but 'not in spirit,' her grudge toward the organization clearly deep and personal. "They will beg," she said disdainfully, "beg for help. But we will have it all."

"All what?" Misty asked, again surprised at her boldness.

Larkin scowled at her as if she were some pig or goat with whom she was forced to coexist.

"They're total morons," she said. "Don't even see it coming. Even old Coppy's in on it. Go figure."

"See what? What are you after?" Misty asked, this time tensing for a blow. But Larkin only shifted to study the girl.

"You're going to die, you know." She twisted her face with disgust. "Are you just stupid? Don't you get it? You're not getting away this time."

Misty sat silent as they pulled off the freeway, making their way back to the farmhouse. Her insides soured, twisting into hard knots.

Larkin had pulled out a small notebook and thumbed through a few pages. When she saw Misty looking, she at first tucked it close. Then she gave her distinctive single huff.

"We've gotten inside," she said, "inside everything. We wrote Whisper." She laughed outright. "My god, they're stupid."

"Whisper?" Misty asked.

Larkin shook her head, giving Misty a cynical glare. "You sure are a nosey little twert."

"If you're going to kill me... at least tell me why." Misty struggled to say all that, her voice cracking as she blinked back tears.

Larkin shook her head but then turned to face the teen. "We're going to destroy the nation, its economy, infrastructure, electricity, water, all of it in a single night. A digital bomb." She smirked. "Then hold our beloved nation for ransom, demanding all its gold." She paused to study Misty's face, her gaze resting on the plush lips. "Now shut up."

She went back to leafing through her notebook, no longer shielding it from Misty's gaze. When they pulled onto the gravel driveway, she tucked it away.

"But why kill me?" Misty asked, her pleas desperate, her voice quavering, dreadful fear rushing her veins. "What have I done to you?"

"It's what you *haven't* done," Larkin said, already undoing her seatbelt. "Just give me what Tallon gave you and your home free."

"Nothing," Misty said, her voice about to break. "I swear, nothing." She took a trembling breath. "Why would Ganny—?"

Larkin spun to face her, hand poised to strike. "Because your little Ganny has poked her scrawny nose where it doesn't belong." She slapped Misty's wounded leg, ringing out a terrible cry. "But that loose end has been tied up tight!" She spoke with vengeful glee, giving Misty's thigh a firm squeeze.

"They won't give it to you," Misty said, teeth clenched, fighting back tears.

Larkin stiffened, both startled and amused by the girl's defiance. "We have everything," she said, her face stern, yet beaming with pride. Withdrawing the leather notebook, she opened it to show a typed page of letters and numbers, letting Misty see it for a few seconds.

"It will all shutdown, all of it," the woman said. "And they will beg." She paused to look Misty over. "A new age is coming, the age of enlightenment."

As they came to a stop in front of the old farmhouse, Misty's gaze lingered on a host of digits. She drew in a quick breath, seeing several sets listed beneath the capital letters—NORAD.

When Misty stumbled into the old farmhouse, pushed by Carloff, she stopped in sudden horror. On the floor, bleeding and bruised, lay Ganny, her hands and feet tied, her mouth dripping red. The little man stood over her, his face livid, a long leather strap in his quivering hand.

He spit as agent Larkin entered the living room, cursing the older woman at his feet.

"Well?" demanded Larkin. The little man shook his head, beads of sweat glistening on his brow.

Cursing, Larkin marched over to Ganny, and with a kick to her ribs, shouted a string of vulgarity, vowing to make her death as slow and painful as humanly possible.

Misty's legs went weak at the sight. How could they beat an old woman like Ganny? What could they want with her? *This is all a mistake.*

When Ganny caught sight of Misty, her eyes shut for a moment, as if in remorseful prayer. Then she spoke to agent Larkin, a feeble whisper, but a signal of cooperation.

"Promise me… you'll let her go… let her live," Ganny pleaded, offering information in exchange.

Larkin just listened.

Misty shook her head, knowing that whatever they promised, they would most certainly kill them both.

Ganny asked that a car take Misty home, where the girl would call, assuring her safety. Misty would promise to speak of this to no one, and Ganny would give any and all information.

"All I want to know," said the woman, "is if you've blown the whistle on our party. Who did you notify at the agency? Spears? Dunkin?"

Ganny shook her head. "Please let her go. She knows nothing."

Larkin huffed. "She knows now. Gave her the ringside view." She put her foot on Ganny's neck. "Who else knows?" she demanded.

"Kill me," said Ganny, "but let the girl live. She can't harm your scheme. Hold her… till you've… ruined the world, then what will she matter?"

Ganny's voice came out weak and desperate, her lips swollen and bleeding.

Misty forced back a sudden heave, her desperate voice now pleading with the woman. "What do you want with her?" Misty cried. "She's not what you think. She's no agent." The sight of Ganny, her face bruised and swollen, seemed to suck all traces of hope and life from Misty's gut.

For a moment, Larkin just looked back and forth between the two, her eyes cold and calculating, hands clenching and opening, her jaw set firm. Quick and strong, she came to Misty and grasped a lock of her hair. Yanking the girl's head backward, Larkin spoke with nostrils flaring.

"Tell me now, hag, or watch me trim the little wretch, starting with these plump, juicy lips." She held a knife in her hand, its shiny blade moving quickly toward Misty's face. Trembling, Misty stared at the knife, its sharp edge now touching her lower lip. She struggled to stand still.

"Please," Ganny begged the woman, "she's only a girl. Have mercy."

"It's your call, Tallon. Talk or watch… your call." The knife pressed hard under Misty's lip. The blade was cold against her smooth skin. She suddenly gasped, jerking backward. A sharp pain burned beneath her lip. Drops of blood hit the wooden floor. For a moment, Misty's lungs had failed, her eyes blurring with tears.

"I'll talk!" Ganny struggled with her bonds. "Let her go. I'll talk."

With a vicious shove, Larkin sent Misty stumbling across the room. She landed hard in a corner, her wounded leg striking the wall. Bits of loose plaster tumbled off where peeling wallpaper hung as if in shame.

"I told them," Ganny said quietly. "They know of your plans."

"Told who?" Larkin stepped closer.

Ganny knew they would kill whomever she named, kill them as quickly as possible. They had people on the inside. She knew some of them, but not all. She had actually told no one, for she had only pieced it all together on Sunday evening. She had tried to contact her handler but knew they were listening. Monday morning, just after Misty left, they had come.

"Told who?" Larkin gave Ganny another kick.

"Stop it!" Misty screamed. "Stop hurting her!"

Carloff pulled out his pistol, pointing it straight at Misty's head. The blood from her lip dribbled down her chin onto the white linen shirt Larkin had given her, a nice material with a satin feel. Over it she wore a fine cream-colored sweater and a soft shimmering jacket.

Cursing Misty, agent Larkin watched the blood drip. "You're ruining my blouse."

Ganny groaned. "I got a message to Benson," she uttered in obvious pain. "But she didn't believe me."

Larkin waited for more, drawing her leg back for another kick. Ganny shook her head. "All the proof is at my house."

"We searched the house," Larkin said coldly. "Nothing."

"It's hidden." Ganny moaned as she spoke.

"Where?"

"Promise you'll let her go, after it's over."

"Okay, I promise. Hidden where?"

"You're lying."

"So are you. Kill them both. And don't mess up this time."

As Carloff lowered his gun to drag Ganny to her feet, Larkin went over to Misty with her hand out.

"My jeans and jacket," she said coldly. "Keep the shirt and sweater, seeing you've ruined them." She groaned with annoyance, cussing the girl even more. Misty stood in shock. The woman pulled off the stylish jacket, careful not to let any of Misty's blood touch the fabric. She then nodded at the jeans. "Come on, hurry up. You won't be needing those. Too nice for your likes anyway."

Misty fumbled with the leather belt, her trembling hands useless, so Larkin undid the buckle with a huff. Carloff held Ganny up like holding a large doll. They stood at the door waiting.

When the jeans were half off, the little man's cell phone rang. Seeing the caller, he quickly handed the phone to Larkin. She stared at the number for a moment, licking her lips.

"Larkin here." She paused to listen for a while. "What do you mean? Why? No, you don't need to… we're fine. We don't need… Yes, sir." She hung up with another string of expletives spewing from her thin lips. "The idiot wants to check up on things. On his way. Take them to the basement. Get the place ready."

Misty quickly pulled her jeans back up, her eyes locked on Ganny. After a shove toward a door, they were soon going down a rickety staircase into a damp, musty basement with old stone walls of crumbling mortar and endless spiderwebs.

No one had passed through lately and so Misty with her bushy head of hair walking in the lead swept the cobwebs like a dust mop. At first, she tried to pull them off, but Carloff shouted to keep moving.

Soon they were tied up tight to a crooked wooden post, a support made from a tree with its bark shaved. With their backs to the post, their hands and feet were zip-tied, while a sock got shoved in each mouth followed by several wraps of duct tape going all the way around their heads.

"You no make sounds," Carloff said, chuckling as he ripped the roll of tape, jerking Misty's head to the side. "Stop bleeding, ha?" He gave Misty a rough pat on the head. He then dusted off an old metal chair with torn vinyl padding and sat with his eyes fastened on the attractive teen.

He smiled. "Legs good. Wish see more the legs. You show maybe more the later, ha?"

Misty shivered. Ganny softly squeezed her hands. Having the post between them, only their hands touched. As sad as it all seemed, it felt good to feel Ganny's hand.

The room was a small back cellar, mostly bare but for a simple workbench with shelving above, and a large chest freezer meant for holding a few years' supply. The floor was old concrete, loose and crumbly. Dust covered everything as did the cobwebs. Tears trailed Misty's cheeks, one side following the duct tape to seep down beside her ear.

Her heart ached for Ganny, who moaned with every labored breath. Fierce hatred roiled, Misty's heart pounding as she stared at the brute ogling her. She had learned raw hatred from her home, torn between the urge to kill and respect the man known to her now as Mr. Grey.

He is no longer my father. How could they let him out?

The damp basement grew cold, the floor even colder. The rough post had a bump right in Misty's upper back. The zip-ties were so tight her fingers grew numb. Carloff just sat, fiddling with his gun, pulling the clip out and pushing it in, undoing the suppressor to then screw it back on.

Twenty minutes passed, maybe more.

When Misty thought she could endure no longer, footsteps tromped and shuffled overhead, mixing with voices. It was hard to make out what was being said, but Carloff filled in the details.

"Boss of she-devil," he whispered. "Fat man, fat head, stupid like that post." He nodded to the post holding the captives. "No clue they doing here in house." He smiled wide, proud of the deception.

When the footsteps went outside and the house grew quiet, he told them how Larkin was assigned to watch a potential terrorist cell, a cell they themselves had set up so they could be positioned here near the towers. The second story housed a control center of computers and networks, all preparing for the 'bomb.'

"Be real freaky Halloween," he said with a sneer. "When kiddies trick the treat, U.S. become… *history*." He chuckled, trying to make eyes with Misty. He then explained how the plan was to strike commerce sites one minute after midnight, followed by power and utilities, then the government.

Through the fog of physical pain and a heart chock-full of agony, Misty tried to focus. *If today is Wednesday… oh God, that's three days!*

"You have the credit card?" he asked Misty. She shook her head. "If you have it, your numbers they have. Everybody's number. Work long time. Now big Whitehouse numbers have." He smiled wide, glancing once more at Misty's legs.

He was about to say more when footsteps returned overhead. This time the voices were only those of Larkin and the little man. Carloff stood and cracked his neck.

"I'll be bauck," he said, trying to imitate the *Terminator* line. Then he left the room to walk the dank basement, his heavy boots trudging up the rickety stairs.

Without delay, Ganny worked with her hands. Misty cried out as a sharp metal object poked her palm. Although muffled and gagged, Ganny's command was clear. "Quiet!"

In half a minute, Misty's hands were free. She spun around to see Ganny, still bound, holding a small pin between her fingers. Misty took the pin and loosened the zip-tie, something Ganny had taught her some time ago, another thing she thought she would never, ever have to use.

She then carefully tried to unwrap the duct tape off Ganny, but the woman shook her head, nodding toward a small boarded window just above the old freezer. She helped Ganny to her feet, then hopped atop the freezer. Kneeling, she pulled at the plywood covering the window. Cobwebs stuck to every hair on her head, clinging to her nose and lashes. One finger already bled, its nail torn.

She wanted to free her mouth, but Ganny grunted, wagging her head. When the woman came back from the workbench with a small pipe smashed on one end, Misty used it as a pry bar, popping a nail out an inch or more. The plywood creaked as she worked the other corner. They both paused, listening, then Ganny nodded for her to continue.

After what seemed like a dreadful eternity, Misty got enough of the plywood loose to yank it free. Exposing an old window so dirty and full of dried out insects, only faint light streamed through. She worked the rusty latch and opened the frail window. Dust rained down from the crumbling mortar above.

Dried weeds filled the small indent outside. It would be a feat climbing out but was doable. Ganny had her duct tape off and with an angry spit, sent the wet sock rolling into a cobweb-infested corner. She undid Misty's gag, yanking the last. The girl cried out with lips tight, shaking her head at the pain. The cut beneath her lip, though small, burned sharp.

Ganny took a second to examine it. "We've little time," she whispered. "We must escape. We need a car."

"Tried that."

"What?" Ganny looked with amazement.

"I was here. They were going to shoot me," Misty said. "I got away, but…"

Ganny nodded, now understanding the bandages.

"Climb out. Quick!"

Pulling at the weeds and grass outside while Ganny pushed from below, Misty finally squeezed through. She quickly turned, leaning back into the window to help Ganny out.

"Where's your locket?" Ganny asked, seeing it gone. "Did they take it?"

Misty shook her head. "Sorry, Ganny. I lost it."

The stairs creaked, then came the voices of Larkin and Carloff.

"Run!" Ganny whispered. "Call this number." She rattled off a string of numbers, giving a code name and a contact with earnest orders to find the locket. "You must get the locket to Bellows. Trust no one but Bellows! Now go!"

For a moment, Misty couldn't move. She knew that the car she had arrived in still sat outside the front door. The memories of the frantic chase still burned painfully clear.

"Not without you!"

Ganny shook her head. The voices drew closer. They would be in the backroom in seconds.

"You must do this. Promise me you'll try. I'll stall them. Go!"

With a word of sincere promise and a painful last glance, Misty left the dear woman who had taught her so much.

Convinced they would kill Ganny, she raced to the car, eyes blurring. Every ounce of flesh protested, her leg and hip screaming with pain. The climb out the window seemed to have torn something in her shoulder. Now it hurt so bad, she feared she'd pass out.

Stumbling several times, she finally turned the corner and stopped. Just ten feet away, leaning on the car near the driver's door, was the little man lighting up a cigarette, his elbow on the side mirror.

Misty froze.

He glanced her way, a look of confused surprise twisting his ugly little face.

Misty bolted, her mind now seeing the little man standing over Ganny, his leather strap in hand. Then she saw her father with his leather belt, his drunken bulk looming above her fallen mother.

Before she knew what happened, the man lay backward, his head having struck the windshield. Misty stood panting, fist raised. But the man didn't move, his head wedged in with the wiper blade.

Did I kill him? Chest heaving, she held her arm back, still poised to strike again. Glancing to the farmhouse, she listened. From the basement window, faint shouts mixed with torturous cries. Her eyes narrowed, now on the lifeless man sprawled over the hood, a pistol glinting beneath his suit coat.

Panting two breaths, she then lowered her arm. Another breath. More cries from the basement. She winced. *Oh, Ganny!* Grabbing the gun, she scrambled into the car.

Fumbling, trembling, she turned the key. Her eyes darted upward, expecting bullets to once more shatter the glass, to scream through like demons of terror.

Slower this time!

But her foot stomped, revving the engine into full roar. And like before, gravel sprayed, the rear fish-tailing as she spun out. Swerving wildly, she cranked the wheel, eyes on the long driveway.

Oh, God! she gasped, the little man now sliding off, tumbling over the gravel. But her face tightened, the image of him beating…

Focus!

She clutched the wheel, trying to stop the stupid trembling. This car handled better than the Cadillac, faster with more control. She checked the mirror, surprised to see the driveway empty.

"Oh, Ganny…" she cried, blinking back tears.

Breathing crazy hard, she squealed onto the main road. Tires bounced and caught the tar, lurching her forward. "Better," she breathed out, pleased to have made it first try. "Now keep it under…" She glanced at the dash, searching for the right dial. She winced, hissing through clenched teeth. Three knuckles bled as she clutched the wheel, hot, sharp pain screaming from everywhere.

Approaching the railroad crossing her whole body stiffened, locking up as if frozen. Using both feet, she stomped the brake. Still loud within her memory, the whistle blew, the car spun, then pain… so much pain.

How long she sat stopped in the road, fear-filled eyes staring at the crossing, she didn't know. Both feet held the brake pedal firm to the floor, her lungs breathing way too fast.

Then the voice of Ganny drifted through the foggy mist, hearing her own voice reply with a promise.

"For you, Ganny," she said, forcing her feet off the brake. When she crossed the tracks and finally turned onto the freeway, she deeply wished it were all just a long horrible nightmare.

"Did I really do it?" She fought to keep the car in one lane, to keep its speed equal with those driving beside her. "Oh, Ganny," she moaned, heart still pounding, the little man's pistol on the seat beside her.

"Blast it!" she cried out, suddenly realizing her mistake. "Stupid signs!" Home was north. She had taken the southbound ramp. Glancing in her mirror, she wondered. If they were following, they would go north, maybe. "Might be my best dumb mistake ever." It was just after three in the afternoon, a partly sunny day, chilly and crisp.

Tears again filled her eyes. "Oh, Ganny, where do I go?" She replayed the woman's last words. "A phone, I need to find a phone… and my locket."

For over an hour she drove south, shivering in her bloodstained shirt and sweater, trying to figure out the temperature controls. After several dangerous swerves, she finally got the hang of freeway driving to safely get some heat.

Several times she passed exits with gas stations and restaurants, but she never felt far enough away. When the 'empty' light came on with a little ding, which startled her, she realized what she had to do.

Pulling into a large station, she sort of parked the car, diagonally taking up two spaces.

For some time she just sat, but then rummaged through the car, looking for any cash or change. Three pennies, two dimes, one quarter.

She closed her eyes, squishing back tears. Ganny's face, bruised and swollen, stared up from the basement. 'Call this number, speak only with agent Bellows.'

Mustering her strength, she tucked the gun under her seat and entered the store, her leg sending stabs of pain with every step.

"I need to make a phone call," she told the twenty-some girl working the checkout. "Can you—"

"Pay phone's outside," the young woman said without looking up.

"I don't have… it's really important."

"Yup, always is. Phone's outside."

"No, I need help." She glanced back, expecting to see agent

Larkin or Carloff. "I need… isn't there a phone I can use?"

The woman finally looked up. She stared at the auburn hair full of cobwebs and the bandaged forehead. Then at the bloodstained shirt and sweater, finally resting on the crusted cut beneath Misty's lip. Two customers had already formed behind the beleaguered girl.

"What happened to you?" the twenty-some asked.

"There's a bunch of…" Misty looked about at the people lining up behind. *Where'd they come from so fast?* "Can I just use your phone?"

The young woman shook her head, a wary look on her face.

After a bit more pleading, Misty turned to leave.

"Here, use mine."

She looked up at a young man holding out his phone. As if straight from a GQ magazine, the well-dressed college-type gave a simple nod, extending his hand closer.

For a moment, Misty just stood looking into his eyes. She had heard of angels helping people, the stories sometimes saying they were handsome young men. She continued staring, his cologne intriguing, heavenly even.

"Are you an a—?" She caught herself and then timidly took the phone.

"You okay?" he asked, drawing her aside from the checkout line. Concern covered his face. "What happened? Need a ride or something?"

"No, just need to make…" She fumbled with the smartphone, her hands trembling, left arm throbbing.

"Oh, sorry," the young man said, taking her hand into his so he could type the unlock code. "Try that."

She looked again into his eyes, a greenish-blue with thick brows and strong lines. Late teens, early twenties, sharp, polite, seemed smart. Nicely dressed, straight back, rather tall and very… attractive.

"You can call now." He smiled with a nod toward his phone. "Need help dialing?"

"No… I can dial." Misty stepped away toward the ATM in the corner. Dialing the number given by Ganny, her heart sped even more.

"Section twelve," a kind female voice answered.

"Hello?"

"Section twelve," came the voice again.

"Is Mr…" For a moment, Misty actually forgot. "Is Mr…" Her heart surged with panic. "My God, I can't remember. That's never happened."

"I think you have the wrong number. Goodbye."

Misty stood in shock, her mouth agape.

"Can I help?" the young man asked, his concern deepening. She looked up into the beautiful eyes.

"No, no, I just…" She dialed again. "Is agent Bellows there, please?"

"Who's calling?"

"Calling on behalf of Ganny, no, agent Tallon. It's urgent."

"Tallon?" The woman's voice rose with surprise. "Sorry, you must have the wrong number."

"No, wait! Code name, indigo bunting."

A long pause followed. "One moment please." Several beeps and then a click.

"Bellows here. Who's this?"

"I'm Misty." She glanced at the handsome man, then turned away. "I'm a friend of… agent Tallon, I think. I know her as Mrs. Quinn. She's in trouble, if not already…" She glanced over her shoulder to see the handsome man listening intently, his face perplexed. She took a few more steps toward the restrooms in the back.

"There's a plot, they call it their digital bomb. They've hacked a ton of numbers, a program—"

"Who are *they*? Where are you calling from? Is this your phone?"

"I'm in… ahh…" She looked back to see the young man still with her but not as close.

"Interstate thirty-five, Koffen exit," he said, his face now seriously perplexed.

"I'm near Koffen," she said, giving him a questioning look. She stared for a moment. "Um, just off thirty-five."

"What state? Never mind, we found you. Stay put. I'll have someone there in forty-five. Talk to no one. Stand by the ATM. He'll ask for a cigarette. Answer, 'I quit years ago.'"

"I'm only sixteen."

"Just give that reply. Got it?"

"Got it."

"Stay put! Talk to no one!"

Bewildered, Misty handed the phone back to the young man. He lightly pulled a string of cobweb from her hair.

With furrowed brow he watched her, eyes going from bandaged forehead to lips and the dried cut beneath, then the red stain on the blouse. "Can I get you something?"

Misty shook her head, glancing to the ATM.

"You sure? A drink, some pizza? Bandages?"

Again, Misty shook her head. She was to talk with no one and wait by the ATM. "Thanks, for… letting me use your phone." She looked away, trying to hide the pain. But her hands trembled as she glanced nervously about.

He stood watching, now very concerned.

"What if you go clean up," he offered. "I'll get you a sandwich and a hot drink. Coffee, hot chocolate?"

It did sound good. He did seem nice, nice like James. *James… I miss you.* Her eyes misted over as she turned toward the bathroom, giving the attractive young man a simple nod.

"Sounded mysterious." The young man, Roman Whitehall, or 'Caesar' to his friends, sipped a coffee as Misty ate rather aggressively the ham and cheese sandwich. He'd bought a box of Band-Aids and some ointment for her lip, offering to apply both, but Misty refused, using the restroom mirror instead.

She cried when she studied her bruised face, her head having several tender spots, the bandage on her forehead dirty from the basement escapades. Dark rings circled her eyes, her hair a tangled mess. If she weren't waiting for whomever Bellows sent, she may have never left the restroom.

"You a spy or something?" Roman asked with a disarming smile, his teeth perfect, his cheeks and jaw perfect, the glint in his eyes…

For a moment, Misty just sat staring. Then his question registered, bringing a startled twitch.

"No… no, but… I can't… well, you know."

"No, I don't know, but that's okay. How's the sandwich? Want another?"

Misty wiped her mouth, blushing as she sipped the hot chocolate. "Thanks. I really appreciate this. I'll repay you." She kept glancing at the door each time it opened, which was quite frequent, and her foot refused to stop tapping.

They talked little, with Misty working hard to keep her answers innocuous. Roman didn't pry, which Misty found amazing, especially with him hearing things like 'code name, Indigo bunting.'

Finally he asked with genuine concern, "Can I ask what happened? I mean, you look a mess, no offense, just, are you in trouble? Need help? Live nearby?"

"No, I'm from…"

A man had entered and now milled about the ATM, his eager gaze searching the convenience store. He wore dark jeans and boots, a thin leather coat with a slight bulge at the back of his right hip.

Misty slowly rose, a look of apprehension on her face as she looked back at Roman.

"Your contact?" he asked.

Misty shrugged, doubtful anguish darkening her face.

"I'll stay close," Roman said. "Just holler if something's off."

Nodding, she stepped toward the man who seemed a bit edgy. She advanced with tiny steps, pretending to need the ATM, but then just stood nearby, watching him.

Has it been forty-five minutes?

He looked her way as Misty stood stiff, her large green eyes staring like a frightened child.

"Do you have a cigarette?" he said, stepping up close, his dark eyes looking her over. He smelled of cigarette smoke, and Misty wondered. *Had it even been a half-hour?* She stood staring. *Is this real?*

He glanced around, then studied her close. "Do you… have a cigarette?" he asked again.

"No… I quit years ago."

The man, mid-thirties, glanced side-to-side, then whispered for Misty to follow.

Shooting an anxious glance to Roman, Misty followed the man out the door. She saw Roman rise as they walked past the windows toward a dark van with the engine running.

Every nerve hummed, her mind fighting a thousand scary thoughts. *Trust no one. Talk only to Bellows. Had it been forty-five minutes?*

Her hand trembled as she touched the small bandage on her

lower lip, her leg throbbing as she hustled to keep up. *It's okay. He's just early. He knew the password.*

"Hop in!"

After a little shove, Misty found herself inside the back of a van full of electronic equipment. The driver glanced back, looking Misty over.

They pulled away and took the freeway north. Before even a mile had passed, Misty felt suddenly sick, her whole insides tightening into painful nausea. *The sandwich?* she wondered, clutching her gut. Then everything swirled as thick fog filled her brain. "Nooo…" she muttered, struggling to breathe, her body floating, her skin numb. Then all around her spun into a deep, murky darkness.

Roman peered out the store window watching the most interesting girl he had ever met leave without even a last name or number. She had a unique, surreal kind of beauty, almost dream-like, even with all the cobwebs and dirt. He chided himself. *A bit young for you, cowboy.*

"Something's off," he muttered, discreetly snapping a picture of the van and its back plate. "What's she into? Being trafficked?"

A middle-aged man in a dark suit and trench coat walked briskly up to the glass door. Being right there, Roman pulled it open.

Without a nod or thank you, the man went straight for the ATM. He spun around, scanning the convenience store, his eyes tight and urgent. He surveyed Roman with a single scan, turning to walk toward the bathrooms.

"She's gone," Roman called after him, skin prickling.

The man spun about, narrowing his eyes even more. "Who are you?"

"She used my phone. Some guy came and took her in a van."

The man stiffened, studying Roman, his gaze now even more

intense. "Which way?" he demanded. "You see 'em leave?"

Roman opened his phone as he described the guy and the van, showing him the photo.

After a muttered cuss, the man read off the plate, then pulled out his own phone.

"They just left," Roman said. "You could catch them. They went north."

He gave Roman a scrutinizing glare. "Who are you?"

"She's kind of battered… and really scared."

The man looked about. "North? You sure?"

Roman nodded. "Can I come with?"

"What? No!"

The man hustled back to his car and sped off. Roman was already on his tail by the time he reached the entrance ramp. Keeping distance, the youth followed with wonder and excitement, hoping he hadn't actually messed things up more.

Entering the freeway, the man's car left a smoky cloud as he punched the car into high speed. Roman followed, his BMW accelerating with little effort. But when speeds exceeded ninety-five miles an hour, he let it go. His father would never approve. Although raised to be a gentleman, always willing to rescue a damsel in distress, going this fast was simply stupid.

With reluctance he slowed, watching the car speed into the distance. He would follow, for he was heading north anyway, and who knows, maybe there'd be some action when the two forces met, whoever they were.

"She's in trouble," he said, scolding himself. "Should have done more."

After only several minutes, a roaring overhead startled him. He peered up through the windshield as a black tactical helicopter zoomed low. Within seconds it slowed to follow a group of cars a mile or two ahead.

"Whoa, that's not normal." Roman sped to pass a line of cars, all decreasing speed, for they too had been startled by the sudden roar. He pulled out his phone, ready to capture the action.

If young Roman Whitehall had known what lay ahead, he would have spun his car around and never looked back.

A flash of light, followed by billowing smoke, rose from the horizon up ahead. Roman swung his visor over to block the low sun. Thick black smoke swirled upward in a mushroom cloud, its dark silhouette clear against the sky.

"That's not just smoke," Roman said, his heart quickening even more. Traffic had slowed as he neared the billowing column, the right lane almost blocked. Roman zoomed along the shoulder until he saw what he had feared.

Twisted and belching out flame, lay the car of the middle-aged man. Upside-down in the ditch, its frame looked oddly mangled. The black van was nowhere in sight.

For a moment, Roman just looked on, his car idling on the shoulder. Three men were moving cautiously toward the burning vehicle, one with a fire extinguisher at ready.

Roman shook his head, a trembling fear rushing through him. No one could have survived that. He pictured the young girl nervously glancing about the store, her foot ceaselessly tapping. "What are you into?" he pondered aloud, his mind searching.

Figuring others had already called 911, he drove off, continuing north, heart now racing.

"They took her!" he said, smacking the steering wheel. "The bad guys took her." He then shook his head, eyes scanning the road far ahead. "No, it's none of your business. Let it go."

He sighed, breathing fast through his nose, his car now passing all others. "She's only a kid. Sixteen, seventeen at most."

He swerved to pass a truck and trailer. "*Bad* guys? What am I talking about? What am I *doing*? This is serious, deadly serious. A missile… from a chopper!" He suddenly slowed to flow with the traffic, his phone still in his hand.

Then, on impulse, he pushed redial.

"Section twelve."

"Yeah, you just got a call from a girl, code name was ah, indigo bunting, maybe. I think she's been kidnapped. I think the guy you sent has been… murdered. Hello? Are you still there?"

"Hold on, please."

Roman was no dummy, in fact, he was top of his class, a junior in law school. Two forces wanted this girl or the info she had. Whoever this was on the other end, had someone listening in. And now they had his voice, his number, his location.

"Bellows here. What the heck is going on?"

Roman quickly told him everything he observed. When he described the chopper and the explosion, Bellows went silent.

"Are you still there?" Roman asked.

"Yes."

"They must be listening in," Roman said. "They were at the ATM in less than half an hour."

"Hmm."

"What should I do?" Roman asked, his voice rising.

"Turn around and go home. And get rid of that phone, immediately! Pretend this never happened. Understand?"

Roman slowed, his mind racing.

"Do you understand? Do not pursue them. Go home!"

"Yes sir, but what about the girl, Misty?"

"Go home!"

The call went dead and Roman drove in silence. Then he quickly disabled the GPS on his phone, wondering if that would be enough. Home was this way. His heart pounded hard. That chopper had come and gone so fast. He glanced at his phone. The fun was gone. "This is real," he said, breathing hard, "too stinking real."

The sound of a chopper rose in the distance. Roman lowered

his window, his arm poised to throw the phone. Then, with heart pounding, he scribbled down the number just called. When the phone left his hand, the chopper could be seen up ahead. Within seconds it passed over, slower this time, slow like a shark searching for prey.

Roman tried to swallow, his throat suddenly dry, mouth sticky. Like a man on the gallows, he awaited death. Why, why had he been so stupid? *She's not your problem!*

The chopper moved on, making its way south. After ten minutes and no sign of the chopper, Roman began to chide himself.

"Well, that was stupid! I just threw my phone out the window. Probably all some huge mistake, some convoluted mix-up. Got played," he grumbled, his heart still beating fast.

He drove in silence for a while, his brain searching. "Forget the whole thing," he finally said, shaking his head. But the girl with frizzy auburn hair, beautiful eyes, and very intriguing lips would not go away. She was in trouble and he had a strange, powerful urge to help her.

Without his phone, he felt a bit lost. After an hour, he was downright mad. "Why in fate's fire did I throw out my phone? Was that car even the same one? Maybe it just went off the road, rolled, and caught fire. Driving so darn fast."

The miles passed as he cruised along, thoughts and feelings wrestling hard. "Digital bomb? What in the world did she mean?"

As he traveled on, moving from anger to wonder and back again, he glanced toward an underpass that led off into endless fields in both directions. To the right, he saw what looked like the dark van making its way east. Having already passed the exit, he slowed to look back, his mind and heart battling hard, logic and passion dueling in full force.

Like with the phone call, he suddenly pulled over and stopped. Vehicles flew by, gusts rocking his car. Knowing he could drive another twenty minutes or more before finding another exit, he put his car in reverse.

With flashers blinking, he slowly backed up toward the exit ramp, asking himself 'why' as cars whirled past, several blaring their horns. "Just need to see the plates."

By the time he took the exit and drove east, the van could have gone pretty much anywhere. Open country spread out in all directions, farms and fields, long dirt roads, a wind turbine on the horizon. But on he went, driving fast, hoping to see it soon, hoping it wasn't what he feared.

Zooming past a long driveway, he looked down toward the small farm just as a dark van stopped in front of an old farmhouse.

"Pandering pigs!" He hit the brakes, stopping just beyond the drive. "Now what do I do?" *If they really killed that guy...*

It was several miles back to the freeway and who knows how far to the nearest phone let alone a police force able to take on these guys, whoever they were.

"This isn't happening. Weird dream?" He shook his head. "No. Just being stupid?" He sighed. "That's a given."

Inhaling deep, he turned down the driveway, determined to prove that it was nothing, to forget the strange girl and get on with his life. But when he pulled into the farm, seeing the very same van, his heart went into triple time. Not only did the plates match, but there she was, standing on the front porch with a man on each side.

The man from the ATM glanced back, his stare intense. Roman quickly circled around toward the driveway, his head turning to follow the girl named Misty.

When he turned back to look forward, he hit the brakes. Skidding to a stop, he stared wide-eyed into the barrel of a small automatic weapon. A husky brute stood blocking his way. Dressed in black tactical gear, the olive-skinned hulk walked over and smacked the window. Roman jumped back, his face blanching. Dark-featured with stubble and neck tattoos, the man looked battle-hard and itching for another fight.

Roman struggled to compose himself, his clammy fingers lowering the glass. "Is this... ah, the Sutton residence?" he asked, his voice squeaking. "I'm looking for... Mr. Sutton. Didn't mean to trespass, sir."

The brute said nothing, looking toward the house for instruction. "Get out!" he then growled.

"Hey, I—"

"Out!"

All blood seemed to drain from Roman's face. He swayed, dizzy as he climbed out into the path of the automatic weapon. Misty watched with sickening woe, the fine young man now being marched toward the house.

When forced inside, they were met by a furious agent Larkin. A long red bruise from eye to chin marred her thin face. A huge bloody scab was forming on her left ear.

"You imbecilic twit!" she screamed at Misty, spewing out a torrent of vulgarity. From it, Misty learned that the little man, a Ukrainian hacker named Vladimir, was the only one capable of running the equipment, but now lay in a deep state of comatose. Viktor's leg wound would not stop bleeding no matter what they tried. Ganny so wounded Carloff, he would probably never walk straight and certainly never bear offspring.

The bruise on Larkin's cheek bore the size and shape of the metal pipe. It seemed Ganny had caught them by surprise, was still alive, but suffered greatly for her actions.

If the two men who captured Misty had not arrived, there would have been only Larkin and the brute, whom she learned was a Spaniard named Alvaro.

Roiling with malice, the woman slapped Misty full on the face, tumbling the girl into Roman. He caught her and stumbled, his eyes so full of fear they bulged.

"And who are you, ya bumbling idiot?"

Roman steadied Misty before answering. "I... I'm just looking for the... Sutton residence, ma'am. I don't want any trouble. I..." He lifted both hands in surrender.

"Score?" Larkin said, looking to the man from the ATM. He glanced up and down the young man.

"Was at the pickup, maybe."

Larkin swore up another tirade. "Unbelievable, for stupid sake!" She touched her face and cursed. "Oh, god! Take them both out back. And do it right this time!"

Misty inhaled loudly, then swooned, both legs buckling. Woozy from whatever they used to knock her out, her guts now wanted to heave. She convulsed, trying to hold it back. Roman reached out, trying to keep her up. Her face had gone ghostly white, eyes wide like a deer trapped by wolves.

She stared up at him, anguish twisting her face. "Why?" she moaned, slowly shaking her head "Why'd you…?"

Roman could only stare back, his body numb.

Misty suddenly slumped to her knees, Roman unable to keep her up.

"Get them out of here!" Larkin yelled. "My god!"

Shuffling over the dusty gravel toward the tool shed, Misty kept muttering apologies, her eyes blurring. "Why?" she asked him again. "Why'd you follow me?"

"Just shut up!" Score, the man from the ATM ordered. He held Misty while the brute, Alvaro, held Roman. "For a stupid girl, you've made a lot of trouble," Score said.

Alvaro looked her way, his dark eyes leering. "Give me girl for a little," he said, his accent unlike the others. "Teach her my way to… you know, have fun." He chuckled at Score who gave Misty a long look-over.

Behind the tool shed, Misty began to tremble, panting shallow, broken breaths. The twisted fate of having escaped here once before, to now be here again—it was obviously her appointed place of death.

The lines of an old poem flashed. *'All things are subject to decay and when fate summons, monarchs must obey.'* She couldn't recall the poet, an extremely rare occurrence for her. Her legs gave way again, bringing pain to her arm, as the man's grip tightened. She glanced at Roman, a shiver snaking through her whole body, her skin suddenly cold.

Roman… the nicest, most lovely young man she'd ever met, besides James of course. *Oh, James…*

The brute shoved Roman up against the wall, switching his automatic weapon to single-shot. He leveled the weapon at Roman's chest. Misty squeezed her eyes tight, tugging to turn away, but Score held her tight.

A second passed, then Score shook Misty. "You know this kid?" he asked, nodding toward Roman.

Misty hesitated. In all honesty, she didn't really know him. She weakly shook her head.

The man looked her over again, his gaze darkening with evil intent. "Not your boyfriend?" he asked sharply.

Misty shook her head, her mind filling with images of James, his warm hands taking hers, his lips—

"He didn't come here looking for you?"

At first, Misty couldn't answer, her mouth hanging open. "I… he… no… he… he's not here for me."

The man drew his weapon, a large caliber handgun, much larger than the one with which she'd shot Viktor. "Prove it," he said, handing the heavy gun to Misty.

"W-w-what?"

Its polished metal glistened a reddish hue, touched by the last of the sun's rays. The evening air had grown cold, the gun's metal colder. She shivered hard as if it had passed into her, its weight like lead. The man watched with a wicked delight. He smelled of cheap aftershave and garlic. These men were clearly mercenaries, hired guns who had no personal interest in the workings of Larkin. Misty glanced up at him, then at the gun, then at Roman.

Alvaro, at first surprised, smiled, his weapon now aimed at Misty.

Score motioned toward Roman. "Shoot him, anywhere you like, and we'll let you go."

Alvaro chuckled, knowing what the man really meant. Score stood dead serious. "Go on. It's a three-fifty-seven mag. Use both hands."

As Misty's trembling hands held the gun, her ears filled with a dull, thumping silence, her heart hitting her chest. Roman stood stock still, face bloodless, eyes and mouth gaping wide.

"Go on. Shoot him, and I'll let you go." Misty didn't see his sly glance to the brute.

She shook her head, eyes watering, everything going blurry.

He helped set the heavy gun between her trembling hands. "I'll count to three," he said, his breath pungent. "Help you out a bit."

As he counted, Misty thought of Ganny, of James, of her mother and Max. She thought of Roman, a young man willing to help her, to feed her, and now… *What is he doing here?*

"Three!"

Like a bomb going off in her hands, the gun bucked her arms upward. A cloud of dust and debris exploded from the stone wall beside Roman's head.

"Oh my gawd!" the brute exclaimed, laughing with great excitement. "You really shoot him, almost." He laughed hard, enjoying the fun.

Misty aimed again, holding the gun steady, straight at Roman's head. No counting this time. Score waited with twisted anticipation. A moment passed, Misty's hands trembling, her finger quivering on the trigger. She tried to breathe, to see through the blur, her lips praying, pleading.

Roman stood stiff, his eyes so wide he looked like a boy at his first haunted house. He didn't move, his fingers dug into the stone behind him.

Misty glanced at the Spaniard, her vision blurring. She then turned back toward Roman, the gun now aimed at his chest.

KA-WHOMPFFF!

As deafening as a lightning strike, the air rippled with exploding force. A wave of thunderous shock rushed over them.

Billows of flame rolled upward from the house. Then debris splattered against the shed. Boards, glass, and stone whizzed about them, peppering their bodies.

Misty turned to see the house a ball of fire, a column of smoke rising high into the evening sky. Alvaro's gun arm had gone limp. A narrow fragment of wood protruded from his left chest, right where his heart should be. His eyes stared blankly, his gaping mouth trying to find air. Thick smoke gathered above the house as flames ate greedily at whatever timbers remained.

Score stood bewildered, his eyes glued to the inferno consuming the house. He muttered something, blinking in disbelief. A blast of heat rushed over them as smaller bits of debris now rained from the sky.

Alvaro crumpled to the ground, his heavy body falling forward, cheek striking a large smooth rock embedded in the sandy soil. Like an awed child, his eyes stared at the burning chaos, his face already pale and lifeless.

Score turned back, quickly realizing his plight. Like a snake, his arm reached for his pistol. But Misty whirled back, bringing it up to aim at his chest.

Glancing at his partner lifeless on the ground, he stepped toward the body. Alvaro's gun lay partially pinned beneath his arm and chest.

"Hey, I… I wasn't going to hurt you," Score said, his gaze going from Misty to the gun on the ground. "Was going to let you go. You know that, right? I mean, come on." He glanced back at the burning farmhouse, then back at Misty and the pistol, his face twisted.

When his eyes darkened, Misty gripped the gun tighter.

He spun. She fired.

Before he hit the ground, she'd fired again unintentionally. One shot ripped through his upper left thigh, the other his hip. Screaming and writhing in anguish, he pleaded for mercy. But the teen girl stood firm, and although trembling, she held the heavy gun toward his chest.

"How did you find me?" she demanded, her voice quivering. "Who told you I was there?"

Blood already soaking his pants, the man only winced, grinding his teeth.

"Tell me or die!" Misty shouted, glancing at the inferno rushing into the evening sky.

"Do I live?" he asked, face twisted.

"Maybe!" she barked, breathing fast through her nose, jaw tight.

"They have people… on the inside," he groaned.

"Who? Names, give me names."

He shook his head. "Don't know. Not my game." He clutched his leg with both hands, sucking air fast through his teeth. "You can't… stop them."

"Names!" Misty demanded.

He shook his head again. "I'm just security." He cussed, groaning loudly. "That's the truth."

Roman remained frozen against the wall.

"Get the gun!" Misty ordered, her glare intense. Roman moved with stiff, shuffling steps, his face ghostly pale.

She looked back at Score. Blood now pooled under his leg. If she'd hit an artery, he would most probably die, and soon.

"You don't deserve to live," she said. "Close your eyes and I'll make it quick."

"No," he pleaded. "I told you the truth." He winced with great pain. "You can't stop them. They'll find you. Find you both."

In a rage, Misty fired the big gun, the bullet slamming into the dirt beside his head. He spun, rolling away, hands covering his head. For some time, he lay scrunched up on his side, awaiting death. When nothing more came, he slowly rolled over.

The girl and boy were gone.

20 "WHO ARE YOU?"

As Misty limped back to the burning house, her mind was all on Ganny. Why had the house exploded? Was Ganny the cause? Was she still alive?

Roman ran straight for his car, pulling a burning fragment off the hood. Misty went straight for the house.

"Come on!" he shouted. "Let's get out of here."

"Ganny!" Misty yelled into the furnace of flame and smoke, the heat intense on her skin. "Ganny! Are you in there?"

Roman ran and grabbed her, pulling her toward his car. "Come on! No one's alive in there!"

Misty shook him off, limping back toward the flames. After calling and shouting into the roaring blaze, she finally slumped to her knees, her face red from the heat. She sobbed as tears wet her burning cheeks.

Grabbing her under the arms, Roman dragged her from the heat, her body limp like a fresh corpse. He struggled to get her inside the car as she continued to sob, making no effort to help.

He tossed Alvaro's gun in the back seat, and gingerly took the 45 from Misty's grip. Breathing heavily, the young man sped off down the long drive toward the setting sun, a cloud of darkness spreading overhead. Not until they reached the freeway, did either speak.

"Which way?" Roman asked, his voice tight, but Misty didn't answer. Her mind had gone numb, her body limp and throbbing.

Then she softly muttered, "I think… I need… a hospital." Her head dropped back and she cried.

As Roman pulled onto the freeway, he kept shaking his head.

"Who are you!" His voice was desperate as he glanced her way, his look so very stern. "You tried to kill me!" His hands shook as he held the wheel. "A house... that car... exploded... my phone..." He muttered like a child, then got stern again. "You tried to kill me... to shoot me... and that house..." He went back to wagging his head, his lungs huffing. "It had people inside."

Misty's cries turned back to sobs.

Roman continued shaking his head. "We have to call the police! Don't we? But that guy, that friend of yours, tells me to throw out my phone." His eyes were wild, his breath fast and shallow. "Answer me. You shot a gun at me, at my head!"

Misty took a deep, staggering breath, then sniffled, swiping a sleeve across her nose. "Wasn't trying to shoot you." She fought to steady her breath. "Was... testing the gun."

The young man raised his eyebrows. Specks of blood dotted his right cheek and ear, wounds from the stone fragments that had exploded next to his face. A dull ringing still resonated.

Misty wiped her nose again. "I'm sorry. Had to make it look real." She then pointed to a billboard advertising a restaurant in a city twenty-three miles ahead. "That one."

Roman nodded, his mind struggling for an explanation. As he drove, he sat stupefied, both at the girl beside him and with himself. Why had he chosen to help her? Why was he still trying to help this girl?

"Are you a spy?" he asked with all seriousness.

Misty shook her head.

"I mean, what the heck is going on? Who's Ganny? And you just... shot a guy! Twice! Doesn't that bother you?"

Misty looked over at him like a little girl being scolded. As if melting, she began to weep, her painful cries coming from deep inside.

"No," Roman said, "I didn't mean it that way. Please, don't..." He huffed, but Misty lost it, her last bit of strength gone. Inside her heart was bleeding. Burying her face into her palms, she wailed as one in painful mourning.

Roman quickly rummaged through his center console to withdraw a pack of tissues. In silence he drove, listening to Misty weep for this person called Ganny.

"I'm sorry," he finally said, after she had somewhat composed herself. "I just…" He sighed, handing her another tissue.

Misty gave brief directions as he took the exit, heading toward the hospital. He pulled into the clinic's lot and parked, exhaling long and slow. "Let me know when you're ready," he said, his voice gentle.

Misty blew her nose, looking about the parking lot. The memories of Larkin and her goons came all too clearly, bringing twitching shivers.

"You cold?" Roman asked.

She shook her head, then reached for the door latch. Roman was quick to hustle around and open her door.

As he took her hand to help her out, she looked up at him with surprise. He was so like James, so kind and considerate, so gentle and sweet. She studied his perfect face now splattered with dust and blood.

"I'm sorry," she said, blinking back more tears. "I'm so sorry." He reminded her of someone, but she couldn't think who—a strange feeling for her. For a moment she just sat in the car studying his face. Then inhaling a ragged, sniffling breath, she softly said, "No, I could never shoot someone like you."

The same doctor she'd had before now stood bewildered, a hundred questions flooding his brain.

"What happened?" he asked, his thoughts on the details of her unstable mental condition. "Where's your mother?"

Misty shook her head. "She's not my mother. She tried to…" Misty sighed as the man gave that fake understanding look. "I'm not whatever that report says. Larkin made that up. She's… I need to call…" Sighing heavily, she glanced up at Roman who now stood discreetly trying to read the open report. A new confusion twisted his handsome face.

When they both looked at her with pitiful eyes, her face and hair still dusted with dirt and cobwebs, she let go a weary huff.

"I'm not what that says. They took me from school. I was trying to escape when I hit that stupid train, or… it hit me." She lowered her gaze. "And now Ganny."

"Who's Ganny?" they both asked in unison.

"She works for the CIA. She's…"

Sudden nausea washed over Misty. The room spun and wobbled as the lights went dim and then bright. Her stomach swirled and her head felt like a large balloon floating all about the room.

"I think, I'm gonna throw up!"

21 ANALYSIS

Thursday, October 29

When Misty opened her eyes, the sun peeked through her window, bringing a soft light of warmth and hope. Slumped in a chair beside her bed, slept Roman, his head cocked to the side in what would surely bring a stiff neck.

He looked miserable. What was she doing to such a nice guy? She thought of James, of his words about love. *What is love?* Her mother loved her. She loved Max. She felt the lips of James, his weight on her body, the pressure of his embrace. She lightly touched the tape on her lower lip. Being such a fine cut, they were able to glue and tape the wound.

"Where are you, James?" she whispered. "Are you sitting in history class waiting for me? Are you out looking for me?"

She had thought to call her mother, to call James, but feared for their safety. The images of Ganny and thoughts of her death brought waves of pain, like sharp, cold needles piercing her heart. She had slept well, the doctor giving her something for just that purpose, but now the overwhelming miseries returned.

What was happening? Why this strange twist of fate? And poor Roman.

She thought of slipping out, of leaving without a trace. He didn't know her real name. Her chart said she was Marie E. Downing.

The memories of all that happened since Monday filed through her mind in perfect order. The challenge for her was to revisit the scenes without being overwhelmed by the accompanying emotions. For with the scenes came every sound, smell, facial expression, every word with subtle meanings, every detail of everything within her perception.

She jerked at the memory of firing the gun. Her chest heaved as she pictured the blood pooling in the dirt behind the tool shed. And the heat, the intense heat…

"Bizarre," she whispered, thinking how she had escaped the tool shed twice, both times having to shoot someone in the leg. *Fate is weird,* she mused. *At least they can't take me back to that cursed farmhouse.*

"You okay?" Roman rubbed his eyes, and then craned his neck, wincing.

Misty tried to calm herself, nodding with a little smile. "Did you sleep there all night?"

He groaned the affirmative.

"Oh, Roman. Don't you have somewhere to go?"

He was due at college soon and knew his friends would eventually notify the authorities, which would cause alarm, especially to his father.

"Need to get you home," he said. He watched Misty for some time, trying to work the kink from his neck. "Where is your home?"

"Good morning." A pleasant nurse, Sara, strode in with two trays full of food. "Are you hungry this fine morning?"

She checked Misty's pulse and blood pressure, reminded her to take her pills after eating, and then happily announced that she had a visitor, a doctor Minsk from the psychiatry department.

Misty shook her head. "Roman, you have to help me. I'm not what that report says. Larkin made all that up to keep me from talking."

Roman just chewed his fruit and yogurt, his eyes searching.

"You believe me, don't you?"

He studied her before answering. "I'm not sure what to

believe." He lightly touched the side of his face, feeling the specks of dried blood and scab.

Misty's eyes moistened. "I'm not crazy, Roman. Ganny gave me something… in the locket. I need to find it and take it to…" Her face lit up. "…to Washington!"

"Good morning, Ms. Downing." A tall, lanky man with a beard like Abraham Lincoln walked in, and glancing about for a chair, nodded to Roman, who quickly got up and stood to one side. After seating himself, the man then looked at Roman and then toward the door.

With tray in hand, Roman left, closing the door behind him.

"Call my mom, Roman!" she called after him, rattling off a set of numbers.

The lanky man opened a file and muttered to himself.

Misty watched him. "That report's a lie," she said with an angry glance toward the door. "My name is Grey, not Downing. She put all that in there to keep me quiet. If you don't believe me—"

The man held up his hand. "Ms. Downing—"

"I'm not Ms. Downing! I'm Marie Grey. Call my mom! That whole report's a lie!"

The man sat quietly still, a little smile so fake it made Misty furious.

"Whenever you're finished," he said calmly, "I have a few questions for you." He waited a moment. "May I?"

Misty just scowled.

"Is your name Marie Elsa Downing?"

Misty's glare could have ignited a fire.

"Do you live at two thirty-two Maplelawn Avenue in Somerset?"

Misty screwed up her face. "Somerset? No!"

"Do you believe someone is following you?"

At that, Misty pulled the covers over her head and bit down hard to keep from screaming.

When Roman asked to use the phone, a nurse led him to a small alcove near the bathrooms. He rubbed his neck, his mind still struggling with all he had seen and heard. *Who is this girl? Why am I still with her?* He dialed the numbers Misty had yelled to him, his pulse increasing, his mind wondering.

"The number you have dialed is no longer in service. Please check the number and dial again."

Roman did just that, getting the same result. Misty must have given him the wrong number, or he misheard or mixed them up. He went back to her room.

Knocking lightly, he waited. "Misty?"

Silence.

"Misty?" He slowly pushed the door open. "What the…?"

Thursday, October 29

When James entered the courtroom, he scanned the crowd, searching for his mother. Mrs. Longmire sat near the front, behind the defense lawyer who presently riffled through a thick file, jotting down notes and numbers. Billy Bonhoffer, a bachelor still living with his mother, never finished law school but managed to complete his degree online, passing the bar exam by a minimal margin. A pudgy man with an oily comb-over, he didn't exactly booster confidence, especially against the city's notorious prosecutor, Charles D. Stein from Stein, Culver, & Stein.

As Mrs. Grey's defense lawyer appointed by the local government, he was doing all he could to hold his own against the overpowering bulldog, Charles D. Stein.

The arrest of Sally Grey had overnight become one of national interest. A woman with two children, having endured years of abuse, finally pulls the trigger.

Women's groups had rallied behind her, calling for media attention to the plight women suffer, often in silence. When murder charges were filed, many of the townspeople who knew the situation came to her support, thus the packed courtroom where James now pressed through to sit beside his mother.

With the added disappearance of Misty, Charles D. Stein had introduced the idea of a double murder, which the media was quick to entertain, although neither a shred of evidence nor motive could be given, for it was simply a ploy to discredit the woman. Billy Bonhoffer fought the vicious accusation like a Pomeranian against a Pitbull, doing all he could, but affecting little.

Twice the day before, James had stood and shouted protests when Stein pointed his finger at Mrs. Grey and proclaimed her a vile criminal not worthy of life. Warned of being escorted out, he fought to keep his cool as others, mostly coworkers of Mrs. Grey would do the same, their voices fraught with anger at the ridiculous charges. James, along with his mother and father, had been asked to verify the police report regarding the night of the murder. They were more than eager to take every opportunity to defend Mrs. Grey, describing her life of abuse while the 'victim,' Mr. Grey was alive.

Judge Mathison, older than the earth itself, just listened, scribbling notes from behind his high bench. He had seen much in his long career, acquiring a strong tolerance for the emotions that surge during murder trials like these. With quiet, drooping eyes he watched the antics of both prosecutor and defense attorney, of witnesses and defendants, of friends and family members, taking in all that transpired during the preliminary hearings of a pretrial.

Some said he could be bribed, others that he was filthy rich. Some said he was fair and just, others that he was evil and mean. Today he seemed uninterested.

James looked over at Mrs. Grey. Like a woman bereaved, she sat in silence, her eyes fixed on the floor. She, like all the others, had no idea what had happened to Misty. Maxwell had been made a ward of the state until a decision was reached regarding his mother.

James had badgered the police and even the FBI in a vain effort to find Misty. *Shouldn't have kissed her*, he kept telling himself. *Screwed up everything.*

"Where are you, Misty?" he whispered. His mother reached over and squeezed his hand. Although perplexed over Misty, she had felt a sense of relief, followed by guilt for such thoughts under the present circumstances. As mothers know things, she had seen all too well the way James followed Misty's every move, how he opened doors for her, helped with her coat, carried her books up the driveway and into her house. She knew it wasn't right to feel such, but it was nice to have the girl gone for a while, at least till James found interest in one of those other girls at school.

She put her arm around him as Bonhoffer questioned a witness from Mrs. Grey's workplace. "Sally wouldn't hurt a flea," the man said staring straight at Mrs. Grey. "Nicest gal to work with if ever was."

Mrs. Grey looked up with a weary smile and then back at the floor. James sighed. He wondered why the police officers' testimonies of multiple domestic abuse visits to the Grey home, coupled with numerous arrests for brawling, drug use, DUIs, etc., were not enough to acquit Misty's mom and so end this charade of justice.

"Why is this still going on?" he whispered to his mother, who quickly shushed him. "They should be out looking for Misty."

For two days, James sat listening to the lawyers do their best to persuade Judge Mathison on their behalf. If Bonhoffer got his way, this all would end with a decision of self-defense. If Stein got his way, the pretrial would escalate into a murder trial requiring a jury, which would put Misty's mother in jail waiting for months, maybe even years before the dust settled and a decision was reached.

"It's so stinking obvious!" he said to his mother, who shushed him again, scolding him for using such language. "They should just let her go. She's been through enough."

A pretrial was never to have gone like this, but for the unprecedented publicity and for Stein being bent on making this 'vile woman pay for her crimes against the very fabric of humanity,' the usual formality had turned into quite an extended ordeal.

With his skillful craft of persuasion well refined, Charles D. Stein seemed to have moved Judge Mathison to a decision. Despite all the evidence in favor of self-defense, the judge began a long-winded speech that clearly revealed his intentions of declaring the case a possible murder and thereby requiring a trial by jury. It was near the end of this speech when a young clerk rushed into the courtroom and up to the desk of Billy Bonhoffer, whispering frantically into the defense lawyer's ear.

After a moment of hushed discussion, the very annoyed judge called him to approach the bench.

"It appears, Your Honor, that we have a problem. My defendant, Mrs. Sally Grey, well…" Billy hesitated, glancing back at Mrs. Grey.

"Well, what?" Mathison demanded.

Without a chance to discuss his new findings with Mrs. Grey, Billy wondered how much to reveal.

"Well, it appears, Your Honor, that Mrs. Sally Elisabeth Grey… was found dead."

The judge drew back, his face all screwed up. "Bonhoffer, what are you talking about?"

"Murdered, Your Honor, 'bout eleven years ago."

Thursday afternoon, October 29

Roman rushed into Misty's hospital room. Bedding lay strewn about the floor, as did Dr. Minsk, his glossy eyes staring blankly at the ceiling. From the side of his neck protruded a small syringe, its plunger pressed fully down. A chair sat pushed beneath the window where the soft curtains blew inward with a crisp breeze.

Misty was nowhere.

Roman stood staring at the body of Dr. Minsk. The look in the man's eyes gave the college boy a flush of cold chills.

"Not breathing," Roman muttered. "He's not breathing."

He glanced up at the window, which was at ground level. "Misty?" His hands began to tremble. This couldn't be real, it just couldn't be. He looked at the syringe, its needle driven in just above the left collar bone. Whatever it was, had killed him, or at least made him look really, really dead.

What have I gotten into? For a moment, Roman couldn't move. Every muscle seemed to have turned to mush. "Should call for help." He glanced at the door, thinking to close it and run after Misty. He looked to the dead doctor, thinking to pull the syringe and make it look like the man fell… or something.

Seriously! Oh, God, what am I thinking? The girl's crazy, a killer! But then he looked again at the syringe. *What was in there? Or had been in there? And who was it for?*

Scolding himself for being an idiot, he rummaged through

the dead man's suit coat. Upon opening the man's wallet, his heart flew into hyper-drive. "CIA?"

"Is everything okay in there?" Sara rapped lightly on the door, peering in before giving full vent to an alarming scream. Within seconds, the hospital staff was on full alert as Roman scrambled out the window after Misty.

"You idiot!" he kept yelling at himself. "What are you doing?"

Within moments he was at his car, glancing about for Misty. After calling her name several times, he jumped in and revved the engine. As he sped toward the entrance, nearing the hospital sign, Misty jumped out, bringing his car to a screeching halt.

"You killed him! My God, girl, you killed him!" Roman shouted as the haggard teen climbed in, her face ghostly white. Speeding toward the freeway, he trembled, eyes shooting glances at the girl beside him as if she were some wild beast.

Misty looked at him, her face truly puzzled. "What? He died?"

"Yeah, he died. What did you do?"

For a moment Misty sat stunned, her whole body going cold. When they pulled onto the freeway, she struggled to tell him what had happened.

"He tried to… to give it to me. 'Help me relax,' he said." She stared wide-eyed at Roman. "Are you sure? Dead?"

Roman didn't answer, his eyes glancing back and forth between the road and the battered girl, the girl who had just turned his world completely upside down and inside out with no hope of ever getting things back to normal. Why had he fled?

"I'm an accomplice to murder," he muttered, his stomach souring. "Where do you live?" he asked harshly. "I'm taking you home! And don't ever speak of me, to anyone. Don't call me, don't… oh, God! What have I done?"

He flashed an angry glance at Misty. "He was CIA! Did you know that?"

Misty's face seemed to sag, her mouth hanging loose. She slowly wagged her head, tears welling.

"Carlton Meed. Securities Branch. Section… something. Oh God, this is bad!"

Misty drew one leg up, hugging it as she quivered. For a long while, she sat whimpering, moaning as she rocked back and forth. She had told Roman where she lived and so they traveled north, the young man checking his mirrors every other second.

After a time, Misty muttered something about organ failure. "Larkin had a syringe," she said softly. "Said it would cause organ failure." She looked at Roman, tears trailing her pale cheeks. "Was that guy going to kill me?"

The handsome college boy didn't respond.

Misty sniffled. "You still don't believe me, do you?"

"I don't know what to think, other than you've messed up my life."

Misty inhaled, stiffening with indignation. "You didn't have to follow me! Didn't have to pick me up." She turned away. "I'm sorry… sorry we ever met."

They rode in near silence the rest of the way, speaking little of what had happened.

When the car pulled up the drive and stopped outside Misty's little house, they both stared in fresh alarm. Yellow tape stretched from porch post to handrail and across the front door. Orange stakes held a ring of tape circling the area directly in front of the porch.

"You live *here*?"

Without reply, Misty slowly climbed from the car, wincing as she struggled to stand. Her bruised head throbbed with every second she stared at the yellow tape. The tied-off ends were gently fluttering, while the black letters screamed: 'CRIME SCENE DO NOT CROSS.'

Misty stumbled backward, catching herself against the car. Her stomach convulsed as cold sweat chilled her skin.

"No, please, no… no…" she moaned, her whole body slumping.

Roman moved with careful step toward the yellow tape, stopping short as he surveyed the simple porch. A large stain clearly marred the wooden planking. Eyes wide, he looked back to Misty.

Face pale, she stared, her chest swelling with labored breaths. She would soon vomit or pass out, or both. Roman rushed to her side just as she collapsed.

Suddenly frightened and ashamed, he helped her up. "I'm sorry," he said, "I didn't… oh, my."

Misty wrapped her arms tight around his strong chest, hugging him as if she were falling off a cliff, falling to her death far below. Pain rifled through her shoulder but she hugged and wept, squeezing him, pressing her face hard into his chest.

"We better go," Roman said looking all about. "They might be watching."

Still hugging tight, Misty pondered his words. *Watching?* Sick with the image of Mr. Grey having killed her mother and possibly Max, she hadn't considered the others, the people trying to kill her. She recalled the warning of Vladimir when first inside the black sedan. '…cooperate without questions… best for your safety and your family's.'

Her gaze then went to the home of the Longmires.

"James!"

Pushing off of Roman, she made a mad limping run to the house next door. A thousand fears swarmed, tormenting her as she hobbled in pain over the cold autumn lawn. Finding the door unlocked, she stepped inside but then stopped.

"What?" Roman came in beside her.

"I… " Misty stood trembling as if freezing cold. "Please… go first."

Roman brushed past and after several minutes came back. "Empty," he said rather relieved, but still very nervous about his car with license plates sitting in the open. "Is this normal? Unlocked and no one home?"

Misty shrugged. "Sometimes."

"Okay, but we need to get out of here… fast!"

Misty made her way toward the stairs leading up to the bedroom of James. Roman followed.

"You went up there?" she asked, to which he nodded.

But lifting her leg brought so much pain, she broke into feeble sobs.

"We need to go," Roman urged her. "There's nothing up there."

But she tried again, and again winced with a painful cry. "Please…" she pleaded, "help me up there."

With care and steady step, Roman scooped her up and brought her to the top of the stairs. He glanced out a window, checking on his car. Misty hobbled straight into James' room.

For a moment, she stood silent, recalling the warm kisses, the strong embrace, the words of love. A terrible ache squeezed her chest, a gush of pain rising from deep within.

Roman followed, picking up a picture of Misty and James, their heads pressed together in laughter as the sun set over a large blue lake.

"Your boyfriend?" he asked rather coolly.

Misty didn't even turn to acknowledge. She had taken a piece of notepaper and was scribbling with trembling hands.

'Dearest James,

I was kidnapped. Ganny is dead. I really, really x1,000 miss you. Is my mom… is Max okay? I…'

The pen trailed off as Misty suddenly felt weak. Her whole head went woozy and once again Roman caught her just in time.

When she came to, they were in the car at a stoplight.

"I'm taking you to the police," Roman said firmly. He wanted to say more, a lot more but was now concerned for his own family.

"No," Misty shook her head. "No, you can't. They'll find out. They knew I was in the hospital. They knew I was with you, at the ATM. Somehow they know." She sobbed, the stretched yellow tape torturously vivid. "Please don't take me to the police."

"Then where do I take you?" Roman grew angry, but not with her. He had never felt such fear. "I'm not taking you to my house. We've already…" He suddenly grew silent, lost in a memory, a memory of pain like the girl beside him, weeping at the loss of loved ones.

He pulled into a McDonald's and turned off the car. For a time he sat in silence, watching the young girl with one knee drawn tight to her chest, convulsing with agony.

Face smeared with tears, Misty looked up at him. Even in her miserable state, the girl held his gaze. She was beautiful, a natural, subtle kind of beauty that drew upon symmetry and graceful lines. Her long lashes, damp with tears, drew him in as if lured into a mesmerizing dream. His gaze rested on her lips, lips designed for kissing, fashioned by the gods themselves in a contest of perfection.

"What?" Misty asked, breaking him from his trance. "Why are you staring at me?"

"Where shall I take you?" Roman asked very gently. He almost reached up to wipe the tear-trails from her cheeks. "I'll take you wherever you want. Are you hungry?"

She shook her head.

"Well, I'm going in." He looked her over, handing her the last of the tissues. "I need a restroom." As he opened the door, he paused. "You really shouldn't stay out here alone."

She agreed and got out. He placed an arm about her waist to help her inside, glancing over his shoulder several times. He then insisted they use the restrooms at the same time so he would know where she was.

They had both cleaned up and came out looking a little better, though their eyes and actions showed the accruing stress. With the smell of fast food permeating the air, Misty's stomach desired food. But the thought of eating while not knowing about her mom and brother felt repulsive.

She squeezed her hands together, trying to still the tremors. When they turned to find a booth, her hip gave out, bringing a stifled cry. The stress and trauma of the last few days had reached the meltdown point. She fought to stay upright, to not crawl under the table and just wail.

As Roman ate, Misty just stared out the window, her eyes distant.

"We don't know what happened," Roman said, trying to sound hopeful. They sat in a corner booth, away from the doors and other patrons. "Maybe..." He tried to think of a possible scenario other than the more likely and dreadful reality of what probably happened. He saw men in black uniforms, a troop of snipers or assassins sneaking stealthily toward the house, all under the cover of darkness.

Then he saw them surrounding his father's home in New York, their weapons aimed with laser dots weaving about, searching for their victims. He inhaled sharply, intense fear surging.

He looked hard at Misty. "Have any I.D. with you?"

"What? I.D.? Why?"

"To book a flight."

Misty shook her head, pondering what the good-looking college boy had in mind. "They took all my stuff." She studied his face. "Where are we going?"

"Away," Roman answered, his breath unsteady. "Anywhere but… home."

"Where's your home?" Misty asked.

He hesitated.

"It's okay," Misty said. "Probably better I don't know."

Roman continued to watch her, his face tight with concern. "Greenhaven," he said softly, "New York."

"New York. That's a long way. Will you drive there?"

"Drive? Well, it depends."

They sat in silence for a while, then Misty asked a strange question.

"Could you get there before Halloween… driving?"

"Halloween? Why?"

Misty studied his face. *So fine, handsome, so nice*, she thought. She swallowed as if preparing to say something difficult. "Could… we… get to CIA headquarters before midnight… on Halloween?"

Roman slumped back, hitting the booth hard. "Are you nuts? Don't they have people on the inside? They'll see you coming a thousand miles away. See *us* coming!"

Misty slumped, sighing wearily. "I promised," she said, her voice breaking. "I need to finish it." She looked up, her eyes intense. "I'm going to Washington! I have no choice."

"Misty, no… that's not—"

"You can stay. I don't want any more bad to happen to you." She stood. "But I have to, Roman. I have to keep my promise."

As she turned to leave, a large, lanky man with dark glasses entered through the glass doors. He quickly scanned the seating and those at the order counter. In the time it takes to blink, Misty had crawled under the table, whispering loudly for Roman to look down.

Eyes and nostrils flaring, Roman fought the urge to turn

around. Slinking down in his booth he brought his hands up to his forehead, sipping slowly through his straw.

"What?" he whispered. "Who is it?"

Misty just jerked on his pant leg, shushing him with urgency.

When the man made a long slow loop through the seating area, Roman stretched out his legs nudging Misty to crawl in as far as possible. Although head down, he followed the man with the corner of his eye, hands quivering at his temples. *They're everywhere!* he screamed in silence. *They... are... everywhere!*

Seconds became long painful minutes, as the man stood eyeing the counter and seating area. He then turned to check the restrooms, entering the women's room without hesitation. Risking a glance, Roman saw the man step briskly into a dark sedan idling in the parking lot. It pulled away slowly, stopping briefly just behind his car.

Everything he'd just eaten now wanted to bail.

"Is he gone?" Misty whispered.

Roman couldn't answer. His head spun in tight busy circles, his breath rapid bursts of useless panting. Never had he felt such fear, such dread, not even when behind the tool shed looking down the barrel of the gun. The trauma now had found its mark. His whole insides went numb.

"We're going to die," he muttered. "My God, I'm going to die."

Peeking out from beneath the table, Misty slowly scanned the restaurant. "Did he see you?" she asked.

Roman sat shivering, his cup bobbling in his frail grasp, his lips muttering things of doom, death, and torture without escape.

Misty moved to a booth away from the window, motioning Roman to follow. She studied him, the fear in his eyes frightening her.

"Are you okay?" she asked, scanning the windows for any sign of the man. "Was he looking for us?"

Roman nodded, saying something about stopping at his car.

Misty inhaled deeply, the dread now spreading into her. How *would* they escape these people? They seemed to know their every move, to find them no matter where they were.

The dread for her mother and brother came again, feeling so heavy she felt to be collapsing inward, to be sinking into something dark and oily.

Oh, how she yearned for James, to call him, to see him, to once again feel his tight embrace. But then they would find him too. These were the times she ran to Ganny's, pouring out her heart in all its vivid detail, details she longed to forget.

"What do we do?" Roman said in a weak whisper. "They know my car." He then narrowed his eyes at Misty. "What do they want with you? What have you done?"

Startled by his accusing tone, Misty stiffened, her gaze intense, both hands fisting tight. For a second she thought to knock him down hard and take his keys, drive away in his car as far as she could go, far away from him, from everyone.

For a time, the two sat glaring, each looking like a bull about to charge. Then Roman exhaled, slumping backward.

"Sorry," he muttered. "But, why do they want you?" This time he spoke with gentleness, his eyes showing deep concern.

Misty sat back, opening her fists. She watched him for a while, her eyes locked on his. The more she told him, the more danger... *But he deserves to know.*

"My locket," she said softly.

"Why? Where is it?"

"Lost. Has information... about them." She continued staring into his eyes. "I need to get to Washington, to tell someone there."

"But why would you have...?" His eyes narrowed again, his face tightening. "If you're hoaxing me... if you really are some delusional freak that—?"

Smack! The slap resonated through the restaurant. Roman jerked back, eyes wide, a hand to his cheek.

Misty slowly stood, her fists tight. Though still between the booth and table, her stance clearly showed she would pummel him if he said one more word.

Seeing the look in the girl's green eyes, Roman scooted against the wall, a hand still on his reddening cheek. Misty thought again to take his car and flee. It might save his life.

A tense moment followed as Roman sat cowering, Misty towering over him.

Then, without warning, she flopped down and buried her face in both hands. A soft, moaning wail came from deep inside, the sound of a soul dying.

Roman slunk low, feeling the entire restaurant was now looking. He yearned to comfort her, but he now seriously pondered the psycho report. For some time he didn't speak, his mind screaming at him for getting involved. Then his heart took over.

"I'm sorry," he finally whispered. "That was wrong. I just… I'm sorry."

Misty just shook her head, her face still buried in her hands.

After what seemed a long time, she sniffled loudly and Roman handed her several napkins. As tensions calmed, she sat up, her face a mess.

"I need to use the…" Misty rose, making her way to the restrooms just as a busload of high school girls came filing in. Like a flood, they crowded the front counter with boisterous jabber. Roman watched with interest, getting looks from more than a few girls.

As they piled in, pushing and jostling to reach the counter, a tall blond strode in last, her hand upon a locket about her neck. She kept glancing back toward the doors, a mischievous smile on her deep red lips. Roman continued to watch, his heart and mind a mess.

The blond flung her hair back as a good-looking high school boy whipped open the door, his face red with anger. Walking straight for the girl, he held out his hand, demanding the locket. The tall blond just smiled, lifting her chin.

"Kiss me first," she said, licking her lips with well-practiced seduction.

"Just give me the locket."

She shook her head, extending her lips toward his.

The battle continued until finally the boy became aggressive and reached to pull the locket from off her well-formed chest. The girl playfully shook a finger at him, saying something about no foreplay in public. The boy's face grew redder and as he was obviously not interested in her game, the girl removed the locket with a frown.

Insisting to place the locket over his head, she quickly pulled him to her embrace and landed a very intimate kiss upon his lips. As he struggled to free himself, Misty passed quickly by, looking the other way toward the doors and parking lot. The boy stormed out as Misty took her seat.

Roman chuckled briefly at the encounter. "Been thinking," he said. "Maybe the police… can protect us. I mean… we can't run forever."

Misty shook her head. "I've been thinking. We should sell your car, trade it for something else."

"What?" Roman gave a cynical laugh. "My dad would kill me. Besides, I'd need the title."

They watched the girls pack out the seating area, loud and lively, scrunching themselves into booths, sitting on tables. More than several had eyes on Roman. The tall blond came from behind and slipped a napkin into his lap, squeezing his thigh. He jumped, bumping his knee into the table. The girl giggled as she passed by, exaggerating her already seductive walk.

"Seems her name is Lyla." He slid the napkin over to Misty. "Want to make a friend?" They sat in silence watching the girls perform their silly antics, each vying for attention, some sitting quietly, their eyes locked on Roman.

When the last of the girls left and sanity returned, they sat talking, unsure of what to do, where to go, who to tell. The afternoon sky had turned a glooming gray, the trees barren, the world looking colder by the moment.

Roman said he would go out first and start the car. If all seemed well, he would flash the lights twice and then swing around to the other door where Misty would get in. If he sensed trouble, he would drive away and Misty would then call the police.

Roman gently took both her hands and gave a gentle squeeze. "If I don't ever see you again," he whispered, "I… just wish it could have been different, you know. I'm sorry for upsetting you."

Misty stared into his eyes wondering if he would simply drive off. She would. Her eyes studied the small scabs on his right cheek, the red handprint on his left. "I'm sorry," she said softly. "Be careful."

With great relief she watched the lights flash off and then on again, her body stiff as she made for the other door.

When they pulled onto the freeway, the sun peeked out from beneath a band of dark clouds. The pale glow lightly painted Misty's face, a silhouette of gentle beauty. Roman smiled.

"You're very beautiful," he said as if stating some common fact.

They rode in silence until all the world was black. Several times Roman took a random exit with Misty watching the cars behind. No one followed and so their tension eased, at least a little.

Misty would still break into sniffling whimpers. Was it her father, or the men pursuing them? Was her mother alive, and Max? Where was Max?

"Where are you, James?" she whispered, staring out the window, the sounds of freeway drumming beneath her feet.

"What's he like?" Roman asked.

Misty sighed. "Kind, handsome, a good heart… like you." She turned, giving him a soft smile.

"Handsome, or the good heart?" Roman asked with a sly smile.

"You know you're handsome," Misty said. She watched him for a bit. He seemed to be everything a young girl could dream of—not only good-looking, but pleasant and kind with such refined manners. A gentleman with style. If things were normal, she knew they could have a fun day together.

Roman glanced over, seeing her studying him, *again*. "So is he?"

"Who? What?"

"Your boyfriend?"

Misty sighed, the very idea tingling her insides. She'd never had a boyfriend, not a real one like James. Until that first kiss, James had been her older brother, her best friend, her confidant. Yet, that night in his room...

She thought how he'd always made time for her, never annoyed, always eager and willing. They had done so much together, been through hard stuff together. Again, she felt the warm kisses, heard his words as if spoken that moment.

"He's my best friend," she said, a bit dreamily. "My very best friend." She glanced his way. "You have a girl, I'm sure. Probably very pretty, and smart."

Roman chuckled. He had several girls pursuing him, but the one he wanted, showed him little interest. "No, still free."

"Any brothers or sisters?"

Roman shook his head. "Just me." But his voice revealed a hint of sorrow.

"Tell me," Misty gently urged. "We have a long drive."

For a good mile or two, Roman said nothing. Then he cleared his throat, like before a nervous speech. "I had a sister, reddish hair, frizzed out like yours." Another mile of dark, empty road passed by. "I was almost eight. She was... really cute and... only four... I think. I remember a lot of policemen and FBI types."

Misty wished she hadn't asked. "I'm sorry. You don't—"

"Collateral damage," Roman said, his tone cynical. "That's what they called it. Mom being the real target."

Misty now deeply wished she hadn't probed.

"Kidnapped. We don't talk of it now. Never."

Misty's eyes moistened, her heart aching as she thought of her own mother and brother. "The world is cruel," she said softly, pulling her left leg up, hugging it close. "Why does it serve up so much pain?"

They traveled on, neither speaking.

Then Roman glanced over. "Why 'Misty'?"

"What?"

"Is that your real name?"

Again, she studied him. "No… but I've always been Misty."

Roman nodded, wanting to ask her real name, but then thinking best he not know. "You remind me of her. Maybe that's why I'm still around."

Misty so wanted to ask the girl's name, but seeing his pain, she pressed her lips tight.

"Wisteria," Roman said quietly. "Her name was Wisteria."

The low fuel light came on, startling them both.

"Next exit's eight miles," Misty said nonchalantly.

Roman wondered how, but didn't ask.

After pulling up to the pump, he first went around to open Misty's door. As he helped her out, Misty gingerly stood, suppressing a painful groan. Surprised by his thoughtfulness, a sudden rush of longing swept over her. She wished to hug him, embrace him and hold him for a long time, for as long as it would take to erase the pain. Beneath the red and yellow neon, they just stood, their faces close.

"You okay?" Roman asked.

"Yes, thank you." She sighed, dropping her gaze, her heart aching. She thought how nice he had been overall, how much she'd put him through, and how much he'd now sacrificed. Then of his family's tragedy. "I'm sorry," she said softly, "sorry for everything." Her hip had stiffened and so the first step was painful. He held her arm as she hobbled to the storefront.

"If anything's off, you scream, alright?"

She nodded, a sweet smile lifting her weary face.

As he went to fill up, she touched her cheeks. They were surprisingly warm. "Oh, James, he's so like you," she said, hobbling on toward the restroom. The image of James being jealous tickled her insides. "You needn't worry, my dear James." But then her heart grew heavy once again. "No… we all need to worry… a lot."

Thursday afternoon, October 29

As Mrs. Longmire drove from the courthouse, James sat beside her in silence, his mind struggling to make sense of Billy Bonhoffer's statement. The court had been immediately adjourned until further notice and the equally stunned Mrs. Grey escorted quickly from the courtroom.

Mrs. Longmire kept shaking her head, mumbling to herself about wishing her Willie, or Mr. Longmire had been there.

James kept running the words over and over like repeating a riddle searching for some clue. 'Was found dead, murdered, eleven years ago.' As the crowd with its protesting murmurs had made their way out the double doors, he stayed, lingering close, catching but a single phrase from Billy's clerk. 'No marriage license either, nothing.'

"What does it mean?" Mrs. Longmire kept muttering. "She's obviously not dead."

"It means, Mother, that there's a mix up somewhere, city records and things, that's all." James knew it was more, but thought to try and convince himself. It didn't work.

As they slowed to approach the long driveway to their house, a blue BMW pulled out the drive and turned south. As it passed them, James gasped. Slumped in the front seat was a bushy-haired girl.

"Misty!" he shouted. "That was Misty!" He hopped about in his seat, fighting with the seat belt that pinned him back. "Turn around! That was Misty!" Then as if slapped in the face, he looked to his mother. "Who was she with?"

Mrs. Longmire just shook her head. "I don't think that was Misty. Wasn't that the lawyer fellow working with Billy, and his secretary?"

James thought for a second. "No! That was not Billy's... Please turn around, Mother. Just for a second. Please!"

Mrs. Longmire made a slow cautious U-turn. If it was Misty, she was secretly hoping the car would turn off somewhere before they could catch up. If it wasn't, then she hoped they would find it quickly and so get back to all the things being left undone because of this unpleasant interruption of life. The Greys had become far more trouble than she ever thought possible when she offered to do the good Christian thing of renting the house to a needy couple. This whole disappearance of Misty was an answer to prayer and she wanted it to stay that way.

"Hurry, Mom! Step on it, please."

"I'm not going to speed if that's what you mean."

"But the light..." James sighed as he watched the BMW pass through on a yellow while he and his mother came to a stop. The light seemed bent on taking forever. When they finally got through, the BMW could have gone a mile in a dozen directions.

With a sick heart, James rode in silence back to their house. He hadn't seen her face, but he knew it was Misty. *She looked drugged,* he thought, picturing her head slumped against the window. *Who was she with?*

When he entered his bedroom, he suddenly stopped. Someone had been here. Then his eyes fell on the scribbled note. Heart jumping into overtime, he read the lines out loud.

"'Dearest James,

I was kidnapped. Ganny is dead. I really, really x1,000 miss you. Is my mom... is Max okay? I...'"

Completely stunned, he stood staring at the note, a million thoughts surging through his brilliant mind. *Why couldn't she finish? Why didn't she stay? Where has she been? Who was she with?*

"Ganny dead?"

Adrenaline rushed as he pulled the card from his pocket and called Detective Yurkowski, a large, lanky man assigned to Misty's case. James had caught the numbers on the BMW's license, maybe. If the car was still in town…

"Two twenty-eight, out of state, that's all I could see. Newer, four-door, dark blue. She looked drugged, you know, her head slumped to the side." In strained voice, he told detective Yurkowski about the note. "They turned up Fourth Street, maybe, I couldn't… if you send out some cars—"

"We'll look into it, son. You just let me know if she shows up again. Thanks for the call."

Just short of begging his mother, James got permission to take the car and look for Misty. He drove for hours, scanning back lots and alleys, places he thought kidnappers would hide. He checked every gas station, every grocery store, every school and park. He went to all the fast-food joints, pulling into McDonald's just as a busload of high school girls from Brenton took their sweet time to unload and file past. Stuck behind the bus, he waited to park. More than a few girls gave him provocative looks, one blowing a kiss, touching it to her tightly formed backside projected straight toward James.

When a tall blond tapped on his window, he blushed.

"Are you coming in?" she asked, with a seductive smile. "You look lonely. I'm Lyla." She proceeded to open his door and then noticed Misty's locket about his neck. Quick as a snake snatching its prey, she had her head inside the car, her hands about his neck, and her lips firmly planted on his.

When James struggled free, gasping for breath, the girl stood back, dangling the locket from her hand, a triumphant smile drawing her lips.

"Now you're coming in," she said, sauntering off toward the doors.

In a fury, James honked at the bus still blocking his way. He jumped out to rush after the girl, but she scooted inside. Daring not to leave his mother's car unattended, he hopped back in to honk once more as the bus slowly pulled ahead. He parked in a frenzy and ran to the doors, his face livid.

Pushing his way through the crowd of girls, he demanded Lyla give the necklace back. Only after being nearly smothered in a wet kiss did he retrieve it.

When James drove off with a flushed face, he never once saw the blue BMW parked just behind where the bus had stopped to unload.

"Where are you, Misty?" he said, his voice pleading as he pulled out onto the main road. He wiped his lips and spat. "Where have you gone?"

27 VISITORS

2:00 AM Friday, October 30

"If you won't let me drive, then at least pull over. You need rest," Misty said, her tone strong.

"You don't have a license. And chill out. You're getting cranky."

"I'm not cranky, you're cranky."

It was two in the morning and Roman had almost nodded off several times. Grumbling, he took the next exit onto an empty road leading nowhere. A red motel sign flickered in the distance, toward which he drove slowly, struggling inside.

Misty watched him, her eyes following the profile as they pulled into the rather rundown motel.

"I'll get two rooms," Roman said. "Stay put."

When he came back, his face seemed stressed.

"What's wrong?" Misty asked.

"They only take cash. What place only takes cash?"

"Then we sleep in the car, for an hour or two."

"No, I got a room, the only one I could afford, a single. I'll sleep in the car."

"No you won't."

"Well, you sure aren't going to—"

"I trust you, Roman. Let's go."

When Misty saw the tiny bed, she had second thoughts. Roman offered to sleep on the floor, which looked like it hadn't been cleaned since the moon landing. After a deep breath, Misty suggested, then insisted they just sleep on the bed. It had been way more than just a very long and trying day. They needed sleep, and needed it bad.

After a bit of awkwardness and vain efforts to keep from touching each other, especially since the mattress slumped inward like a bowl of mush, they both conceded and lay with backs together.

As Misty lay as still as she could, listening to the boy beside her breathing slow and steady, she once more viewed the images firmly locked inside her mind.

'Crime Scene. Do Not Cross.' What had happened? Had her father finally… no, no it couldn't be… but maybe…

When her muffled whimpers and not so muffled snivels awakened Roman, he rolled over and with gentle kindness whispered that somehow things would work out.

"You need sleep," he said groggily. "Try to… think of something else… like James."

Feeling the body of Roman now directly behind her, she at first tensed, thinking to jump from the bed. But for some reason, she stayed. When the slow and steady breathing came again, she sighed, a measure of stress lifting. He was a gentleman, a rare find in a world of jerks and twerds.

She did think of James. He too was a gentleman. She thought of Ganny's advice for dealing with the bitter things. 'I think he's… well… rather sweet.' His kisses sure were. The last image of him in math class defending her brought a sudden deep longing, a sickness of heart. She wanted him close, to be near him, with him. Pulling up every memory she could, her mind swam with scenes full of feeling, of friendship, of comfort, but always, like persistent mosquitoes, came the memories of guns, of Ganny suffering, of explosions, of hypodermic needles, of trains and pain.

She jerked when her finger pulled the trigger, the loud report numbing her ears, the blood oozing on the ground behind the tool shed.

Roman hadn't budged. She sighed with sorrow for him, such a nice guy, dragged into her mess.

Ganny's mess. Everyone's mess. Can we really stop them, get to Washington, alive? Find the right people… convince them without the locket?

For a time, she contemplated sneaking out and driving away without Roman. *He can call his dad, get a ride, live another day.* Could she safely drive the rest of the way? Roman said they were still over twelve hours away.

In slow, gentle movements, she lifted the covers, pausing to let him fall back into sleep. Climbing from the bed, she made her way toward the door. She paused to listen as she felt for the keys inside his coat. Then she thought of money. How would she buy gas and food? How would he fare if she took his wallet? What if someone asked for I.D.?

She slumped, a heavy sense of woe sweeping over her, its weight pressing. Standing at the door, with keys and wallet in hand, she whimpered inside. It was all too much, way too much for a sixteen-year-old girl.

Why me? What have I done? I don't deserve this, do I? She glanced at Roman still sleeping soundly. *He doesn't deserve this, any of this.*

And with that, she opened the door.

Thud! The door stopped short, the safety chain rattling taut. Misty looked back at the bed. Roman hadn't moved. But as she went to lift the chain, she saw through the open crack, two men standing near Roman's BMW. He had parked it away from their room and directly under a light.

Car thieves! From a glint of light, she caught the sight of something like a shoebox in the hand of a smaller man. He looked left and right, then dropped to crawl under the BMW. After two full minutes, he was back up and the two men walked off into the darkness where a car sat idling. As they drove off toward the freeway, Misty's chest thumped like a bass drum.

Those… weren't… car thieves.

For some time she sat on the edge of the bed, keys and wallet still in hand, a hand that wouldn't stop trembling. She knew what they had done. They had been following, waiting for the right moment. They no longer cared about the locket, whatever it had. They wanted her silenced.

"This is too big," she whined, lying down at the feet of Roman, her heart trembling. For what seemed a long time she lay there, her face buried in the covers, the pain within so overwhelming she wished to die, to fall asleep and never wake, to finally and forever... just forget everything.

Friday morning, October 30

When she awoke, bright light filled the room. Rolled in covers, she sat up and blinked, wondering for a second at her surroundings. Then it all came back. She looked about for Roman. He was nowhere in the grungy room and the sun already shone high in the sky.

Standing, she called his name and then seeing the safety chain undone, ran to the door. Just as she opened it wide, Roman shut the door of his BMW, his eyes on the dash.

Covers tangled about her feet, Misty hopped out, arms waving, lungs screaming.

"Nooo! Roman, nooo!" She stumbled, trying to run. Finally shaking the covers loose, she hobbled toward him, her head wagging wildly as she continued to scream. "Don't start the car!"

Roman inserted the key, his mind still perplexed at finding the sleeping girl with his keys and wallet. Was she going to leave him? At first, he thought her a deranged thief, taking her time to create this elaborate scheme. But just to steal his wallet and car? Then he figured she was desperate and confused, having possibly lost her family, and so wasn't thinking clearly.

He turned the key, powering up the dash and lights. The seatbelt warning chimed. *Maybe trying to protect me,* he thought, *leave me behind for my own good?* For a second he paused, glancing up to ponder.

Wham! Misty stumbled, falling hard onto the hood, her head

striking the windshield. The look of terror in her eyes sent Roman squirming back. He stared in wonder at the young girl pounding on his windshield, yelling for him to get out.

Misty yanked open the door. "Get out!" she screamed, grabbing his arm and wrenching him out onto the pavement. Bewildered, Roman tried to stand but Misty kept pulling and tugging, trying to slide his butt over the weed-infested asphalt. He struggled, but her nails bit into his flesh.

"Stop!" he shouted. "What are you doing?"

Crazed, she kept tugging till they were several yards from the car.

"Misty!" He broke his arm free. "What has gotten—?"

BA-WOOOF! As if a ball of fire had fallen from the sky and landed smack on top of Roman's car, flames shot out in all directions, rolling over each other, tumbling outward right up and over Misty and Roman.

Knocking them onto their backs, the flames spread out and upward, scorching the asphalt with black and orange heat. It sucked the air from the parking lot, pulling it upward into a cloud of oily smoke. Within seconds the blast was over, leaving a mangled pile of metal burning with flames dancing wildly toward the late morning sky.

For a moment, neither could breathe. The air had disappeared. Soot and smoke filled their lungs with burning pain, their faces flushed and singed. Now Roman was the one dragging Misty, stopping only when he bumped against a car at the far end of the lot. He helped her stand, his red face wide with terror.

He stood holding her, trembling and speechless. Misty gasped for breath, her eyes stinging.

"Oh, God," she whimpered. "Your car. Oh, God, I should've..."

Roman stood huffing, his face fully perplexed. Anger, bewilderment, fear, all swirled about wildly inside. "How'd you know? How in the heck did you know?" He sounded angry. He looked around, searching for answers.

Misty stood panting, eyes watering. "Oh, God. Roman… your car."

Their brows and bangs were singed, their faces stinging warm.

Glancing about, Roman hustled Misty behind a low brick wall, a landscape feature with a flag pole and lights. He pulled Misty down beside him, hunkering as if in battle. He stared hard at her, his eyes wild. His clothes and hair smelled awful.

Fearful panic had gripped his heart. "A bomb!" he said incredulously. "How did you know? Did *you* put…?" He shook himself, realizing how stupid that sounded.

"I saw them," Misty said, "last night. I… oh my." She swallowed hard, her throat painfully dry. Slowly wagging her head, she murmured, "I was going to… oh my. Oh, Roman, if you'd…" Still winded, she slumped over into him, her head on his neck. Her warm tears wet his skin, her arms limp at her sides.

For a moment Roman didn't know what to do, his shaky hands taking one of hers. She softly cried, muttering the words, "Could never, ever forget… I'd never forgive…"

Then she flung her arms around him. Her singed hair smothered his face, her wet cheek pressed to his. She sniffled loudly, her nose nearly in his ear.

Awkward, yet somehow natural, he put his arms around her. Her jerking sobbing shook them both, her hands trembling like his. For a time they sat behind the low wall, held there by overpowering fear.

When Misty finally told how she had planned to leave without him, to protect him, Roman's face darkened.

"You'd never have made it," he said sternly, sounding like a parent. "Ever driven through a major city? Oh, that's right. You don't even have a license."

Misty stiffened, his tone quite cynical. But then he looked at her with the most sincere and loving gaze. He studied her reddened face for some time, his eyes seeming to memorize every feature. Her long lashes were curled back, her brows, almost gone.

"No, you probably would have made it," he said, sighing. "And I would have followed, mad as hell, grumbling the whole way, but following."

He offered up a silly smile, then glanced over the wall at the crowd circling the mangled pile of burning metal.

"And both of us," he said sardonically, "pursued by guys who plant bombs under your car." He shivered, the stark fear returning. He shook his head, exhaling another sigh. Then, as if completely natural, he reached up and brushed aside a strand of Misty's hair. A little crispy, it hung over one eye. His arm and hand shook as he tucked it back into the disheveled spirals.

"Are you hurt anywhere?" he asked, his voice soft.

Misty shook her head, looking into those perfect eyes. "I'm sorry," she said with a sniffle. "I should have told you. Please forgive—"

"No," he said firmly. "You saved my life… again." He tried to sound calm, but his whole frame quivered, his heart still thudding.

"What do we do, Roman? Now we've no car."

"Maybe…" He looked off toward the freeway. Sirens sounded in the distance. "Maybe we let the CIA handle this, like they're supposed to." He sighed again, his breath jagged. "We're just… it's too big for us. I mean…"

"I promised Ganny," Misty said, staring at the dry grass between her feet. "You… should go home… be safe."

Roman let his head drop back against the brick wall. He didn't know what to do. He wanted to go home, but dark fear hung over that thought. Tell the police? *How did they follow us?* he pondered, the sirens now exiting off the freeway.

"No," he said, "I'm going with you." After heated discussion, Roman giving all the reasons why he needed her, Misty giving all the reasons she should go alone, the fire trucks arrived, bringing with them three police cars, two sheriffs, and a highway patrol, followed by an ambulance and lots of onlookers.

"We need to tell them," Roman insisted. "We can't do this alone."

"If they found us here…" Misty suddenly paused, then yanked Roman back down behind the wall. "No! If we talk to the police, they'll know we survived. Like this, we're dead." She held his arm tight, her gaze intense. "No, we stay dead and keep going." She loosened her grip, studying his face. "Well, what'd ya think?"

When the last remains of Roman's car were loaded and being hauled off toward the freeway, Misty's stomach growled. Several blocks away they found the dingiest café on planet earth, where they took a booth, only after sharing time in the world's dirtiest restroom, trying to undo the damage of the explosion.

Misty had pulled her hair back, binding it with a rubber band. Her red cheeks looked tender, but not so burned as to need treatment. It was mostly the brows and lashes that suffered, the crispy stubble looking rather strange.

Misty ate like a teenage girl coming off a long arduous fast. Four eggs, five pancakes, and six strips of bacon, with a large sweet roll to 'hold things in.'

Muttering apologies for a sudden unpredicted burp, she wiped her curvaceous lips and smiled a silly girly kind of smile that made Roman chuckle.

Then his face went somber again. "This is real, isn't it?"

"Of course it's real!" For a moment, Misty took offense. Ganny was dead, her family possibly dead, she ached with constant pain, and now Roman's car was burnt rubble, a horrible fate intended for them.

"And the 'digital bomb'?" Roman asked.

Misty watched him processing the heaviness of it all. "Ganny gave her life to stop it," she said softly. "It's real."

"So what's in the locket?"

Misty shook her head. "Ganny just said, info on the bomb." Misty thought for a moment. "She knew there were moles inside the CIA. Larkin talked of big money. I bet… their names are in the locket! The moles!" She vigorously nodded her head, some loose strands bobbing in rhythm. "That's why they want it so bad, want us dead."

Roman slumped back with a sigh. He glanced about the café, scrutinizing the overweight elderly farmers faithfully munching their pancakes like cows chewing cud.

"I don't want to save the world," he said. "Can't someone else do it?"

Misty watched him. She enjoyed staring at him. He didn't mind, didn't get goofy like boys in high school. He rather enjoyed her focused attention. Again, she looked at his lips, now curved in a smug little smile. Without realizing, she lightly wet her own.

Roman's smile went flat, his gaze going straight to her lips.

"We better go!" she said, standing suddenly. "We need to tell them. We need to get to Washington. Halloween's tomorrow night."

Roman stood slowly. "We don't have a car, Misty. We need to get home."

"D.C. or northwest?" a large man with a chest the literal size of a barrel asked as he passed by en route to the restroom.

"Ahh… D.C." Roman sputtered, totally caught off guard.

"Ya see that car burst aflame over yonder," the barrel-chested man said, shaking his head, a large head with a very full beard, to which scraps of breakfast still clung. "All them computer parts they be putting in cars these days…" He paused to look them over, large brown eyes scrutinizing the two.

"Well, if ya need a lift, I'm doing D.C.," he said. "Could use the company." He paused to look them over one more time, puzzled, but then shrugged. "But no pot smokin' ya hear?"

Before they knew what had happened, they were rumbling east in an eighteen-wheeler rigged for long days on the road.

"Been driving truck since I could spit tobacca," Corby Dan Dankow said with a near toothless grin. "This rig's me honey.

Been to every state but them islands that want to be American." He nodded to a hula doll dangling from his visor.

After tons of questions, each followed by loads of advice, Corby noticed Misty dosing off. "No nappin' in the control center, missy." He nodded over his shoulder to the sleeping compartment behind some very dirty curtains that did more than hint at the filthy blankets that lay beyond.

Without even noticing the filth, Misty fell fast asleep as Roman nestled in for a long, lively ride to Washington D.C.

"She could be in the movies," Colby said.

"Huh?" Roman glanced over.

"Your little sister. She got some looks to her, don't she?"

"Sister?" Roman straightened.

"Oh, ain't she?"

For a brief moment, Roman sat staring off into the road ahead.

"Well, is she, or ain't she?"

"No," he said, shaking his head. "Just a friend… that needs help."

Corby's eyes became slits. "Looks a bit young, boy. You better not—"

"No!" Roman shot a protesting look. "No, she's just a friend. Not my sister, and… not anything else."

Despite the rule of no dozing in the control center, Roman too had succumbed to the stress and trauma of the last two days. After several hours of troubled sleep, he awoke with a jerk, yelling something about his car and a bomb. He wiped the drool off his chin, rubbing his head, which had been wedged between the seat and the window. The sun hung low in the western sky.

"You two pups sure be mighty sleepy," Colby said, rather suspiciously. "What's the real deal? Ain't one for prying, but you got me fiddling."

Roman massaged his neck with a groan. "Been on the road, that's all. Driving through the night. I'm sure you know what that's like."

Colby gave a satisfied nod and proceeded with a bounty of instructions on staying awake during long night drives.

"I gotta pee." Misty poked her head through the grungy curtains, her bushy hair a tangled mess. "Are we stopping soon?" She rubbed her eyes, giving Roman a pleasant smile.

Without shame, Colby told them how he used the bottle when time was 'of short supply,' offering it to Roman who drew back so hard his head hit the window. Chuckling, Colby said they would stop at the next 'trucker's inn.'

Both Roman and Misty were surprised at how long they had slept and how far they had traveled. With Washington now just five hours away, Misty felt a sense of both hope and anxious tension. She motioned for Roman to crawl back into the sleeping bunk with her. Colby eyed him suspiciously.

"What's the plan?" Roman asked, still rubbing his neck. "We just walk in and find this Bellows guy?"

"Is that a bad plan?" The lost puppy look on Misty's face both amused and disturbed Roman. He thought of how she'd shot that mercenary in the leg, and then the dead CIA imposter at the hospital. He touched his face, feeling the shrapnel-scabs from the old stone wall, then touched his bristled eyebrows. Who was this girl?

He shook his head. "You are so..."

"So what?" Her face became a scowl.

"Like no girl I've ever met." He looked rather forlorn. "I wish... I wish you were..."

"What?"

"Nothing."

"You wish I were nothing?"

"I wish..." He paused with a glance to her lips, "a little older."

Misty looked away, toying with the image of being older—a college girl in class with Roman, walking the campus by his side, his arm around her, holding her close. Her cheeks warmed and she cleared her throat.

"So, is that a good plan, or do we do something else?"

"What if they don't believe us, or…?" He saw the flames billowing upward, the guy combing the McDonald's, and again, the dead CIA agent on the hospital floor. "We need to be careful, Misty." He lowered his voice to a faint whisper. She nodded, taking a deep breath.

"You two pups behavin' back there? No funny stuff, ya hear."

Misty poked her head out. "I'm too young for funny stuff." She gave Colby a big smile, hiding the pain and dread building inside. "How far can you take us?"

"My trail ends in Winchester."

Roman poked his head out. "How far is that from Langley?"

"About an hour, I reckon. You live in Langley?"

"No." Roman said. "New York. Greenhaven, in Rye."

Colby nodded. "Never been there. What ya need in Langley? Visiting the CIA? Y'all secret agents or something?" He laughed, his belly bouncing. Neither responded, which brought his laugh to an abrupt halt. "What you pups up to? In trouble or something? That burned-out car…" He frowned. "I don't pry, but would I be right in thinking it was yours?"

"Ahhh…" Roman tried to answer.

Colby's gaze grew stern. "You ain't working for no liberal commies are ya?"

"Commies? No!" Roman replied adamantly. "We need to find… a friend. Get some stuff sorted out."

"It was our car," Misty said, offering a pleasant smile. "And you've been a great help, Colby. If you can get us to Winchester, that would be great." She closed her eyes for a second. "Is sixty-six the best route to D.C.?"

"Could take that, but seven through Leesburg be a heck-a faster coming from Winchester."

Roman scrunched one eye, cocking his head at Misty. She gave a little shrug.

"If you're in trouble, little one, you let ol' Colby know, ya hear?" Misty assured him they were okay, wondering if James would consider it a lie. "Only trouble I'm in," she said, squeezing her legs, "is needing a restroom."

Thursday evening, October 29

After searching for hours, James returned home, his heart sick with despair. Dusk had come with a chill, its gloom settling over his soul. As he pulled up the driveway, he noticed his house unusually dark. He had his mother's car, so where could she have gone? His breath condensed as he walked to the front door.

Then he froze.

The front door sat slightly ajar, something his mother would never allow. Slowly James pushed the door inward, his steps creaking over the old wood floor of the entryway.

"Mom? Dad? Anybody home?"

He paused, thinking he heard something. Listening to the silence, his own breath sounding too loud, he stood wondering. *Must have gone out with someone from church,* he thought, trying to calm his anxious nerves. He went to flip on the lights, expecting to find a note.

What he found left him speechless.

As when straight-line winds scatter lawn furniture, topple grills, and fling debris into every corner, the Longmire house was a horrendous mess.

Smashed dishes seemed to be everywhere. Papers, files, books, lamps, sliced cushions, even food items lay strewn about as if sent through one gigantic fan—the entire contents of the house, blended up and spewed out in all directions.

James stood in silent shock, his eyes trying to behold the mess that lay before him. Then came the sound. As before, he thought he heard something, something very muffled, but when he listened, only his pounding heart and heavy breaths filled his ears.

"Mom! Dad!" he called out in a frantic voice, horrid pictures pressing to come forward. Then racing through the house, he went from room to room, fearing most to open his parents' bedroom.

When he stepped into his room, his heart sank. Everything that was anything, lay smashed, broken, disassembled, or ripped in shreds. Either someone hated everything he owned or they were looking very meticulously for something—something small.

He picked up a piece of broken pottery, a fragment of an oblong ball that Misty had made for him, leaving a small slit in the top. 'For hiding secret things,' she had said. It lay shattered as if hit by a hammer.

Sudden, violent dread washed over him, his mind seeing the bloodstains on the Greys' front porch. His heart beat so hard his ears felt plugged.

He rushed downstairs, searching for the phone. Then the sound. He froze, listening.

The basement!

Flicking on the light, his blood tingled through his fingers. The first stair creaked. Like an ornery raven squawking in protest, the old wooden tread announced his approach. Then the sound came again—a muffled cry.

"Mom?"

With tearful relief, he undid the zip-ties and duct tape holding his mother to an old metal chair. Her eyes, wide with terror, gave James a good image of what had happened. She burst into hysterics as he held her tight, trying to comfort her with words of safety, but his own heart screamed fear and doubt.

What was going on? All hell had broken loose and they hadn't a clue why. Hands quivering, he dialed his father.

When Mr. Longmire arrived with the police, the house soon became a whirlwind of activity. Four policemen filed in along with a photographer, two detectives, (one being Yurkowski,) a lab guy and gal gathering fingerprints, too many questions about this and that, all while Mrs. Longmire sobbed and bawled, her eyes red with endless tears. It seemed way into over-kill.

What is going on? James wondered.

"Anyone you know," asked Detective Schmidt, "have a grudge or reason to do this?" The fact that nothing valuable was missing left them all perplexed. It was obviously more than just a prank.

"They were searching for something," the tall, lanky detective Yurkowski said, his eyes narrowed as he scanned the wreckage. "Something small is my guess." He held up a tiny wooden case smashed to splinters, once an antique box for a small folding eyeglass.

"That was my father's," said Mr. Longmire. "He'd made that as a boy. What a shame. Could've just opened it."

"Angry," said Yurkowski. "Frustrated, not finding their quarry."

"What *was* their quarry?" Detective Schmidt asked Mr. Longmire rather accusingly.

"How would I— I don't know!"

James watched his father confront the man. *What had they been looking for?* he wondered.

"They seem to be professionals, Mr. Longmire," Schmidt continued. "Sure you don't know what they were after? Information? Smuggled diamonds? Drugs?"

"What! You're kidding!" Mr. Longmire looked about the room. "He's kidding, right?"

As the chaos continued, James returned to his room, his heart now so heavy, he let the tears roll. He stood before his window, his mind struggling to recall the memory of holding Misty. He longed for her ability to recall events as though seconds fresh.

He pulled her note from his pocket. 'I really, really x1,000 miss you.' Reaching up, he withdrew the locket from beneath his shirt. He popped the tiny latch and stared at the little black and white of Misty. Warmth and pain simultaneously flushed through his veins. The hustle and bustle downstairs drew to a close as the flashing lights outside grew fewer and fewer.

As James went to close the locket, something small fell to the floor. He looked down at the piles of junk, once his precious belongings, scanning for what may have fallen. Seeing nothing, he closed the locket and tucked it back beneath his shirt.

"James," his father called. "Come downstairs, please."

For some time the family sat on what chairs could still hold weight. His father said they would spend the night in a hotel, to which James shook his head.

"You two go. I'll stay here."

"You will not!" his mother protested. "What if those horrible men return?"

"I don't think they will, Mom." James didn't seem to care either way. Never had he felt so sick of heart as he did that evening. *Why would Misty leave? And with some guy in a BMW? Was he the kidnapper?*

Willie Longmire shook his head. "I just don't understand what they could've been looking for. At least they left your jewels, dear."

Mrs. Longmire found no consolation and went into another fit of bemoaning tears.

"Take her to the Smithton, Dad. I'll be fine. I'll call if anything's up."

As James climbed into bed, he wondered if he'd made the right choice. Alone in a quiet, ransacked house, he battled the fears that tried to arise. "Come kill me," he whispered. "I don't care." Self-pity overwhelmed his soul, filling his mind with rancid thoughts of misery and gloom. Just days ago, the girl of his heart had lain here in his bed. He had held her tight, his lips smothering hers, his mother coming up the stairs.

He chuckled. "That was crazy, so bonking crazy." Then all

went sad again. Was this all a nightmare, punishment for kissing the girl next door? Was he just a twerd taking advantage of her?

"I would die for her." His voice sounded strange in the stillness of the empty house. He lay with hands behind his head, a tear making its way down his face past his ear. "I'm sorry God, sorry if I've done something wrong. I shouldn't have kissed her, shouldn't have made her enter the contest. She's so—"

He bolted upright.

Something had crunched downstairs. James sucked in a breath and held it, his heart leaping into panic mode. Nothing more came. He lay back, chiding himself both for being afraid and for being so stupid as to stay in the house alone.

Then it came again. Footsteps this time, footsteps slowly making their way over shards of dishes and broken glass.

James flew from his bed, pulling out the junk he'd shoved underneath, searching for the rope ladder. The footsteps ceased. They too were listening. James tried to move silently, but when broken stuff covered every inch, he finally just went for it.

Yanking out the ladder, which caught and tangled, he scolded himself as he pulled.

The footsteps quickened.

Jerking hard, he freed the ladder, then flung open the window. As he dropped the rope ladder, securing it to the sill, he suddenly stopped.

The heavy steps had entered his room.

"Leave it!"

James turned to face the gruff voice. A short, stocky figure filled the doorway. Enough light shone to reveal a gun in his left hand, a long suppressor on the barrel.

James tried to breathe, to swallow. "Who… what do you want?" He tried to sound brave.

For a moment the figure stood silent. Then the man came near. James pressed against his desk, eye on the gun.

"Where is it, kid? Where's the locket?"

"What?" James touched the locket beneath his t-shirt. "You want what?"

"The girl's locket. You have it?"

"But why? It's my girlfriend's. Why—?"

"Shut up and give me the locket." The man came forward so quickly that James fell back onto his desk. A sudden yank, and the man had Misty's locket in his hand. "Tell anyone and you're dead, understand?"

James nodded, his whole body quivering.

As the car drove away, James slunk to the cluttered floor, limbs like noodles. Never in his life had he been so scared. It seemed a long time before his heart and lungs settled down, but he couldn't move, his cheeks tingling with numbness.

What do they want with Misty's locket? he pondered. Is that why she was kidnapped?

For half an hour he sat on the floor, his mind a mess of fears and worries. He so wanted to call his dad, but then what would happen? Who were these guys? How much did they know?

Oh, Misty, what have you gotten into?

It was almost eleven in the morning when James rolled over with a groan. He hadn't left his room, hadn't called anyone, and surely hadn't slept, at least not until sometime after 5:00 AM. As the late morning light spread over the broken junk, he rubbed his eyes, searching, as he had all night, for answers.

Angered at how late he'd slept, he also wondered what he'd have done different.

Upon returning from the bathroom, he stopped, suddenly remembering the sound of something falling from the locket. On hands and knees he searched, careful to move each piece, his heart hoping, yet anxious for what he might find.

Like solving a riddle, he knew it as soon as he saw it—an SD card as small as they come. "Why would Misty...?"

"James? Are you home?"

"Of course he's home, dear. Where else would he be?"

In revived agony, Mrs. Longmire bemoaned the destruction of her home. They had come by earlier, only to find James sound asleep, so they went out for breakfast.

After setting the SD card on his desk, James dressed and went downstairs. Every fiber in him wanted to tell of the visitor and now his discovery, yet something greater caused him to hold his tongue.

"Everything go okay, son?"

James hated lying. "Should've gone with you guys. Would've slept better."

After a bit of scrounging, he managed some breakfast, then returned to his room where he sat staring at the tiny card. *Why would Misty have this in her locket? She doesn't even have a cell phone. Why did that guy—?*

He bolted upright. "He'll be back!" With heart and mind once again plunging into panic mode, James scurried about his room like a flustered squirrel looking for a place to hide his only acorn. After a moment, he stopped with a forlorn sigh, his shoulders drooping as he stared at the tiny card resting in his palm.

"They'll just torture me till I talk." He plopped into his chair. "Why do they…? What's on this thing?"

"James, we're going to meet with the insurance agent," his father hollered up the stairs. "Mother notified the school. Don't touch anything until they take pictures, okay?"

"Okay, bye."

Since the shooting and now the burglary, SAT testing for James had been deferred.

As he watched them drive away, he turned the little card over and over in his hand, his mind filling with dreadful thoughts of torture scenes from movies, the image of Dustin Hoffman getting holes drilled through his teeth made him twitch and shudder.

"Kidnapped, for this? They wanted her locket, for this. How did they know… why would she have…?"

He sat for a long time, afraid to go anywhere or call anyone. A dozen times he went to call the police, and then detective Yurkowski, but each time set the phone down in fear. 'Tell anyone and you're dead, understand?'

"Just give it to them," he finally told himself. "Wait for them to come, and give it to them. Then they kill me!" A dreadful woe washed over him, that kind of dread that presses down, smothering every flicker of hope.

The longer he stared at the card, the more he yearned to know its contents. If he knew the contents... "Numbers probably, or a list of bad guys. I need someone to open this, someone I can trust." He smiled, just a little. "I need... a nerd!"

Friday, October 30

"Oh, fat fanny!" Roman stopped suddenly as he and Misty walked back to Colby's rig.

"What?"

For a moment, Roman stood speechless, his eyes staring off into nowhere.

"What'd you say?" Misty asked again.

"I am so stupid!" His mouth just hung as he wagged his head. "Misty, I'm so sorry, so totally stupid!" He ran a hand through his thick hair. "That guy... in McDonald's! Misty, that was your James! And I think that was your... Oh, fat fanny!"

"My fat what?" Misty asked with agitation.

"No! Not your..." Roman spun in a circle. "Misty... no way, no stinking way. The guy kissing the blond... that was James... your James!"

Misty stiffened, her mind searching.

"Don't you remember? You walked right past them at the counter. I knew I had seen him somewhere but, how was I to think...?"

Misty stepped back, her face contorting. "James wouldn't kiss..." The dread overtaking Misty's face brought Roman to a start.

"No! No, no, no. She was kissing him. She had your locket. Is your locket silver, real small on a thin chain?"

Misty nodded with eyes blinking fast. "He gave her my

locket?" she asked, her voice faltering.

"No! Listen." As Roman explained the whole scene, tears pooled in Misty's eyes. "He was furious, Misty. He was about to rip the locket off her neck. She grabbed him. He didn't kiss her." Roman then covered his face with both hands, shaking his head. "Maybe it wasn't him, maybe I'm going nuts. Why would your James…?"

Misty looked off into the distance. "My locket… kissing James…?"

"You pups ready to roll?" Colby walked up with both hands full of snacks and drinks. "Next stop, Winchester, Virginia."

The air inside the rig was far from pleasant. Not only did Colby's fast-food binge create enough methane to seriously damage the ozone, but Misty's silence grew heavier with each passing mile. She refused to discuss any of the ugly details regarding the incident at McDonald's.

Misty had no trouble recalling the scene. The problem was that she had not paid any attention to the kissing couple for her memory to grab details. The other problem was that when she did focus, it seemed more and more like James had taken advantage of her disappearance and found himself one of those 'nice girls.'

But my locket? Why would he give that long-legged…? A slew of nasty adjectives filled her mind, bringing her blood to an even higher boil. At one particular moment, she poked her head through the dirty curtains and yelled an incoherent string of sentences at Roman, which left him staring blankly through the windshield. He had told her over and over, describing the scene a dozen times, until Misty screamed at him to stop.

"I think she ain't in the mood for listening," Colby said with a nod, as if he had some great insight into the female brain. "Needs time to process. That's how gals work through stuff like cheating boyfriends and all. I remember when…"

As Colby went off into a monologue of all his encounters with females, giving more advice and information than any twenty-year-old guy would ever want, Roman sat pondering.

If James has the locket...?

The miles rolled by to the sounds of country music and Colby's relational advice. Roman gave up on Misty, figuring it was more the stress over her family and Ganny and all the other crud. He never thought the connection with James would bring so much agony. For a good hour he scolded himself, believing it to be all a mistake. "Wasn't her locket, wasn't her James." But then he'd shake his head, knowing in his heart it was the guy from the picture.

Approaching Winchester with only an hour or two of daylight, he tried to plan out their next move. *Is the building always open? Who has access? Will Bellows be in on Friday night or Saturday morning? Will anyone answer his phone? Can they stop the 'bomb' without the locket?*

Over and over he considered scenarios, wondering if Misty would even cooperate now. She had remained silent in the sleeping compartment for several hours, causing no little concern, but he resolved to just let her be.

"She's been through hell and back," he said to himself.

"The little missy?" Colby caught his words.

Roman glanced over, his eyes dark and weary. He nodded, giving no further details.

"Got someone to meet ya?" Colby asked. "Pick ya up in Winchester?"

Roman thought for a bit. The idea of calling his father had come to mind many times, but fear for his father overshadowed the yearning to call for help. With horrid memories of losing his mother and sister, he wasn't going to take any chances, not with the singed hairs on his head still giving fresh reminders of how thorough these guys could be.

"No," he said. "Not sure if we'll continue on tonight or stay in Winchester."

He had barely finished speaking when Misty popped her head through.

"We're going to Langley tonight!" she said firmly, looking at Roman for a moment, her eyes very red and swollen. Then with a swish, she pulled the curtains back together and the miles rolled by as before.

"Women!" Colby shook his head. "Don't let 'em fool ya. What they're saying, ain't ever what they're thinking. Be heaven and hades all wrapped in one."

Roman silently chuckled at Colby's analysis, but then stopped, lest he incurred the wrath of Misty any more, if that were even possible.

As the signs for Winchester became more frequent, he wondered how paranoid he should be. If they knew his car, or what had been his car, then they knew his home address, his father's name, his college, his…

If they have credit card numbers and names, he mused, *they now have mine.* He had used his card for gas and to buy food for Misty and himself several times. He would need to use his card to get them to Langley, and if they needed another hotel…

He chided himself for not using an ATM earlier and so travel without a trail. *But they'd find us anyway.* He sighed as hopeless despair moved into his heart. He wished Misty wasn't so mad. Despite all the trauma, she had been incredibly strong, unlike any girl he'd ever known. Even in the face of death, running from unseen dangers, he had found himself relishing her presence. He loved being with her.

She seemed smart, very observant. On more than several occasions, she left him spellbound by her recollection of trivial details, remembering things that no one could or should remember.

She had an alluring beauty of innocence and natural grace, was fully formed and well proportioned, with lips and eyes that made any guy struggle to keep from staring.

Again Roman sighed. How would he tell his dad about all this? *Hey Dad, I befriended this high school junior while on my way back to college… a girl. She'd gotten herself mixed up with some high-level conspiracy and oh… did I tell you my car blew up?'*

"What am I doing?" he muttered.

"You ain't doing squat, boy." Colby glanced over. "Like riding with a wooden Injun."

Roman smiled at the trucker. *'And did I tell you, Dad, about the truck driver named Colby?'*

Friday afternoon, October 30

When James stepped into the room of the infamous nerd, Stanton T. Froulinger, he stopped in amazement. Lining every wall, mounted on makeshift desks and plywood constructed platforms, were at least a dozen computers and monitors.

"My word, Stanton, what do you do in here, monitor the U.S. government?"

Stanton smiled his quirky smile, shifting his weight back and forth. He had rushed home from school to find James waiting outside his door. The idea of helping James on something connected to Misty ignited every cell within the teen's scrawny frame.

"Those are for gaming, and those for browsing, those for homework, those for—" He quickly blacked out a screen full of scantily clad women, his face blushing bright red.

"But can't you do all that with just one computer?" James asked.

"Just one?" Stanton went off into a hee-haw laugh, his quirky smile growing quirkier. He was about to tell James the minute details of each computer and why they were best suited for each designated purpose when Dreldon and Buckham walked in.

"What are you guys doing here?" James asked rather annoyed. He had hoped to keep this after-school meeting with Stanton secret for fear of endangering anyone else. "I told you not to tell anyone." He gave Stanton a serious frown. The skinny boy just shrugged.

"You need us," said Bucky, "if you're ever going to find Misty."

Bucky was a nice-looking kid with dark features. Being small for his age, he struggled in sports and finally gave up to pursue a 'career in hacking,' which he said could pay very well, provided you 'leave no trace.'

As the nerds and Bucky took to examining the SD card, James wondered if he'd made the right move. His hope was to crack the mystery of this card and Misty's disappearance before his midnight visitor returned. He knew that the infatuation, or rather ardent worship, these boys had for her would drive them nonstop until they ensured some form of resolve.

"Got an SD reader?" Bucky asked the two nerds.

Stanton rooted about in a top drawer full of technical junk, his hands quivering with excitement. James had not shared about his house destroyed or the dark visitor with the gun, but he had told them it came from Misty's locket and that was enough to fire their hormone-driven engines.

Within moments, they had the card in a reader and were syncing it with the 'mother of all computers.'

"Just a word doc," Stanton said, looking up, quite disappointed. He had been hoping for some revealing selfies of Misty or something of the sort. But when he tried opening the file, his eyes lit up with zeal. "Encrypted? Whoa, Misty my babe, what is this?"

"Can you crack it?" James asked, his eagerness elevating with the nerds.

"Is it her diary or something?" Stanton asked. "Afraid she's cheating on you, snooking it with—?"

"No, it's not her diary, at least, I hope not." A sudden fear flushed through him. He was putting Misty, and so himself, in great danger, revealing something secret to the nerds and Bucky of all people.

"Serious shh… ssnot," Stanton said, knowing not to swear in

front of James. Once he'd said something inappropriate in Misty's hearing and James had subtly inflicted enough pain to impress his memory cells with rapid reminders whenever the urge came again. "This is big-league code," he said. "How does Misty generate—?"

"I don't think it's Misty's," James reluctantly said, his thoughts recalling the dark form with the gun. "Maybe we should scrap this."

"Heck no!" Both nerds shot him a look of disbelief. "This is awesome shh… sstuff."

As James looked on, each nerd took to working feverishly fast on computers designed for this kind of 'shh… sstuff.'

Bucky went online in a search for Misty. Unknown to James, the boy had incredible skills at hacking into sites and systems. He pulled anything and everything even remotely connected to Misty.

Shots from security cameras began to appear from around town. After an hour or two, he tapped into gas stations and fast-food joints. When he spotted James at McDonald's, the room lit up like a box of fireworks in a fire.

"Wow! Dude! What a babe! What the fffudge? Oh man, that's not fair."

Then the room went silent, but only for a millisecond.

"That's Misty!" Every boy shouted the name simultaneously, as Misty passed behind James and the tall blond eagerly smothering his face.

James stood speechless, his stomach souring. She had walked right past him, right when the blond… He turned to leave the room, thinking he might be sick.

"Hey, look who she's with."

When James saw Roman, he recognized him from the BMW leaving his driveway.

Dreldon shook his head. "Hot dung!" His long greasy hair flopped over his classic black-rimmed glasses. "Some guys have all the luck. Ain't fair."

"I need to know what's on that card," James said. "She left me a note. Said she was kidnapped. I think that card has something to do with it." His words came out weak and feeble as he fought with the thoughts of never seeing her again, and if he did, she would never speak to him.

How evil can fate be? He shook his head at the irony, the crazy odds of her walking past him, of being there and not seeing each other all because of that stupid floozy from Brenton.

Bucky sped the surveillance into fast forward. "She sits there a long time, dude. Check this out." They all watched as Roman left through one door and Misty out the other. After patching cameras together, Bucky showed her getting into Roman's BMW. "Don't think she's there by force, is she?"

The hours dragged on without any more breakthroughs. When James thought to give it all up, preparing to hand it to his midnight visitor, Bucky called out with excitement.

"Hey, got something!" He motioned for James. "I checked each cam leaving town, but found nothing, right? Well, I found one with plates. The beamers registered to a Sterling Whitehall of Rye, New York. I wager my… ahh… you know, that Mr. Good-looking is his kid. He's snagged Misty and they're on a pleasure ride to meet his daddy. What do you think?" Bucky flung his arms back behind his head and smiled wide at his success.

"You're amazing, Bucky." Although fighting a horrid war inside, James admired the boy's prowess. "How do you do that?"

"Skills, dude. I've put in my ten-thousand." He shook his head at James. "But I'd trade it all to be in your shoes, even just a day. Living next door to Misty Grey… come on!"

"What about his credit card?" James asked. "Could you track him that way, like in the movies?"

Soon Bucky had a purchase for gas and snacks, a meal, more gas. "Heading east, like I said." He smiled wide. "Just pulled cash from an ATM, eastside of Winchester, Virginia."

James slumped in silent misery. He turned to leave, his heart sick, his mind and body tired from lack of sleep. He couldn't go home; his visitor would surely return. Needing less effort than expected, he had persuaded his parents to spend another night in the hotel. Never in his life had he felt such tension, such dread and confusion. So many questions, so many feelings—such unpleasant feelings, such horribly nasty feelings.

"I need its program," Stanton said, rubbing his frizzy head, slurping the last of his off-brand energy drink. "I need to know who this is for. How did Misty code this? And for who?"

After a junk food break and a stint of YouTube viewing, they got back to work.

Dreldon found a password-protected file tucked far away within the data. "Any guesses," he asked James.

"I really don't think this belongs to Misty," he said. "I think she got it by mistake."

Dreldon shrugged and started typing a random password.

"Wait! What if you only get three tries or something?"

"Fine, what do you suggest?"

Bucky swung his chair around. "Let me see it." He pulled up a program he had transferred from a personal drive online. Loading the program, he gave some commands and then sat back, letting it do its thing.

"Wrote this last summer. Piggybacked a Russian program for hacking passwords. Got it off an Asian guy who stole it from a dude in France who got it from the Chinese, who stole it from the Russians." He glanced up at James. "Spent a whole summer working on this while studying the psychology of passwords." His smile left James wondering if he were kidding or serious. "It's both coding genius and a psychological wonder."

"Maybe it's her birthdate backward," Stanton said. "Try September four, two thousand four." The other two just huffed, both watching Bucky's program slowly find the secret characters, sending a little chime with each successful ping.

"You know her birthday?" James asked, the room taking on a whole new dimension of peculiar.

But when Dreldon uttered some strange nerdy phrase, his eyes bulging at the screen, the room filled with renewed gusto and shouts of adolescent triumph.

"Buckham, you are the biggest…!" Dreldon gave Bucky a palm-burning high five as he spewed out a string of bizarre superlatives.

But as the contents of the file were displayed, the room became eerily silent. Numerous names, departments, and alleged affiliations with what was continually referred to as 'Black Caldron' filled the screen. Below those came a string of dates and numbers with brief notes and abbreviations that ran down several pages of spreadsheets ending with Wednesday of last week.

Before the last page had loaded, Bucky was searching names and places, snatching files like a mongoose on Red Bull.

"CIA?!" He stopped to jiggle his hands, breathing deep. "Now we're snortin' digital smack." The fire in the boy's eyes seemed uncanny. "Come on baby, feed me more." He shot James a quick glance before delving back into high-speed keyboarding.

"Hey, butt-heads!" Dreldon sat upright as if shocked. "Look at this!" A page of small black and white mug shots filled the screen, each with names and numbers. His finger soaked in pizza grease, Dreldon tapped the screen. "That's the guy who took Misty from school! Ain't it?"

As they all stared in wonder, he read the brief notes beneath the picture. 'Vladimir Talichuk. Ukrainian Mafia: '97–'05. Black Caldron: '05– Present.' "I think we found your napper, James." He paused, turning back to look at the boys crowded around him. "I think Misty's in some deep… ah… doo-doo."

The 9:25 night bus to McLean-Langley, carrying a total of thirteen passengers, left the station right on time. As if selected at random from the lost souls box, the occupants did little to ease Misty's tension. From homeless types to businessmen-wanna-be's, hookers, single moms, and teenage runaways, the riders all found their seats, mostly near the back. Misty and Roman sat second from the front.

As Misty watched the Winchester station fade into the background of streetlights and colorful neon, she suddenly had a distant memory flash by, but only for a second. Rising from a dark and hazy time where no memories dwelt, she saw an image long forgotten. In the window reflection beside her sat a little girl with bushy red hair, her eyes wide with wonder and fear. Beside her sat her mother, hands trembling.

Misty stared at the bus window, her mind struggling to stir up more of the memory. She had very few, if any, memories of her early childhood. Her memory curse hadn't started until sometime late in first grade, and almost everything before that was a dark flickering screen.

"Ride the bus much?" Roman asked.

Misty turned to stare into his beautiful eyes. The look on her face alarmed him.

"You okay?" he asked with sudden concern.

Misty only stared, her eyes questioning and fearful.

"Misty? What's wrong?"

She shook her head. "I don't know... I just had a... my

mom…" She looked back into the window hoping for more of the scene. *Where were we going?* she pondered. *Why was Mom so frightened? Why can't I remember?*

Without realizing, she slid her hand into Roman's, her fingers entwining with his. A look of surprise touched his face, but he silently watched her, wondering.

"I have ridden a bus before," she said dreamily, "when I was little, I guess, with my mother."

"Where were you going?"

Misty just shook her head.

As the bus rolled onto the highway, Misty let her head rest on Roman's sturdy shoulder. Her hair tickled his ear and cheek, but he just smiled, uncertain of how long this moment may last.

"Tell me again," she said softly, "about James and the blond."

As Roman once again described the scene in minute detail, avidly expounding the noble character of this guy he'd never met, Misty listened in silence, her hand still entwined with his, her head upon his shoulder.

"He was adamantly resisting," he said again, "but her hand was on the locket. If he would have pulled away…"

Misty thanked him, her heart sick. "I must have lost it that night in his room." She lifted her head. "I wonder if he knows what's in it, and who wants it?"

"Do they know he's your boyfriend?"

Misty stiffened, her whole body going rigid. Of course they know. It was something she had tried to push down deep, to ignore, telling herself he'd be okay. But now it gushed to the surface, filling her with sudden dread.

"What if they take him!" She drew her good leg up to her chest and hugged it with both arms. "Torture him like—" The images of Ganny brought horrid waves of anguish, which led to thoughts of her mother and Max. Then she bolted upright. "We have to warn him!"

"Misty, in warning him, we may endanger him."

She glanced about. "Call or text, or something… message

him… or…"

Sure, Roman mused, *instant message him—for all the world to see.* "What would you tell him? 'Hide it? Hide yourself?' Does he know of any of this?"

Misty shook her head. "We last talked in math class, before they took me."

"Will he search for you?"

"James?" She thought for a moment, and though her brow tightened, her lips formed a weak smile. "James will turn the world inside out."

Roman stared at the dirty floor, silently laughing at himself, at his foolish envy of this boy James. "So… is he the one?" he asked.

Misty looked out the window again, the words of James fresh in her ears. 'I love you, Misty… I will always love you.'

She turned back to look longingly at Roman's hand. "May I?" she asked, touching his hand. Giving his perfect smile, Roman took her hand, holding it tight between his two strong hands. She let her head fall back onto his shoulder.

"I think I love him," she whispered. "But… not really sure… what that means."

They rode in silence for a while, Roman thinking hard about their next move. He had grown tired of keeping a wary eye as they traveled, suspicious of anyone coming their way. At a gas station, he'd pulled Misty into a janitorial closet after seeing a large man with dark glasses coming their way.

Seeing how it frightened her all the more, he learned to be discreet. He'd glance back when she wasn't looking, turning corners ahead of her, or always stand where he could view the doors.

He sighed. After first being in a state of denial, he had finally come to accept their predicament. Like Misty, he had stumbled into a mess. Now he had to buck up and do whatever necessary to survive and maybe even bring this mess to a close.

They would spend the night as near the CIA building as

possible, with plans to taxi there first thing in the morning. Misty wanted to go as soon as they arrived. Roman had to argue against it for fifteen minutes, telling her it would be dangerous with only security guards alerting whomever of their presence.

'Better in broad daylight,' he had said. 'The more people around, the better.' Under the promise of a nicer hotel and two beds, she consented. He had withdrawn a good amount of cash, which Misty insisted would be repaid by her personally, for her share at least, when this was all over.

He chuckled at the girl nestled beside him. Why was he so drawn to her? He smiled. Everything in him wanted to protect and help her in this quest. Never had he felt this way for a girl.

His thoughts went back to contacting James. The safest might be from within CIA headquarters, or it would be the worst! Maybe it doesn't matter, just warning the CIA might be enough to shut the hackers down. *Will they believe us?* he wondered. *Was that old lady really a spy?*

Misty shifted her head, her hair once again fluffing into his face. An old memory suddenly shot through his mind, a memory long-forgotten. He was young, playing with his sister, running and skipping, singing songs together. He had worked hard to push those memories away, yet another part of him worked equally hard to draw them out.

As the long-suppressed yearnings stirred within, he let the memories rise. Never had he fully dealt with the loss of his sister, never had he fully accepted the fact that he would never see her again. The little boy within still secretly longed to once again run and play, sing and dance with his silly red-haired sister.

Maybe that's why I've stuck around, he thought, moving his head back and forth, letting the twisted strands caress his face. A stream of affection filled his heart. Was it love, or just missing his sister? *Aren't they the same?*

With a single nod, he made a resolution.

James may be your boyfriend, he said within his heart, *but I can be your brother... provided we live through Halloween!*

As Misty stepped into the shower, Roman flicked on the TV. The upscale hotel room had lifted Misty's spirits. Although relentlessly troubled over Ganny and her family, she felt safe with Roman. Being alone with such a fine-looking boy in such a nice hotel brought a bit of warmth to her soul. Then guilt would prick her thoughts. *I'd rather be with you, James.*

Into this mix of feelings would then come the worries and fears over what tomorrow may bring. She'd see the look on Ganny's face, hear her pleas of urgent warning, fresh as the moment spoken. 'Trust no one but Bellows!'

Roman turned up the volume as the shower went full force. Flicking through the endless channels, he paused on a local news station as he got up to check the mini-fridge.

"And more exciting news today on the murder trial of Sally Grey," a female voice announced.

Roman rushed back to face the TV just as a picture of Misty's mother disappeared from the screen.

"It appears there has been even more of an upset, as a witness today claims he has known the defendant's true identity for over eleven years. Authorities have given no indications regarding his claims until they can make further investigations."

Roman's mouth fell open. "Defendant? Her *mom's* on trial? Did she...? Oh, my God!"

The female voice continued. "The witness claims he's kept silent all these years for fear of his safety." A brief recording of a man's voice played. 'Clay told me that if I uttered a peep, he'd put a bullet through me head.' The female voice came back on.

"As this testimony confirms the previous suspicions regarding Ms. Grey's identity, the court has postponed, pending investigation. But with the continued disappearance of sixteen-year-old Marie Elsa Grey, the judge has refused to withdraw the murder charges."

"Misty?" Roman called toward the bathroom, his eyes fixed on the screen. A picture of Misty's mother appeared for a few seconds, her face bruised and swollen, one eye completely shut.

"Oh, my word!" Roman glanced back at the bathroom door.

"Women's rights groups are storming the courthouse with this recent testimony," the news story continued. "Some say it'll become the trial of the year." The camera switched to a male newscaster with slick black hair and fine features.

"If that judge had any common sense," he said, "just voicing my opinion here. Hasn't this woman been through enough?"

"There's rumor she's an heiress of some kind," the female newscaster added. "Wouldn't that be something? No wonder the whole nation is watching this."

"For sure, Bree. It'll be exciting to see how this turns out. In other news today…"

"Misty!" Roman pounded on the door.

"I'm in the shower!"

"Misty, listen! Your mom's not dead. She's… I'll talk to you when you come out."

The shower shut off immediately and Roman could hear Misty whip the curtain back. In a heartbeat, the door flung open, and there stood Misty wrapped only in her towel, her fiery auburn hair hanging limp with little spirals dripping. A pool of water formed beneath her feet as she stood wide-eyed waiting for Roman to speak.

Roman stood as equally wide-eyed at the girl wrapped only in a towel. Without realizing, he looked her over head to toe.

Misty frowned, her lips drawn tight.

"Your mother!" Roman stepped back. "Your mom's alive,

Misty! She's on the news… on trial." He stepped further back, as if wary. "I think she…"

"She what?"

"I think she… killed your dad." Roman winced, struggling to find some other way to rephrase it.

Misty's legs weakened and she fell back against the door, her face going suddenly pale. "Mom… killed…?"

"No! Your mom's alive. On trial." Roman wondered how much to tell her. "But listen to this. They're saying she's not really Mrs. Grey. Something about her identity being someone else from eleven years ago, an heiress or something." He paused for his words to sink in.

Standing with her right hand loosely holding her towel together, she held the doorframe with her left. She stared in bewilderment as she steadied herself. She had wondered, but only briefly if maybe her mother had turned the tables, no longer the helpless victim, but had defended herself. She knew her mother would never have intended to kill him.

"Heiress?"

"Yes. Something about a guy who knew, but… Is Clay your father?"

Misty swayed, her face pale. She nodded, then shook her head. "I've… disowned him."

"But his name is Clay?"

She nodded.

Roman went on to tell her everything the news had said. As he talked, Misty went and sat on the bed, her mind oblivious to her lack of apparel.

"Does your mom have a secret identity?" Roman sat on the other bed, his eyes falling naturally to her legs, which were now quite exposed.

Misty shook her head, her mouth still hanging open, her eyes staring blankly at the bathroom floor where her dirty clothes sat in a heap.

"They say you're still missing and think your mom had

something to do with it."

Misty looked his way, a shaky hand wiping droplets off her wrinkled forehead. "I need to call her. And where's Max?" Misty stood and walked numbly to the hotel phone.

For a moment Roman sat watching, wondering what number she would call, wondering if he should tell her to wait just one more day.

Without thinking of their safety, Misty dialed James. Still dripping, she looked back at Roman, one hand holding her towel, the other holding the phone, her eyes searching his. He shook his head.

"One more day," he said gently. "We should wait one more day."

As the phone of James rang, the eyes of Misty stared at the young man on the bed. Suddenly aware of her near-naked state, a flood of guilt washed over.

"Hello, this is James."

The eyes of Misty went wide, her mouth hanging speechless. It had been five days since she last talked with James, her constant companion. Now she stood in a towel, alone in a hotel room with a college boy and the voice of James at her ear.

"Hello? Who is this?" Roman could hear the voice, assuming it to be James.

Just as Misty prepared to answer, to tell James everything, a corner of the towel slipped from her hand. With a loud gasp, she dropped the phone.

Grabbing at her towel, she struggled to bring it back up, to cover her naked left side. Roman just sat stunned.

"Don't look!" she shouted. Pulling up her towel, she stormed into the bathroom leaving the phone and James dangling.

"Hello? Misty? Is that you?"

As the bathroom door closed with a bang, Roman stood, staring at the phone. Still in shock from the news report, and then Misty in her towel, then without her towel, he wasn't quite sure what to do.

Walking to the phone, he picked it up and examined it like it were some strange object from outer space.

"Misty? Are you there?"

"She's okay," Roman said in a daze. "She'll call you tomorrow. Bye."

As he hung up the phone, his mind suddenly swung in a totally different direction. When the corner of the towel had fallen, it revealed a brownish birthmark on her left hip. It could have been a bruise, but…

Roman shook his head, his heart and mind swirling. The bruised skin around her wounded arm and right hip were dark blue, for he had been monitoring her wounds. This mark was brown. He put his hands to his face, his mind terribly perplexed. "It can't be," he muttered. "That's stupid. Impossible."

For a long moment, he stood in total bewilderment, his mind fighting to grasp the ends of a dozen random thoughts. *Coincidence? No. But the name, the hair… no! But… No way! No… stinking… way!*

As in a brain fog, he moved slowly toward the door. "Misty?"

"You shouldn't have looked!" she shouted back.

Roman went closer to the door. "Your name… is Marie Elsa," he said, his brain feeling scattered. "Why do you… go by the name, *Misty*?"

"Cause that's who I am! I'm Misty! Always been Misty."

"But you have a mark on your hip… the shape of a leaf."

"You shouldn't have looked! I thought you were a gentleman."

"A ginkgo leaf."

"So what?"

"When were you born, Misty?" Roman's voice suddenly became adamant. It frightened her. He sounded like… Mr. Grey when he was angry.

"Misty, when's your birthday?" he demanded.

"Don't speak to me like that."

"Were you… no, no way, never mind. I'm sorry… sorry I

was looking." He stood shaking his head, his heart pounding. "Do you have your bandages?" He tried to soften his tone, but waves of adrenaline gushed through his veins. Pulling a bag of bandaging material from his pack, he rapped lightly on the door. "The bandages, Misty."

As she opened the door just enough to take the package, Misty fought a host of feelings. By the time she finished dressing, numerous fears had filled her heart. What was she doing, trusting herself to a stranger, staying alone with him in a hotel far from home? She remembered the boys pinning her down that day after school, the day the old man came to her rescue. She stood with her hand on the knob, a plan forming. This boy, no matter how nice he had seemed, was not going to get his hands on her.

Flinging the door aside, she rushed into the room, the cord of the hotel's curling iron wrapped tight in both hands.

36 MISTY… A SPY?

Late Friday night, October 30

James had answered with fumbling eagerness. The unknown number coming from Virginia had thoroughly alarmed the room of nerds. Fearing it may be his midnight visitor, James had waited with bated breath. When he heard what could only be the voice of Misty, his heart went into triple time. But like a lifeless mannequin, he stood there staring blankly at his phone.

"Was it Misty?" all three boys asked excitedly.

James nodded.

"Call her back! Hurry!"

"She seemed to be in trouble, maybe," he said, still staring, "then a guy ended the call."

"Call her back!"

Coming to life, James hit redial. It seemed to ring forever. His heart was doing some ka-whoomp thing, making his chest hurt.

"Front desk. How may I help you?"

James blinked. "Ah… front desk where?"

"This is the Grand. Would you like to make a reservation?"

"Ahhh, do you have a Misty, or Marie Grey staying there? She might be with a Mr. Whitehall."

"Sorry, can't give out guest information. If you have her room number, I can put you through."

"No, she just called. This is the number that came up."

"Misty Grey? Isn't that the girl they're looking for? Is this a prank?"

"No! She's my…" James looked at the nerds peering up at him. "She's my friend. Yes, it's the girl… no wait. How do I reach the person who just called from your hotel?"

"You need the room number."

"I don't know her room number. It's very urgent. Can't you check your registry?"

"Can I put you on hold?"

James shook his head at the nerds and Bucky, the latter punching keys like a mad scientist at the zenith of his experiment.

After a minute the hotel line went dead.

"Disconnected," James said with a disgusting sigh.

"Room five-one-two!" Bucky flung himself back away from his computer, tossing his hands up high. "Am I good or am I exceptional?"

"Five twelve? Are you sure?"

"Roman A. C. Whitehall, Rye, N.Y. Room 512. Checked in 11:21 p.m." Bucky put his hands on his head. "Just say it. You're amazing Buckham, simply amazing."

James smiled. "You are amazing, Bucky."

Again, the phone rang for a long time before a male voice answered. "Grand hotel. How can I help you?"

"Room five-one-two please."

"Sure. I'll put you through."

Heart thumping, James licked his lips, his mouth going very dry. After a dozen rings, the male voice came back on. "Would you like a different room?"

"Ah, no… she just called."

"Is there anything else I can help you with?"

"No, thanks."

James slumped. The lack of sleep, the destruction of his home, the news of Misty running away with a guy from New York, all left him weak at heart. The rush of adrenaline at hearing her voice had not helped matters.

"She's in trouble," Stanton said, nodding his head, affirming his own conclusion. Bucky kept working the keys, his brow tight and strained.

Dreldon went back to viewing the files. After a moment, he called everyone over. "Butt-heads, come look." He sat with mouth open, his eyes scanning the words across the screen. "Heavy stuff, very, very heavy."

"Is it real?" asked Stanton. "Could they do that? Wipe it out?"

Bucky affirmed the reality of the 'digital bomb' as briefly defined in the report by Ganny. Dreldon had found her compilation and assessment of information regarding the plot.

"Doesn't say why or when," James mused. "Just an act of cyber-terrorism… immediate threat." After scanning the document, he stared at the name compiling the report. "Tallon… V. S. Tallon. Why would Misty have this? Why would it be in her locket?" Then his face went suddenly wide with alarm. "The locket! Ganny's locket! She always called it Ganny's locket."

"Who's Ganny?" Stanton asked.

Before James could answer, Dreldon spun around.

"Where's that hotel?" he asked Bucky.

"Seventeen hundred Chain Bridge Road."

"No, what city?"

"McLean, Virginia."

"Oh yeah, baby!" he exclaimed, looking like a child on Christmas morn. "That's a turd-toss from the George Bush Center for Intelligence! Misty's a wonkin' spy! No wonder she's so hot!"

"Misty?" Roman stumbled backward onto the bed as Misty rushed toward him, the cord tight like a weapon for strangling. The look on her face struck real fear into Roman, his stunned eyes fixed on the cord.

In a heartbeat, she had his feet between her legs, her hands working the cord into a knot. Before he could struggle free, his feet were bound tight.

"What the heck are you doing?" he cried. "You gone nuts?"

Grabbing the bedside lamp and yanking its cord from the wall, she held it high above her head.

"Roll over, or… or…!" She spoke with teeth clenched.

"Misty?" He thought of the psych report from the clinic. "Misty, it's me, Roman."

"Roll over!"

But Roman didn't move. He studied her scowling face, thinking of the birthmark. "Misty, listen to me. When were you—?"

"Roll over, or I will smash this lamp!"

"No! You listen to me! There's a birthmark on your hip."

"My hips are none of your business! You should've looked away."

"Misty, listen, please! I've seen that mark before."

Misty stood poised, her nostrils flaring like an enraged bull.

Roman had both hands out in defense. "Misty, please, I need to know—"

Bang! Bang! Bang! "Open up! Police!"

Before either could move, the door swung open. Rushing in like bursting water, six police officers, dressed in protective gear, pushed through the door. With guns and tasers aimed, they all shouted different commands.

"Freeze! Don't move! Hands on your head! Put the lamp down!"

Holding the lamp still over her head, Misty stood staring in shock. Roman slowly put his hands on his head.

"Put the lamp down!"

For a second, Misty just glared, her jaw set, her face tight with anger. Years of physical abuse had solidified within her the resolve to never back down. Resistance meant more pain, but surrender meant death, death on the inside, enslaving oneself to fear. Only as a ruse, would she feign surrender.

"Put the freakin' lamp down!"

"Misty," Roman spoke tenderly, pointing his hands toward the officers. "Please put the lamp down. Don't make them hurt you."

She glanced his way. "Make them? I've never made them hurt me. Never has it been my fault."

"Misty, they're here to…" Roman looked at the guns and tasers. "Why are you here? Don't you need a warrant or something? We haven't done anything?"

"Hands on your head! Last warning." The man up front readied his taser, stiffening his stance. Another aimed his at Roman.

Hissing, Misty flung the lamp onto the bed, her eyes locked on the officer in charge.

"Cuff 'em both," he said, lowering his weapon. "You have the right to remain silent. Anything you say, can and will be used against you…"

After three calls to Ganny's house, James conceded to Misty's note.

"Maybe she's gone… on vacation," Stanton said.

Not until now, had James realized Ganny's absence. If anyone, she would have been either at the trial or helping him find Misty. They had seen no sign of her since Misty's disappearance. But actually dead… and connected to this cyber-terror threat? No, she couldn't be, or have been, but somehow the locket and Ganny seemed connected.

"But how?" he wondered out loud.

"Wanna find out?" Bucky swung his chair around, his hands once more behind his head, signally accomplishment. "Want to ask her yourself?"

"Ask who?"

"Misty, in person."

"What? Like face-time her or something?"

"No, I just booked us two seats to D. C., Delta airlines, leaving at 6:40 tomorrow a.m."

Unable to detect if Bucky were serious or joking, James stood silent, not willing to fall for a gag and be the joke of the nerds and Bucky.

The young Italian smiled. "I'm serious. We fly free! You and me. Checking up on Misty. Together we'll take out this guy, Roman Whitehall."

"You booked us tickets? Seriously? I can't go to D. C. Fly free… how?"

"I've always wanted to hack my way somewhere, get out and see the world."

"No, Bucky, I can't. Are you serious? You're not serious."

"I'll go!" said both Stanton and Dreldon simultaneously.

For a second, James considered the proposal but then shook his head. "I should leave. Give me the card. Thanks for your help, guys."

"Dude, it's no big deal." Bucky stood. "It's like standby, seats that would be empty. I just bypassed the system and scheduled us on some empty seats."

James shook his head, his hand still poised for the SD card. "You guys are amazing, but cancel those tickets."

As he left the home of Stanton T., his mind filtered through all the startling information, desperately seeking links and probable solutions. The challenge was thinking clearly without feelings for Misty clouding everything.

When he slowed to turn up his driveway, his heart sped into triple time. Parked with the engine running was the car of his midnight visitor.

Driving on past his home, he took the road that circled back around to Ganny's. When he pulled into her long driveway, he suddenly realized it was almost midnight. Chiding himself for being so stupid, he put the car in reverse but then stopped. Something wasn't right. Ganny's property was on the edge of his family's land and sat alone, nestled in the woods. She had a large security light that lit the drive and garage area, as well as yard lights on motion sensors.

But all was dark, very dark.

For a brief time, he sat watching, thinking. *The bulb is out, that's all. No, something's wrong. It's midnight, of course it's dark. No, seems darker than usual... no lights anywhere.*

Back and forth he argued, finally getting out and walking around the house. When no yard lights came on, his blood surged.

"Her power's out, that's all," he muttered, trying to calm his nerves. But when he passed the garage, the argument ended. The side door into the garage looked like it had been hit with a medieval battering ram. Splinters lay everywhere. The scant remains of the door hung lamely from its hinges.

Robbery? James stepped through the broken door, telling himself it was stupid and he should call the police. The fragrance of cedar still hung in the garage where Ganny's husband used to turn wood into bowls and things. Beside the door into the house, hung a rechargeable flashlight, its small location light blinking brightly in the somber darkness.

Hands trembling, he opened the door into Ganny's house. One brief pan of the flashlight's beam told him the story. Like in his home, everything with any possibility of hiding something small was smashed, broken, torn, or ripped to shreds. Detective Yurkowski's words came back, 'They were searching for something. Something small is my guess.'

These guys are thorough. His hand went to the SD card in his pocket. In great trepidation, he checked out the bedrooms and bathroom, fully dreading the thing he sincerely hoped he wouldn't find.

When he found no signs of Ganny having been there, alive or dead, he wondered and hoped that maybe she too was on her way to Langley. *Misty would do anything for Ganny.* He touched his pocket again. *But she'd lost the locket. Wouldn't they need this card?*

He made his way back toward the garage, turning back to survey the devastation. *Somebody wants this thing, and wants it bad.* As he turned to take the steps into the basement, a flicker of headlights shone on a far wall—a car had pulled into the drive.

James froze. Then like a frightened cat, he ran toward the glass doors facing the woods. Just as he reached for the handle, a black silhouette appeared.

Turning back, the sound of footsteps came up from the garage. Trapped like an animal, he spun left and right. The footsteps came closer, the sliding door rattling. Having nowhere to run, he raced down the hall to the far bedroom. Struggling with a window, he scolded himself for coming inside. By the time he got it to slide open, heavy footsteps thumped down the hall.

As the heavy footsteps entered the room, James slid the rest of the way under the bed. *How original!* he chided himself. *You are dead-meat!* He fought to control his breathing, to calm his thoughts, which were presently rebuking him for not having called the police. He watched the boots rush to the open window. Splashes of light came, as a flashlight beam shone out over the north yard.

At any second, he knew it would shine under the bed.

"See anything?" A second set of footsteps came down the hall. "Murk says it's the kid's car."

"What's he doing here?" the one near the window asked, his voice husky.

"Got a call from the girl, half-hour ago."

"What'd she tell him?"

"Nothing, really. 'Don't look,' is all she said."

"Then why's he looking?"

"Don't matter. They got the girl. Almost made it. Cops found her in a hotel just blocks away."

"So she ain't dead."

"Don't matter. Fish will cover it. Be dead by sunup."

The boots at the window turned about, a light panning the room. "Do I chase the kid?"

"No, just watch his car."

"And if he shows?"

"Make it accidental."

When the boots and voices went back down the hall, the

whole body of James Longmire shook as if terribly cold. He now knew why Misty hadn't called him—they were tapping his phone, whoever 'they' were. He now knew why she was traveling east. She and Ganny must have stumbled onto this information and found it necessary to deliver it firsthand.

'Dead by sunup.' James had not cried for a long time, but that night under the bed, with heart racing, tears trailed from his eyes. What had Misty gotten into? How could he warn her... save her?

For an hour or more, he lay beneath the bed. They were watching his car, and so watching the house. If they really thought he'd already gone out the window, then that would be the place to escape.

Inch by inch, he crawled out and crept to the open window. When he dropped to the cold ground outside, he knelt in silence for several minutes. Then, without looking back, he dashed toward the trees. He kept to the far edge of the woods, sometimes running between the rows of standing corn that bordered the woods. Coming up behind his family's old barn, he crawled into the hayloft and watched the house.

Peering and shivering, he touched the tiny SD card in his pocket. Whoever 'they' were, sure didn't want this info reaching CIA. Black Caldron was indeed real... way too real. "Oh, Misty," he said with eyes moistening. The words, 'Dead by sunup,' kept replaying, a constant droning like a stuck song that won't quit.

"God," he softly prayed, "please help me find her, and soon."

The long, lonely run to Stanton's house seemed unusually dark and cold. James glanced over his shoulder every thirty seconds and then some. Only twice he had stopped to catch his breath, each time reaching for the tiny card in his pocket.

With thoughts of capture tormenting his troubled mind, he took out the card and shoved it into his right sock, but after a dozen steps, it made its way down under his arch. He stopped near an old maple to dig it out. A car drove slowly past. He ducked behind the maple, watching the car roll by, his side burning as he panted hard.

Putting the card back into his pocket, he ran on toward Stanton's, still a good two miles, if not more. He had resolved to fly out with Bucky in the morning, if the boy hadn't canceled the flights. He felt terrible, having no way to contact his parents without endangering them, knowing they would worry themselves sick if he just disappeared.

His mind worked with fervor as he ran, always glancing backward, stopping only briefly to listen for any trailing footsteps. He rummaged through all he had learned since finding Misty's note. *How did they know I had the locket? Why was she in my room? And who is this Roman guy? A digital bomb… and… dead before sunup?*

He stopped to look back and listen, hands on his thighs. Taking a deep breath, he held it, listening and scanning the street. It was nearing 2:30 a.m., and all seemed quiet.

"Like a weird dream," he whispered. "Except it's stinking real!" Despair settled over him. 'Dead by sunup,' kept its bleating rhythm. He fought back tears, his heart sinking. "Oh Misty, how can I…?" As he looked about, he suddenly realized he stood only two blocks from Stanton's house.

When he launched a stick up to the nerd's window, James called in a lame whisper. After seven or eight sticks, which brought no response, he finally found a broken piece of a stout branch. Soon the light came on, and a sleepy head poked out through the window.

Stanton opened the door with a huge yawn. "What are you doing here?" Keeping the lights low and voices hushed, James sat in Stanton's room, telling him all that he had heard.

"Dead by sunup?" Stanton said weakly, his voice quavering.

"Try him again," James said, referring to contacting Bucky. He had resolved to fly out on whatever flight he could get, with or without Bucky's help.

Stanton had texted and called Bucky numerous times, but

he'd probably turned off his phone and was now sound asleep after his evening of intense hacking and spy tracking.

"Misty… dead?" Stanton said again, looking like a child who just learned Santa was only a figure of folklore. "Misty can't die. How would I…?"

For a time, James sat staring, his thoughts like those of Stanton's, which was a bit unsettling. But, like Stanton, the picture of life without Misty did feel very, very dark. His words of love to her, the night in his room, all now fading memories of a surreal past. He questioned if he really had kissed her, that maybe he was no different than Stanton or Dreldon, living in a dream world with Misty at its center.

"Text him again," James said, asking to see the documents from the SD card. For fifteen minutes, he studied the names and numbers, the bios and information gathered into files, the compiler obviously trying to find links and clues.

Two times he had taken out his phone to call the local police, but each time a gush of fear stopped him. Then he thought to call the police stations near Langley. *They've tapped my phone*, he'd mutter in frustration. He then thought of using Stanton's, but he'd already put the nerds and Bucky at risk.

Rocking back and forth, fingers drumming, he ran through countless options, from finding a payphone, to contacting his parents, to calling CIA directly. But clouding every thought was a dark fog of dreadful gloom.

Stanton pulled up Bucky's search history but found little of any use. "Leave no trace," he said, reciting Bucky's motto. He then looked up at James, his eyes forlorn. "How would you get to the airport? You need your car."

James sighed, for he too had been trying to figure that out, when suddenly a pebble hit the window. Instantly, James clicked off the desk lamp.

"They followed me!" he muttered, his heart failing. Both boys sat in terrified silence, neither willing to stick their head up and look.

Again, a pebble struck the glass with a startling clunk.

James slowly rose, inching toward the window. "They wouldn't throw stones," he finally said. Lifting the sash, he peered out, heart beating wildly. He squinted into the darkness, straining to see the thin figure silhouetted by the street light.

"Misty, is that you?"

12:38 AM Saturday, October 31

"You can't hold us here without cause," Roman called through the jail bars. "And we're entitled to a phone call."

Misty sat quietly in the adjacent cell where two other young gals lay sleeping on bunks. Somehow the call to James had brought the police. From Roman, she learned there was a search for her, but why lock her up? Were Larkin's people behind this?

"What's my crime?" Roman yelled out to the officer sitting calmly at his desk. The man must have heard this question ten thousand times, for he neither looked up nor seemed annoyed. "You can't just lock someone up without charging them. This is illegal. I want a lawyer."

Two other men were locked up in Roman's cell, and both were awake, their attention mostly on Misty.

When the man rose to get some coffee, he walked by Roman's cell. He paused to look the college boy over. "You booked a room, alone with a minor. You're going to prison, perv."

As Roman stood speechless, the two men within his cell came near. "You messin' with kids?" They eyed him head to toe. "Rich boy, aren't ya? Think ya own the world?"

One man, a large, greasy-haired beast with several days' growth, gave Roman a shove, knocking the boy into the bars.

"Hey," Roman turned to face them, fearful eyes scanning the two ruffians.

Misty watched the scene, glancing toward the police guard who now sat with his back turned.

The large man gave Roman another shove, sending him hard against the cell door.

"Hey!" Roman called to the guard. "Aren't you supposed to do something?"

"Get used to it, kid," he growled without turning.

The men chuckled at the guard's response, giving Roman yet another hard shove. Just as the boy readied himself to strike back, the guard finally called out.

"Knock it off!" His bellowing command echoed in the warehouse-like room. The larger man spat while the other gave a mock punch. Then both went to their bunks.

Fear knotted Misty's gut. She whispered for Roman to come close. "Something's not right," she said.

"Misty, I'm sorry for looking, but…"

"No, listen," Misty continued. "They didn't take our fingerprints." She glanced at the guard. "Or even ask our names. Roman, something's really off." She looked around. "And look at this place. Like it should be condemned. Is it even a real police station?"

A sickening dread spread over Roman as he looked around. Paint peeled from walls and doors. Boxes filled a far wall. The place smelled old and musty, and numerous stains mottled the jail floor, some dark like blood. The only desk was the guard's, and it too looked like a discard.

They had taken his wallet and other personal items, but hadn't even asked his name. *What is this place?* he pondered. He'd never been arrested, but Misty was right, this was off, way off.

Her anger toward him had dissolved, her thoughts appearing focused. Roman looked over at the two smiling goons, each making threatening gestures.

"We have to get out of here," he whispered.

She nodded, her face tight.

"Misty," he said softly, "I just want to say I'm sorry for—"

"No… it's my fault. I shouldn't have called."

He straightened. "Of course, the call."

She nodded. "They've been watching, waiting for us to show up." She reached through the bars and held his hand tight. "I'm scared for you, Roman. For us. I'm so sorry… for everything."

"Misty," he said, glancing back at the goons. "What I was trying to tell you at the hotel… the birthmark…"

Her nostrils suddenly flared, and she dropped his hand, for the whole scene flashed with all its jumbled emotions. She took a few deep breaths through her nose.

"Misty… please listen. That birthmark…" He glanced back once more. When he looked at her again, pain marred his face. "When I was little, I couldn't pronounce my sister's name."

"Wisteria," Misty said.

Roman paused to study her face. He then nodded. "So I called her… Misty."

The teen girl drew back, a sorrow darkening her face. "I'm sorry," she whispered. "I… didn't know. You should've told me."

"No, listen. That birthmark…" He paused, his expression of deep consternation. "It's exactly the same… as my sister's."

Misty stared for a moment, following his thought. Then she seemed to fill with pity. "No, Roman," she said, shaking her head. "I'm sorry, but that's impossible." She continued shaking her head. "I'm so sorry about… No, it's… it has to be coincidence."

The main door opened, and a loud, boisterous woman came shuffling in, pushed along by two male plain-clothes officers.

"Ya lame goats!" the woman shouted, swinging at the officer holding her arm. "Ya lock a woman up for doing nothing but sharing love." A tall silvery-blond with long legs and reinforced bosoms, she sauntered toward the cell, smiling at the guard seated at his desk.

When the cell door swung open and the woman walked into Misty's cell, her expression turned suddenly grim as she locked eyes with Misty and Roman. A devious smile then touched her bright red lips. She took a seat on a lower bunk beside one of the other women.

Misty watched with growing fear. All three women seemed to be employed in 'sharing love.' She turned and whispered to Roman, "We have to get out of here."

They remained together, whispering over possible plans of escape, asking questions that held no answers.

"But Misty," Roman asked, still thinking of the birthmark, "how else can it be?"

"I can't be your sister." She paused to study his face. *Though that would be nice,* she thought. The idea of a big brother, especially one like Roman, warmed her deepest soul.

He told more of what he had seen on the news. "It's become a big deal," he whispered.

Misty scrunched her face. "They actually think my mom might have killed me? That's absurd!"

Roman glanced back at the two thugs now both reclining. "It's holding things up. Women's groups are protesting outside the courthouse. There's a big search for you, it's all gone nationwide. And now some witness says—" Roman suddenly gasped. He stepped back from Misty, his expression frightening her.

"What? Roman, what's wrong?"

He put both hands to his mouth. "That would explain…" He narrowed his eyes, looking her up and down. He moved close, intense eyes studying every inch of Misty's face. Still shaking his head, he kept muttering, "No way… no… no way…"

"No, what?"

He uncovered his mouth. "Am I going crazy?"

"Roman?"

The birthmark and arrest had so caught Roman off guard that he hadn't processed any of it. Now a single, perplexing thought emerged. He stared at Misty, his look distraught.

"It's too bizarre," he said, eyes still wide. "And the odds of

us meeting up… after all these years? You and Mom being…”
He continued to study her face, his head slowly wagging.

"Hey!" the blond called from her bunk. "Ain't you two gonna sleep?" The woman rose and paced toward Misty like a wolf sizing up its prey. She reached out suddenly, giving Misty a firm slap on the butt. "You got a bod, girly. Could make good money out there." She flung her head to the side with a sly smile. "You come work with me. I'll teach you how things happen."

Misty shuddered, reaching for Roman's hand.

"Leave her be," Roman said, squeezing Misty's hand.

"You're a fine looker," she said, reaching straight for Roman's face. She laughed as the two teens broke apart. Licking her red lips, she smiled at Roman. Then again, her face became grim as when she had entered.

"Break it up!" The guard came over and with a severe warning, told them all to separate, his hand on his stun gun. "Go to sleep."

For a moment, the blond just eyed them both, her face stern. Slowly she turned away, climbing into a bunk with the youngest gal, who just rolled over with a groan. The woman's eyes didn't leave the two for some time, causing Misty more apprehension.

"Forget about her," Roman said, trying to encourage Misty. "It's going to be okay. I'll call my dad in the morning." He continued to study her face, his own tight with consternation. "But how?" he said softly. "How?"

41 FOR LIFE AND DEATH

A black mobile phone buzzed atop a large wooden desk. Nicotine-stained fingers picked it up.

"Tallon's alive. Keep things secure or say goodbye." A family photo then appeared on the screen.

The man lowered the phone with a sigh, pulling out a cigarette. A string of curse words followed and then the fingers picked up the office phone.

"Get me Parks."

*　*　*　*　*　*　*　*　*　*

Misty stood near the cell door, her eyes drooping. She regularly moved her vision from Roman, to the two thugs, over to the blond. Her legs ached from standing. Her heart ached for her mother and brother. Where was James? Why was he kissing that girl? *My locket James... why?*

No matter how many times Roman tried to reassure her, she could not overcome the image of the boy and girl kissing. How could she have walked right past? What was he doing there?

Roman had told her he was probably looking for her, but Misty just couldn't get past the image. She sighed, sliding down the corner to sit on the floor, one leg drawn up tight. She so wanted to cry, but her eyes kept moving around the circle—

Roman, thugs, blond… Roman, thugs, blond…

An hour passed, the guard shushing them whenever they tried to speak, even in whispers. He seemed bent on keeping them silent and apart. He routinely made rounds from coffee machine to desk, then to the toilet, coming over to peer inside the two cells, then back to his desk.

At around three a.m., a slick-looking man got shoved into Roman's cell. His nose looked like a little ski jump, flat and curving upward. He wore a nice leather jacket, designer jeans, and shiny black shoes.

He smiled at Roman, revealing a gold tooth that glinted in the dull light. He immediately took a bunk, and with a deep sigh, seemed to fall fast asleep.

For Misty, fear seemed to creep up from the floor like clammy shivers crawling up her skin. She looked to Roman, her eyes pleading. She thought she saw tears in his. *I'm so sorry… so, so sorry.*

She glanced at the blond who now rolled over, her eyes locked on Misty. The cold fear squeezed her chest. Something was wrong. She could feel it. *Why hadn't they taken even our names? And this dump… It isn't right.*

Then it came like a flash. She sat up, motioning for Roman to come close. The guard's last warning had been quite vulgar with promises to zap them both if they didn't stop jabbering. Misty mouthed the words to Roman, moving her lips slowly and pronounced.

"They don't… want… any record of us… being here."

Roman stiffened, fully understanding.

Misty edged closer, eyes on the guard. "It's… a… set up," she said, her words breathy, a new terror in her eyes.

Roman glanced over at the recent arrival. The slick man had fallen asleep way too fast. He looked over at the guard. It was about time for him to make his toilet round. He mouthed his question back to Misty. "Any ideas?"

She shook her head, her weary face distraught. "Get

zapped?"

Roman frowned. He rose just as the guard got up and made his way toward the men's room. Mr. Slick also happened to wake just at that moment, sitting up in his bunk. When the silvery-blond rose with a moan, the air seemed to electrify.

Like two hungry wolves, Mr. Slick and the boisterous blond made their way toward the teens. Misty shrunk back into her corner, her hand reaching through the bars toward Roman.

Roman had stepped away, giving himself room. Since childhood, he had enjoyed sports, a gifted athlete with many awards, including a few trophies in Jeet Kune Do. After seriously injuring a friend, he vowed to never compete again.

Mr. Slick moved slowly toward him with a twisted smile. Roman glanced over at Misty. The blond moved toward her at the same rate. It was clear the guard would not be coming out any time soon.

Out from his leather jacket, Mr. Slick withdrew a black boxcutter. Hacking up a sick chuckle, he slid the razor blade out, slashing playfully at Roman. The boy swallowed hard. A thousand times he'd practiced for things like this, but never this real.

"Hey!" he called, glancing at Misty. "He's got a knife!"

Before he could say more, Mr. Slick rushed him. Misty saw it and tried to scream, but the tall blond came at her with claws out, barred teeth hissing like a deranged cat.

Clawing and scratching, the blond drove the startled teen into the corner. She slapped and clawed, pummeling Misty downward. The weary, battered teen girl employed nothing of Ganny's training. She'd never been attacked like this, especially not by a woman trying to kill her.

The blond now punched and kneed Misty, her teeth still hissing. Striking a heavy blow, she knocked the girl to her butt, finishing with a kick to the ribs. Pressed into the corner, Misty coughed and gasped. But the woman kicked again, driving Misty down hard onto the concrete floor.

The teen couldn't breathe, the blow paralyzing her lungs. She raised a useless arm, her mouth open, trying to find air.

Cold eyes glared down. The blond paused to catch her breath, smiling as her busty chest heaved. Squatting down, she placed a knee over Misty's throat, her long leg pinning the girl's arm.

Seeing Misty gulping for breath, she slapped the girl's face. Somehow it worked. Misty sucked in desperate air, eyes wide with fright.

"Don't know... what you did, girly... but someone's... paying big to have you... silenced." She put her other knee into Misty's stomach. If the girl struggled, the knee over the throat pressed harder.

Misty's left arm lay painfully pinned behind her back. She tried to free it without invoking more of the knee crushing her throat.

Then the woman reached up into her black bra and took out a tiny packet, tearing it open with her teeth.

"They say it's painless. Ya just fall asleep... and forget everything."

Misty fought, trying to speak, but the knee crushed her throat. Using both hands, the woman forced Misty's mouth open. The teen shook her head and bit down hard. The woman leaned, pressing her weight into the girl's throat, snickering as Misty's eyes bulged, face reddening.

Placing the small red capsule between her own teeth, the blond tried again to force Misty's mouth open. The beaten girl could hear the struggle ensuing beside her. Roman wouldn't go down without a fight. And neither would she.

This wasn't the first time Misty had been pinned beneath someone bent on doing harm. Nor was it the first time she had stared into the eyes of death.

Fingernails dug into Misty's cheeks. A thumbnail pressed her eye.

"Open up, or I gouge it out," the woman hissed, her face reddening. She then plugged Misty's nose.

Though fighting hard, Misty weakened. The thumb in her eye burned, as did her lungs and neck.

She gulped in a breath.

The woman squeezed, pressing the cheeks painfully inward. Like a snake about to swallow its prey, the blond lowered her red lips over Misty's open mouth.

'Feign weakness before you strike.' The words of Ganny came clear. Misty relaxed, feigning surrender to the inevitable.

As Misty relaxed, the pressure eased, just enough to free her left arm. The blond smiled, letting the capsule drop into Misty's throat.

She then clamped her hands over the girl's mouth and nose, forcing her to swallow.

But Misty had been waiting.

With arm free, and fingers rigid, she swung upward, stabbing the woman's throat. Like a wounded monster, the blond floundered backward, clutching her neck. Crumpling to the floor, she lay clutching her throat with both hands, her body convulsing.

In silent gasps, she stared wide-eyed at Misty, who now spat the capsule onto the floor.

Scrambling backward toward the other gals who watched in silent horror, the blond fought for breath that would not come.

Misty watched with alarm. She had not planned to kill the woman. She glanced over at Roman. The young man stood panting over the moaning body of Mr. Slick.

For a moment, Misty just stood, lungs heaving, pain everywhere. Then in a burst of rage, she went toward the wheezing blond. The woman tried to scurry away, reaching for the others to protect her. Already her face showed shades of blue, her eyes bulging.

Jerking her up, Misty grabbed the woman's arm and spun her around, bringing her into a Heimlich hold. After several very violent hugs, Misty let the woman go.

The blond dropped to her knees, then crawled onto a bunk

where she collapsed with a moan.

Misty turned toward Roman, tears welling.

His hands trembled, blood dripping from a broken lip. She rubbed her throat, glancing back at the blond. The whole ordeal hadn't lasted long, but both stood very winded.

The two thugs rose and inspected the body of Mr. Slick.

"Is he dead?" one asked.

"Had a knife," the other said.

Roman went to Misty, taking her hand through the bars. "You okay?" he asked urgently. She nodded, stooping to pick up the capsule. Wincing hard with pain, she rubbed her hip.

"We have to get out of here, Roman," she said, her voice quivery. "Get out now."

He nodded, gingerly touching his lip. He glanced down at the body of Mr. Slick who now groaned, his right arm bending strange.

"May have broken his arm," Roman said to Misty. But then he nodded. "I broke his arm."

The man moaned, trying to rise. Roman kicked the box cutter toward the cell door as the guard emerged from the men's room.

"Hey!" shouted one of the thugs. "This guy's hurt. Had a knife and…" He looked over at Roman with renewed respect.

As the guard neared the cell doors, it was plain he bore a look of surprise, not so much seeing the body on the floor or the blond moaning on the bunk, but on seeing Misty and Roman still standing… alive.

Using well-practiced expletives, he asked the two teens what they had done. Roman motioned for Misty to remain silent.

"We were both attacked," Roman said with bold frankness. "We're asking you to move us to a different cell."

"Ain't got no more cells. What'd you do to that poor man?"

"He tried to kill me. I stopped him."

Misty stood amazed at Roman's calm yet firm tone. He had just fought for his life, as she had, but other than his heavy breathing, he bore a sense of authority.

The officer looked over at Misty and then at the blond still rubbing her throat. Misty dropped the capsule into her jeans pocket.

"You need to move us or there'll be more trouble," Roman said.

The guard gave Roman a scowl, then wagged his head vigorously. "Won't be any more trouble from you two." He unclipped his stun gun and opened Roman's cell door.

Misty's heart surged, seeing not the dirty cop, but the vile Mr. Grey. As Roman backed away, Misty's anger fumed into fury. Without realizing, she followed the movement of Roman as he backed away over the body of Mr. Slick. Her hands felt each bar, her gaze intense. Like a hungry lioness, she stalked in silence.

"Hands against the bunk!" The officer moved cautiously, his zapper out front.

"I haven't done anything. You need to get us out of here."

"You were molestin' young girls, perv. Now you're gonna pay."

"I was not!" He nodded to Misty. "She's my sister. We're just traveling. Since when is that a crime?"

"Nice try, kid." The man thrust the stun gun toward Roman's groin.

The smaller of the thugs studied Misty, then called out. "You really his sister?"

Misty had followed the action, her eyes keen on saving Roman. Without giving it any thought, she nodded.

Before her hair finished bobbing, the large thug gave the dirty cop a violent shove. The man stumbled sideways, tripping over Mr. Slick, who still lay struggling to rise. Slamming into the bars directly in front of Misty, the man hit with an umpf. Like cat claws upon a mouse, Misty had the stun gun within her grasp.

In half a heartbeat, the man was down, flopping and twitching, the smell of burnt flesh wafting gently through the bars.

"Roman, the keys!"

"Thank you," Roman said to the men as the cell door swung open. When he asked if they wanted to leave, they both shook their heads. So he closed it, locking it on Mr. Slick and the still quivering guard. After doing the same for Misty's cell, he tossed the keys onto the wooden desk. The blond and Mr. Slick just watched as both teens stood pondering the lack of personnel.

"Where is everybody?" Roman asked, expecting officers to come pouring in.

"Cameras off?" Misty said, seeing no light on either device. Her face grew stern. "Whoever planned this… is someone with power."

Roman looked about. All the windows were barred. The doors leaving the confinement area were of heavy metal with digital locks. As Roman tried to find an escape, Misty rummaged through the desk drawers, quickly crumpling papers once she found what she wanted.

In seconds a fire blazed atop the dirty cop's desk, igniting all that came within its hungry grasp.

"What about them?" Roman looked to their former cellmates who now watched with alarm.

"Just get more paper," Misty said. She had a plan, and it involved fire, so Roman scooped up a large wastebasket full of papers. He stood baffled at the empty silence.

"Where is everybody?" he asked again.

"They'll come," Misty assured him. "More! We need smoke."

Already a layer of smoke swirled against the ceiling tiles. At any moment, alarms would sound, and sprinklers would spray.

Misty kept mounting anything flammable upon the dirty cop's desk. She would glance his way every so often, checking to see if he needed another treatment of shock therapy. As if with a vengeance, she flung things into the growing flames. Its fiery snapping tongues now rose several feet, reaching for the ceiling.

Then all hell broke loose, or rather, preventive measures to keep hell from breaking loose. Alarms blared as sprinklers shot fine streams, forming nice even umbrellas of spray.

As the smoke swirled and billowed, filling the ceiling, Misty pulled Roman toward the metal door.

"Quick!" she said, standing on the hinge side while avoiding the spray. When the electric locks in the door turned, it swung open, hiding them behind it.

Three officers charged into the room, each shouting something different. Misty waited until all came through, tugging on Roman's arm as she bolted out from behind, dashing into the hallway.

She took the second door on her right.

"Where are you going?" Roman asked.

"Shhh. Find the light."

When lights came on, the two looked about. It was the furnace room, an old boiler system with pipes running everywhere.

"Misty…?" Roman asked dubiously.

"I saw this coming in. A guy entered with trash."

"Yeah?"

She looked down, her eyes following a worn path leading back around the boiler. "This way!"

It led to a small metal door three-foot square and several feet off the ground. Without hesitation, Misty opened the door and flung herself through. She landed with a muffled cry into the dumpster below.

When Roman landed beside her, he fought with the smelly

bags of garbage, as several tumbled in around them. He started to climb out, but stopped as voices shouted from nearby. Distant sirens wavered through the blaring alarm, their howling wail like wolves closing in for the kill.

"Stay or r-r-un?" Misty whispered through chattering teeth. She was suddenly shivering hard, her face tight with pain.

The dumpster was three-fourths full with bags of mostly fast-food packaging and coffee cups. The sharp smell of coffee grounds prevailed over the pungent odors of grease and spoiled food.

For a brief moment, they both sat pondering their next move. The urge to run was strong, but the alley was well lit, and the sounds beyond told of growing activity.

"They tried to kill us," Roman whispered, his voice tight.

"Shhh." Misty shifted further down, pulling several bags up over them. One dripped, reeking of coffee and fried food. Though their hair and shoulders had gotten damp, they could hide while maybe staying somewhat warm.

When two fire trucks pulled up, voices shouted commands, the flashing colored lights strobing the buildings overhead. The alarm had finally gone silent, and so they nestled in, listening to the commotion around the corner.

For some time they just sat shivering and listening, hoping to not be found within their reeking hideout. After an hour, the trucks rumbled off, leaving only a few distant voices.

As their nerves began to calm, and the shivers less and less, Roman leaned close to whisper.

"You okay?"

Misty gave no reply, her body hurting everywhere.

"When I saw you down," he continued, "I felt so... so stinking helpless." He swallowed, his throat dry. "If you had... I would never—"

"Shhh," Misty whispered. "I'm sorry I got you into this." She winced, hissing as she inhaled, her ribs crying in protest at every breath.

"You're really hurting, aren't you?" Roman said. "Your hip, your arm, your neck?" He shook his head, muttering some harsh words directed at the blond. "You need a doctor?"

Misty blinked back tears, but then buried her face into his shoulder. For the next few minutes, she fought hard to stifle the sobs rising from deep within.

Roman put an arm around her, shuffling them downward even more. He held her close, but not tight, as she was clearly hurting with each breath. In the smelly darkness, they sat huddled together, struggling to stay warm, to stay strong, to stay alive.

After a quick shiver and several deep breaths, Misty calmed herself, her head still on Roman's shoulder.

"I'm sorry," she whispered once more.

"Should we go?" Roman asked. He held back a bag of garbage, creating a little tent, but the rancid odors stayed strong.

Misty thought for a moment, wiping her eyes and sniffling softly. As unpleasant as the dumpster was, it felt good to be tucked away, hidden from those seeking to end their young lives. She shook her head, pressing into him.

After a time of silence, Roman spoke. "I used to believe in God," he whispered, "when I was young. But when my mom and..." He sighed.

Misty stared into the darkness of garbage, her heart feeling his pain.

He sighed again. "My father paid the ransom, in gold, my mother's weight in gold. They said she would be on a certain bus, arriving at a certain time. For days, my father waited, long past the set time. She never came."

Misty listened in silence, then softly asked, "Did he remarry?"

"No, though many have tried."

She squeezed his hand and he continued. "When were you born, Misty? And why Misty instead of Marie?"

Misty just sat, still gazing into the smelly darkness, her heart struggling with a dozen different feelings.

"Your birthmark," he continued, "it's the same as my little sister's." He paused again. "Am I nuts?" He let go a sudden sigh. "Am I just so… so hopeful, so naïve?"

A tear trailed down Misty's cheek. Somehow she felt his pain, like really felt his pain. To hope for something so hard, so far away, so impossible, yet…

A siren squawked from the end of their alley. They both tensed, but nothing more came.

Misty… Many times her grade school teachers tried to correct her name, encouraging her to use her real name. 'But I've always been Misty,' she'd reply. She now pulled for memories, anything from those early years. But like before, all those memories had retreated into a foggy darkness.

"But how could that be?" she finally asked, her voice weak.

"This guy's testimony," Roman said. "Something about knowing your mom's true identity for the past eleven years. That she's not the legal wife. Eleven years, that's when my mom and—"

"Check the alley!" someone shouted. "Might be hiding." Beams of white light shot about in the darkness. The teens held their breath, listening to the feet and voices.

When a beam of bright light shone into the dumpster, Misty gasped, pressing her lips tight. She dared not breathe, but it felt like torture.

The light moved on.

They waited a long time before Roman continued his hushed proposal.

"They only showed a picture of her face badly beaten. If I could see your mom…"

"But why would my mom stay?"

"Fear. A lot of battered women stay out of fear."

"So you're saying he's not my dad? What about Max? He's almost eleven."

Roman shrugged. "I don't know. I just find it…" He wagged his head. "Agh, maybe I'm crazy. Sorry."

Misty took his hand. "I want to believe with you," she said, ending with a hard shiver. Then after a moment, "You've seen my birthmark before?"

"Lots of times, on my sister. She loved running around naked. Hated to wear a swimsuit." He chuckled, but then his eyes moistened. "If... if you are... and I'm not just going nuts, Misty May... I've missed you every day of my life."

"May? That was her middle name?"

Roman nodded. "Wisteria May Whitehall."

"Girl's gone! With the boyfriend. Delete this problem or else."

The smoke-stained fingers set the phone down with a weary sigh. "One more day," he muttered. "One… more… day."

* * * * * * * * * *

Planning to leave the dumpster before daylight, the two huddled close, shivering, but eventually falling into troubled sleep.

When Misty awoke with painful aches, rays of warm sunlight streaked through the bags. She gasped, sitting up with alarm.

It's day! The fears returned with a dark foreboding. She had no idea where they were, nor how far it was to CIA headquarters. *We're fugitives,* she thought, now shivering. For a time, she listened to Roman's steady breathing, again feeling sorry for him. She scolded herself for dragging him into this.

But it's not my fault. And not Ganny's. Greed, she mused, *greedy people enslaved to… greed. Should just let them have their way… let them destroy everything.* She groaned, fighting back the pressing despair. She knew poverty. She knew hunger. This 'digital bomb' would do more than disrupt, it would devastate hundreds of millions of lives, destroying families, leaving little girls and boys to fend for themselves, crying with hunger as they sought a safe place to sleep.

"No," she whispered, "we're so close." Her love for Ganny

had driven her this far. She wouldn't quit now, not till she gave her all, gave it all as Ganny had.

Roman stirred beside her, his eyes opening with surprise. At first, he wondered where he was, rolling his head about, trying to see through the garbage.

"We escaped from jail," Misty said quietly.

"Oh, yeah." Then he bolted upright. "It's light out!"

Misty held his arm, trying to calm him, to calm herself. He pushed some bags aside, raising his head to peer into the full morning light. Misty sat up with him, her hair a snarled nest. As Roman tried to stand, she held him back.

"Roman," she said with somber earnest, "if something happens today…"

"No, don't talk like that. We've made it this far." He looked about the alley. "Looks clear." With some effort, they climbed out and made their way cautiously toward another alley that led away from the dilapidated police station.

The air felt crisp, but the sun's warmth refreshed their spirits. Coming out onto a small side street, they walked for some distance, trying to find anything familiar or friendly looking. Afraid to stop and ask directions, they just kept walking, putting as much space between them and the station, if it even was a legit police station.

When Misty caught the smell of pancakes and bacon, her stomach growled so loud a passing young man glanced at her with a chuckle.

"I'm starving," she said quietly to Roman, taking his hand in hers. When they found the source of the compelling aromas—Pappy's Café—they went in and took a booth near the back door.

It felt surreal, sitting in a small diner, knowing their lives were in serious danger, but they were hungry, very hungry.

After each downed a full platter, they ordered one more to split. A sense of hope returned with their bellies full, very full. Roman sat back with a sigh, his eyes gleaming as he studied the girl across the table. He chuckled, wondering once again if he were simply driven mad by his desperate desire to see his sister again. *But the birthmark, her name, her hair... and now that guy's testimony.*

Misty returned his smile. She too marveled at the words of Roman, wondering if it were all a dream, if maybe she had fallen and now lay silent in a desperate coma.

Desperate... that was the word for them. Without a phone, without direction, without knowing what the day would bring... what reception they'd find at CIA, and...

"Oh, crumb!" Roman's eyes went wide. "My wallet! I don't have my wallet!"

And... without money.

He glanced toward the counter and then the back door. Misty shook her head.

"What else can we do?" he said, leaning close to whisper. "I don't even have my watch."

The police had taken everything except their clothes. Misty looked about. No way would she leave without some form of payment.

"We just tell them," she said.

"Tell them we escaped from jail? We'll wash dishes till closing time?" His tone was cynical, and Misty drew back with tight lips.

"I'm sorry," he said, seeing her response. "I'm just a little..." He couldn't find the words, his fingers tapping the table like a hungry woodpecker.

Misty sighed, scolding herself once more for getting him into all this. She watched him for a moment, then gently put her hand over his, silencing the nervous tapping.

Their waitress, Rose, appeared with the check. A short, plump middle-aged gal with a contagious smile. "Anything more for you two darlings?" she asked, looking them over.

They both shook their heads. The smell of smoke and garbage emanated from their clothes and hair, which the woman had noticed at first whiff. Misty looked a mess with a dirty bandage on her forehead, bruises on her face, and the scab beneath her lip crusted dark brown. Roman's fat lip had puffed up nicely, turning purple like the bruise on his chin.

"Big party," Roman said. "Bonfire… all-nighter. Got a bit rough."

The woman slowly nodded. "But Halloween's tonight."

"Pre-party," Roman said, trying to smile. "Tonight's the real deal."

For a moment, Rose didn't respond, other than her dubious expression. "Yeah, but one can party too much, ya know."

Roman nodded. Misty just watched in silence, the idea of lying still a conundrum.

"How we gonna pay?" Roman asked after the woman left, his eyes again going for the back door.

Suddenly Misty lit up. "Your card. We can use your card."

"My credit card?" He shook his head. "It's in my wallet, at the jail." He quickly lowered his voice.

Misty rose with a smile, approaching the little counter with their bill in hand. Rose stepped over to take payment.

"My boyfriend forgot his wallet," Misty said, her insides tickling at the words. "But I know his card number."

Rose looked at them both questioningly. Roman stood very perplexed.

"Can we do that?" Misty asked. "It's a long walk back home."

Rose shrugged, punching in the numbers as Misty called them out, ending with the month and year.

"And security code?" Rose asked.

Misty turned to Roman, her eyes searching his face. He was still standing like a wooden statue, his face contorted. Misty nudged him.

"You know that number, I hope."

"On the back of the card," Rose said, still very dubious.

"Ah… yeah. Eight twenty-two." His mouth hung open as he sized her up. "Or is it——?"

"Okay, that works. Sign here."

Roman took the pen, his head shaking.

"Don't forget the tip," Misty said, smiling at Rose, who shut one eye, aiming her finger at Misty with a smile of female camaraderie.

"You birds get some chill time. Ya look plumb worn out."

"Thanks, Rose. You have a great day," Misty replied with a smug smile, taking Roman's arm as they left Pappy's Café.

"How'd you know my card number?"

Misty just shrugged.

"Misty?"

"Don't ask… please?"

He put his arm around her waist, his head still shaking, his belly full. Misty smiled, enjoying his embrace, enjoying the idea of actually having a big brother. She breathed a silent prayer. "Please, God, if it can be true… please?"

With renewed vigor, they stopped to ask directions, learning they were an hour's walk from the George Bush Center for Intelligence. The food and sunshine quickened their step, an ember of hope pulsing timidly in their hearts.

"Should we call Bellows?" Misty asked. "Let him know we're coming?"

"They've tapped his line," Roman said frankly. "And it's Saturday. He's probably not even there."

They cut through a clothing store to shorten their distance and stay off the open streets. Roman paused at a rack of women's coats.

"You need a new jacket," he said.

"We need to stop the hackers," Misty replied, feeling the fine fabric, thinking of her wardrobe always made from secondhand clothes.

"You sure?" he said, eyeing her tattered jacket. "I'd be happy—"

"Roman! If we don't stop them," she paused to look about, "this will... all be gone."

He sighed, sobering at the idea and the daunting task before them.

When they stepped out onto the street, a police car passed slowly by. Roman quickly turned, pushing Misty up against the wall, tucking her frizzy mop behind her head as if they were lovers preparing to kiss.

She stared up, searching his eyes. *Could he really be my brother?*

He glanced to watch the car roll past, his face tight. "I'd make a lousy spy," he said, exhaling a nervous breath.

They moved on with the frightful trepidations all returning, their brief moment of hope drifting off with the patrol car.

"It's still a ways," Roman said. "Can you make it?"

Misty nodded, taking Roman's hand once again. Her hip now hurt more than ever, making each step add to the angst growing inside. The scuffle with the blond had not helped matters in the least. Roman had previously gotten her some pain pills, but they too were at the station.

"You really don't have a girl?" she asked.

"Nope."

"There's a bunch that want you, though."

Roman chuckled. "Except the one I want."

"What's she like?"

He looked over at Misty and smiled. "You."

She squeezed his hand. *A big brother…* It brought a trickle of joy that seeped through the darkness into her burdened heart. Having always carried the load, the grief, protecting Max, caring for her mother, defending them against Mr. Grey… to now have someone so strong and smart like Roman. She drew his hand in closer.

"If it turns out," she said slowly, "that… well, if I'm not…" She sighed a little. "Well, could I still… you know…?" She blushed, scolding herself for even thinking it. From beneath the bed, she heard the words of Mrs. Longmire. 'I just don't think she's the girl for you, James. Think of your future. I mean, really James?'

Misty slumped. Like James, Roman came from a different world, a world of happy people, successful people, people who just didn't mix with the likes of… She sighed again, her steps slowing.

Roman squeezed her hand. "Whatever comes," he said, stopping to look her square on, "from now on, I'm your brother. Not sure of much right now, but I know this…" He paused to study her beleaguered face. "…I'd be honored to call you my sister." Then he straightened. "If it's okay with James."

Misty stared up, her eyes misting. She so longed to hug him right then, to squeeze him so tight and never let go.

Roman glanced about. "We better keep moving."

Misty smiled, her heart singing. It didn't matter what happened today. She had a big brother, an *awesome* big brother. Things were going to work out. She could feel it. All would be okay.

They turned onto a busier street, her limping gait slowing.

"You sure you can make it?" Roman asked. "Maybe I should call a cab."

A sudden squawk, followed by a piercing siren, made them both jump. Two male police officers sprang from their car, both drawing guns as they shouted for the teens to get down.

Roman backed away, asking what they had done. Misty looked about, her hip hurting so bad, the idea of running brought sudden tears.

"On the ground!" shouted the officer approaching Roman. Misty stood stunned, her eyes staring at the gun aimed at her chest. She slowly put her hands on her head.

"I'll go peacefully," she said, limping toward the car.

"On the ground!"

"Why? It hurts to…" She held the officer's gaze. "Can I just… get in the car?" She continued limping slowly forward. After a tense moment, he stepped aside, opening the door, his gun still poised.

Roman followed suit, his hands on his head.

As the officer slammed the car door shut, another squad car pulled up. For a moment, all four officers stood talking, only occasionally looking their way.

Inside, the hard plastic seats felt cold while the lingering smell of vomit mixed with fresh aromas of coffee and fast food.

Listening to the engine idle, Misty glanced back. "Keep watch," she whispered, squeezing her slender hand between the metal barrier and the driver's door.

"Misty?" Roman watched with dread. "What are you doing?"

"Just keep watch."

Grimacing as she shoved her arm further in, one fingertip found its mark. When her window slid down a few inches, Roman spoke with stern protest.

"No, Misty! Stop!"

She glanced back at the officers, now engaged in conversation. Slipping her hand out the window, she trembled as she found the door latch.

When a large bus rumbled by, Misty pulled the latch and slunk out the driver's-side door. In two seconds, she was in the driver's seat, dropping the car into gear.

The squeal of smoking tires drowned the shouts of alarm, as squad car 702 sped off toward the intersection.

"Which way?" Misty shouted.

"Not that way!" Roman called from the back. "Turn right!"

Misty swerved but couldn't make the turn, grazing a parked car as she dashed through a yellow light.

"Next right!" Roman shouted, struggling to stay upright.

With strobe lights flashing, Misty spun the wheel, drifting into the next intersection. Bumping two cars, which then bumped others, she spun the tires, leaving a trail of chaos behind her.

At the next block, she swung the car again to the right, the tires squealing. Speeding past cars like they were frozen in time, she held it steady as sirens blared behind them, lights flashing into her mirrors.

Roman tumbled into the door, his head bonking the window with a pumpkin-like thump. "In three or four blocks," he called out, "take Dolley Madison Boulevard."

"Which way?" Misty screamed back, her hands tight on the wheel.

"Left, left, go left!"

The light ahead turned red. Misty paused, then gunned it,

hoping they'd see her flashing lights. Three cars pulled into the intersection, two stopping short. Swerving like an Indy track pro, Misty dodged the third, shooting past with only a side mirror as collateral damage.

It left a pile of confusion, blocking their pursuant. But no sooner had she cleared that one when the next light turned red. Seeing the blockade of stopped cars, she swung onto the walkway, slowing to avoid pedestrians, horn blaring.

"Look out!" she shouted as a man dove over the hood. An oncoming car screeched as Misty plowed into the street, cranking the wheel to aim back up the intersection.

A truck grazed her rear end, pointing her straight into the oncoming traffic. A row of flashing lights approached two blocks away.

She spun the car back, pressing the pedal to the floor. Misty knew only two speeds—full throttle, and two-footed braking.

The light ahead had turned green, and all the cars were through. She glimpsed a sign for Dolley Madison Boulevard as she bolted through, cranking the wheel to follow the arrow.

As Roman bounced about in the back seat, he felt certain they would both die at any moment, or at best, be injured beyond repair. If the nation's infrastructure didn't end tonight, his world surely would. Even his powerful father, an attorney for the state of New York, wouldn't be able to rescue him from this.

He too saw the sign for the boulevard. Pounding on the metal grating, he shouted for Misty.

"Take it, and stay on it till I tell you."

She nodded, her eyes darting up to the mirror for only a heartbeat. The fire in her eyes spoke volumes to Roman. Though often shy and timid with plenty of self-doubt, she also had a power and strength like no one else he knew, no one… except his father.

Misty over-steered the corner, slamming them into a curb that bounced them back across into oncoming traffic. Swerving and dodging, they somehow got onto the boulevard, albeit not a path anyone else had ever taken.

Behind them, more lights flashed, horns honking, shrilling sirens growing louder. Smoking the tires once more, Misty pulled away from the pack, her eyes on the road far ahead.

As Roman fought to keep his breakfast down, Misty called out, "Almost there! Next exit!" She had seen the sign, which prompted her to go all out, a desperate, insane dash for the ramp.

Exiting way too fast, her tires squealed, hopping and sliding till they hit the curb, swerving over grass and gravel. She completely missed the entrance to the George Bush Center for Intelligence, which had security outposts and plenty of signs warning against unauthorized vehicles. Taking a sharp turn, she followed a narrow road that seemed to circle the compound.

Before Roman could catch his breath, they were speeding straight for a security barrier arm, its black and yellow stripes just yards away.

"Misty!" he shouted, ducking behind the seat. Unlike the wooden gates that easily splinter as in the movies, the metal barrier arm bent backward only to snap up over the hood, smashing the windshield before sliding over the roof.

Instantly the windshield clouded up, a web of cracks blinding her view. Misty stomped the brakes, skidding to a stop just fifty yards from the security outpost. Roman glanced back, just as three shots zipped through the rear window, shattering the broken windshield.

Glass shards rained down over Misty, collecting in her hair, filling her lap. She screamed, shaking the glass from her head and neck. Two more shots thumped into the rear of the car as sirens sounded from all directions.

"Go, Misty! Go!" Roman shouted, now convinced they would soon be dead.

She followed the road, which seemed to meander, taking them nowhere. Catching a glimpse of the main entrance, she cut over lawn and shrubs, bouncing and flopping till her tires found concrete. Speeding hard, she skid to a stop, a front tire thumping up onto the marble steps.

For a moment, she just stared at the huge building towering above. The sirens were now distant, her ears ringing. Then she whipped around, a chill of fear knotting her gut.

"Roman! Are you…?"

Roman sat up dazed, his face ashen. Then he spun to look behind, his eyes wide.

"We better… keep going!" he huffed, crawling out the door, his head bleeding in several spots.

Dazed and wobbling, Misty crawled from the mangled remains of patrol car 702. A quick glance back told her they better run.

"You okay?" she called to Roman.

"No! Are you?"

"Roman, your head is—"

"Hurry! They're coming!" Roman grasped her hand. "Can you run?"

As alarms and sirens blared, the two battered teens ran together, hand in hand up the glossy steps. Limping and wincing, Misty tried to blink away the tears blurring her vision. She glanced back to see armed guards running from all directions.

Passing silently above them, a short communication traveled the airwaves, to then be collected by a tiny earpiece.

"Delete at will," crackled a firm command.

"Roger that."

Black crosshairs followed Misty's back as she hobbled up the marble steps. A subtle click… a finger moving to a fine-tuned trigger… a near-silent exhale… then a well-practiced squeeze.

"Hurry, Misty!" Roman held the door as Misty hobbled up the steps.

With that refined squeeze, a steel pin slammed into a small primer, igniting a cartridge designed for death. A precisely fashioned lump of lead weighing less than half an ounce, sped from a long black barrel, spinning as it cut through space and time.

Life is fragile. Death is cruel. Some see it coming, awaiting its long bony arm as they lie helpless in bed. Some are taken without warning, yanked mercilessly from everyday life, so unexpected, its sudden grasp feeling all the more cruel.

As the bullet left the long black barrel, Misty stepped toward Roman, her eyes on his. Little did either know the death that spun its way toward her, its lifeless eye set upon her heart. She would never know what took her. At least it would be quick.

A blob of pigeon poop squished beneath her foot as she clamored up the marble steps. Fresh as an egg on a buttered pan, the poop compressed and slid her sole off the step as if she'd tread on grease. As she dropped to her hands, the step just above her head exploded. Shards of marble plastered her face and neck.

Screaming, she jerked away.

"Run, Misty! Run!" Roman stretched to grasp her hand, his other still on the large glass door. He scanned the distance behind them, urgent fear choking his heart.

Stern lips issued a curse as the gloved hand yanked back the bolt, ejecting a hot casing that tumbled from the chamber. The hand slammed the bolt forward, the fine black crosshairs once again finding Misty's back.

Again, the well-conditioned squeeze, again, the rifle bucked. This time the little mass of lead couldn't miss. Misty pushed herself upward, her eyes on Roman's face. His cries for her to run seemed to drift into silent space, his mouth slowed by some malfunction of time. She strained to push upward, to run up the last few steps, but now gravity and time conspired against her, turning her movements to sluggish, fruitless efforts of frozen silence.

A black van sped past, eleven grams heavier, a flattened clump of lead lodged within its upper frame.

Misty clasped Roman's hand, his arm jerking her up through the door.

"Someone's shooting at us!" he yelled into the lobby. He flung his arm out toward the building across the courtyard. Two armed guards met him with trained response, their strong hands taking him to the floor.

"No!" he shouted, looking back through the glass doors, his face pressed to the cold, polished marble. "They're shooting! Hide her!"

Metal detectors and security scanners blocked any forward progress from the doors. Without hesitation, Misty bolted through, a security guard quickly taking her down.

Hands bound behind them, faces to the floor, they cried out in protest, stopping only when tasers were drawn.

"Bellows! Urgent!" Misty tried to say, blood from her cheek smearing the marble. "Call agent Bellows… please!"

Guards from outside poured in, their weapons drawn. Orders were shouted, words exchanged, tempers flaring.

"Call Bellows!" Misty shouted, her voice ringing with heightened anger. "Quit arguing and call agent Bellows. It's urgent!"

After a tense moment, they were jerked up and shoved into a room marked, *Security*. Roman shook his head when asked for identification. Misty just kept insisting to speak with agent Bellows, and that it was urgent.

After an officer came and questioned them, they were left alone within the securely locked room.

Still panting from the run, they both sat in silent shock, haggard and weary. Roman started to speak, but Misty quickly shook her head, her lips compressed. He nodded, dabbing several bloody spots on her face with an old napkin from Pappy's Café. She thanked him, then gushed, her sobs deep.

It was good that no one came for a while, as Misty was a blubbering mess, her sleeve collecting snot and tears, her eyes red and puffy. The morning had been hell. Last night's struggle with death still brought shudders. And the pain in her arm, ribs, and hip now screamed for attention.

When the door opened, a casually dressed man with a tight face and thick shock of dark hair entered as if wary, his tired eyes quickly searching the two captives. For a moment, he just stood there, studying the bloodstained faces, the little room silent. Then he cleared his throat.

"You asked for me?" His voice sounded like a smoker.

"Are you agent Bellows?" Misty asked with a loud sniffle.

The man's eyes flittered up to a security camera, then back at the two. "Depends who's asking?"

"Ganny sent me!" Misty said quickly. "They…" She blinked back tears, struggling to stay strong.

"Agent Tallon?" he asked with alarm. "Is she…?" He glanced again at the security camera. "Tell me what happened."

Fighting back hysteria, she gave a quick disjointed account of their traumatic ordeal.

"Hold on!" The man held up his hand, his eyes again darting to the security cameras overhead. "Let's take this to my office."

Misty nodded, then looked to Roman, her hand reaching for his as they eagerly followed the man to his office.

She had not given up, nor given in. Although they didn't have whatever was in the locket, she did know some names and still had all she'd seen at the farmhouse tucked firmly in her mind.

After a silent elevator ride, they stopped outside an office door marked B. C. Bellows. He went to swipe his keycard, but then stopped, his brow tight.

"No, let's go somewhere… safe." He glanced around. "This way."

He swiped a nearby office with the name W. T. Parks, and the lock opened with a loud click. Glancing about, he ushered them in.

A simple one-room office with cabinets and shelves, it smelled of smoke and sort of musty. He took a seat behind the desk, motioning for them to each have a seat.

"Okay, start from the beginning." He lit a cigarette, took one long draw, but then looked at the two and doused it in a paper cup.

Misty glanced at Roman who encouraged her to speak first. In shaky voice, but coherent detail, Misty told of all that happened, from her day at school until the run up the steps. The man listened intently, asking only precise questions, giving no indication of alarm or concern. By the time Misty told the last harrowing details of the car chase and chaos that followed, Roman had to pee so bad his feet were tapping like a sewing machine at high speed. Reluctant to leave Misty, he finally asked for a restroom.

"Down the hall on the left." The man pointed casually to his right.

"Just leave?" Roman said, a bit perplexed.

"You planning to run somewhere?"

Roman shook his head. "No… no, I'll be right back."

The man gestured again with his hand. "Can't miss it."

Misty watched him leave, her chest lifting with breaths of relief. She watched the man scribble the last of his notes, his eyes dark and tired. He looked up at her, his mind obviously in a quandary.

"Without solid proof," he said, shaking his head, "I can't do much. We actually get a lot of these. Most are false alarms. Can waste good funds and manpower trying to track them down, only to look like fools."

"But it's tonight, at midnight!"

He shook his head. "If you had that locket you spoke of..." His voice trailed off.

Misty watched with growing consternation. Surely the man could do something. "But can't you call someone," she asked, her voice rising, "have them check into it? Can't you...? Did Ganny...?" Her face tightened. "Did she die for nothing?"

He sighed. "No, she was onto something, I'm sure. I just need that locket, or whatever's inside." He stood. "Sure you don't know where it is?"

Misty shook her head. She had left out telling him of James and the locket, and that hussy blond, her heart still messy with all that.

"Tell ya what," he said, opening the office door, "let's wait on this. I'll keep a close eye." He stood waiting for her to leave. Misty sat confused. "Trust me," he said with a smile. "We'll keep our eyes and ears open. If anything comes to the surface, we'll take care of it, okay?"

Misty shook her head. "What? Forget the whole thing? But Ganny's dead!" She pursed her lips, her face strained. "I... well, that's just it," she said boldly, as if declaring a hidden secret. "I can't forget... anything. I... remember everything. But I'm not a freak. I just remember stuff more than other people."

The man slowly closed the door, his face lengthening. "What kind of *stuff* do you remember?"

"Well, everything... I saw Larkin's notebook. It was on the table. I wasn't spying. There were passcodes and usernames. Ah... stuff like... well, NORAD kind of stuff, and the Whisper program, and... I tell you, it's real. I saw a bunch of names, lists of contacts and... I'm not making this up."

For a second, the man stood as if pained by something. Then he made a call from his desk phone, turning his back to Misty as he spoke, his voice low.

"Be right there," he finally said, then hung up the phone. "Follow me." Returning to the door, he swung it open, glancing both ways down the hall, his arm beckoning for Misty.

Stunned, she stepped through and glanced toward the restrooms. "What about Roman?" she asked, angst rising.

"Just follow me." He walked rather briskly, taking her down a hall to a flight of stairs. Two floors down, they walked another hall, to finally stop before a sealed door. Misty's hip hurt so bad, she fought back tears. Glancing both ways, the man then punched a numbered keypad.

Before they stepped inside, Misty's stomach turned, an empty hole of some kind forming deep within. Her mind had been poking, prodding, trying to tell her something, something she knew, but it just couldn't get through.

The small room looked like a simple laboratory with shelves and vials, tiny cages and a long white table. Several machines with numerous dials and gauges sat on movable racks with multi-colored wires hanging down in tight bouncy spirals. Two large stainless-steel refrigerators stood against a back wall, but most alarming was a heavy-duty dentist chair with leather straps attached to the armrest.

And ones for the feet! Misty's gut twisted, her body stiffening.

The man watched her and laughed. "No, no," he said, chuckling. "It's not like that." He wagged his head, offering a yellow-stained smile. "Sorry, it's for teaching field agents how to escape from such chairs. Agent Tallon was rather good… a real escape artist."

Misty tried to relax, but again, something inside kept poking at her beleaguered brain.

As Misty stared at the sturdy chair, a man suddenly appeared within the room. She saw no other doors and wondered from where he could have come. Dressed in a white lab coat, the tall, lanky man approached with a queer smile, his face gaunt and angular. He looked every bit a nerdy scientist, even wearing black-rimmed glasses with white tape holding the frames together.

Misty glanced at the locked door. "Roman…?" she said in a quavering whisper.

"Don't worry," the man said. "My staff will bring him down." He motioned toward the chair. "Sit, take a rest. This is Dr. Weltz. He studies memory and such, working with our field agents. Tell him what you told me, about your memory, please. He's an expert in neurological phenomena. If your memory thing is legit, then I may have the proof I need. Understand?"

Misty nodded.

The doctor introduced himself, giving Misty a bony, dead-fish handshake. He too encouraged her to not fear the imposing chair, but to sit and rest.

With great trepidation, Misty lowered her aching body into the white padded chair. She warily lifted her feet onto the metal footrest where the leather straps and tarnished buckles hung limp.

It did feel good to sit, as every muscle seemed to throb with pain. She took a deep breath, trying to calm her nerves, her mind and body frazzled beyond repair. "What do you want to know?" she asked slowly as Dr. Weltz wheeled over a rack of wire-infested equipment.

"Just tell him what you told me," the man said, resting his rump on the white table that sat across from the chair. As Dr. Weltz worked behind her, Misty studied the middle-aged Bellows, a red light suddenly flashing in her brain.

No… no, it can't be. The voice on the phone…

Her eyes went wide, her mouth dropping as she stared up at the man. "Your voice… you…"

Before she could finish, a steel collar snapped shut about her neck. It had come from nowhere. She reached up, too stunned to even scream.

The man leaped to her side, grabbing her right arm as two bony hands grabbed her left. Within seconds, the wrist straps bound her hands tight. She jerked and kicked, pleading for them to stop, but the neck strap clutched only tighter. Then the man pulled a small handgun, its barrel suddenly pressing her brow.

"Shut up!" he barked. "Just… shut up!"

"Hold still!" the nerdy doctor snapped, struggling to attach an electrode patch to Misty's right forehead, one already on the left. She trembled as the man posing as Bellows just stood watching, gun now aimed at her chest. Several more electrodes got placed at the base of her neck, temples, and scalp.

"What are you doing?" Misty tried to ask, her voice quavering. "Who are you?"

"Parks," the man said with a scowl. "You've made a mess, ya little snake!" He cussed at her with pent-up rage. "Should give you what you deserve."

"But I—"

"Keep your mouth shut," he ordered, raising a hand to strike. Misty flinched. After more curses, he made his way behind her. She tried to follow his movement, but the wily doctor stomped his foot, yelling at her to sit still.

"Now, for that memory of yours," Parks said. He came back around to stand over her, a slick smile twitching his smoker-lips. He lifted a leg to sit partially on the table as Dr. Weltz pushed buttons, mumbling merrily to himself.

Misty just stared at the small gun, her heart pounding with the dreadful memories from behind the tool shed. She fought to think, but images streamed in from all directions, scenes of her mother and Max, of Ganny and James… of Roman…

Roman! Where's Roman?

Parks then swung the wheeled cart around for Misty to see the dials and gauges. Wires hung like party string, all connected to her wagging head, her curly mop flopping about as she tried to shake the wires loose.

"This, my little twit, will help you forget." He flashed his yellowed smile.

"Can do more than that," the doctor said with delight. He fiddled with some more dials, flipping switches like he had done this a thousand times.

Misty stared at Parks with eyes wide. "Forget what?" she tried to ask, her voice a mousy cry.

"Was thinking along the lines of… everything. Even your own name."

"No, no," said the lanky doctor. "Mustn't do that." He pushed a large button that made the whole rack light up and hum. "More like a neuralizer," he said with a quirky grin. "You know, from Men in Black." He coughed up a hollow chuckle.

Forget everything? Misty's eyes went wide. For as long as she could remember, remember everything, Misty yearned to just forget, forget the bad things, the mean things, the dumb things.

But *everything?*

"Thank you, Weltz," Parks said coldly. "You can leave."

"Leave?"

"Yes, leave!" Parks became quite stern, his face souring.

After tense hesitation, the lanky man shuffled from the room. He glared back over his hunched shoulder as he closed the heavy metal door.

Frantic with sudden rage, Misty fought the bonds, her legs kicking wildly. She shook her head side-to-side, but the metal collar seemed to only tighten.

The man just watched, his face going through a mix of contractions and scowls, as if in conflict. "Walter," he said, studying Misty. "Walter Thormand Parks." He rose to once again walk around behind her. Misty craned her neck to follow, but before she could see, he grasped her jaw from behind, forcing a rubber disk into her mouth. Yanking her head back, his hand under her chin, he held her jaw shut as he slapped a wide piece of black duct tape over her mouth and nose.

Wild with panic, Misty fought, kicking and screaming, her muffled cries going nowhere. Lunging and jerking, she tried to rock the chair, but its legs held fast, bolted to the floor.

Parks swore at her, finally clutching her jaw to tear a piece of the tape off her nose. "Just sit still, you stupid twit. It's for your own good. So ya don't bite off your tongue." He stepped back to look her over, holstering his handgun. "I don't like seeing blood."

Nostrils flaring, Misty fought to fill her desperate lungs. She watched his every move, her eyes glaring.

"Was told to neutralize you, make sure you didn't interfere." He sat again on the desk, his hand on the machines facing Misty. "I'm not like that psycho, Larkin. Was going to let you go. Keep you under eyes till this whole thing was done."

He moved a large circular dial making the machine whir into a buzzing hum. "I think up here, in the red zone, it wipes your brain clean." He turned it back a notch. "Maybe here you can still remember your name." He looked Misty in the eyes, then her whole body filled his gaze. "You're a fine piece of work. Plenty of boyfriends, I hear. A real hussy."

Misty screamed through the gag, her face reddening.

"Shame you didn't just stay home," he continued, his face again constricting as if pained.

Misty fought at the straps about her wrists. She tried hopping in the chair, flailing her head back and forth. Parks raised his hand to strike her. She stared him down, her eyes daring him.

Then he chuckled, turning the dial all the way into the red. "I don't kill. Not my style." He put his left hand on a single toggle switch. "It only takes a minute or two. Then you'll be wandering the halls of Misty's private asylum, searching endlessly for your own name."

He shook his head with an irritated snarl. "Goodbye, Misty Grey. It *wasn't* a pleasure meeting you."

As the needles bounced with the increasing hum, Misty's eyes again filled with tears. She had so longed to forget, angry at God for making her remember everything. Now her prayer was about to be answered. She shook her head, her gaze on the nicotine-stained finger poised to flip the main switch.

"Please… nooo…" she pleaded through the gag.

Parks stiffened, his face darkening. Slowly he wagged his head as he glanced at the switch. "Should have stayed home, Misty Grey," he softly muttered. "Should have stayed home."

The sudden sound of the door's keypad startled Parks, his left hand still on the toggle switch. He drew his gun with the other. When the door swung open, two security guards burst in with guns aimed. For a moment, time seemed to stretch. The guards quickly took in the scene. Parks stood firm, one hand on the switch, the other aiming his gun at Misty.

The girl sucked air and held it.

"Freeze!" shouted both guards. Behind them came a tall man with broad shoulders and firm-set jaw, face and clothes like a James Bond kind of guy. He glanced at Misty bound in the chair, her mouth taped shut.

"Drop the gun, Parks!" he ordered, calm but very firm. "And step away."

Parks didn't move, his wild eyes darting back and forth between the guards and Misty.

"Take your hand away, Parks, now!"

The hum of the machines seemed to grow with intensity, as if sensing the tension within the white walls. The tall, lanky Weltz stuck his head through the door.

"Oh my!" he exclaimed, seeing the bouncing needles. "You'll melt her brains!"

"Parks…"

Agent Parks clenched his jaw, nostrils flaring, gun arm quivering.

"Doggone it, Parks! She's just a kid!"

With that, the Bond guy moved toward Misty.

"No!" shouted Parks. "Don't come any closer!" He now

trembled, his chest sucking quick, shallow breaths. "Stay back or I'll shoot."

"Come on, Parks," pleaded the other. "It's not worth it."

A stained finger twitched. A surge of bright light burst inside Misty's head. Gunfire split her ears, the deafening sounds rippling around and around.

Flashes of colored light mixed with spatters of blood. Sharp acrid smoke filled the air, like singed hair and melting plastic. She tried to scream as her eyes went dark. The stench of burnt flesh came, then cries of anguish that rang in her ears.

When Misty's sight returned, smoke hung so thick, the guards and Weltz were coughing, waving their hands at the dark gray smoke.

"Can you hear me?" The James Bond-looking guy held an electrode in each hand, his voice urgent. "Can you see me?"

For a moment, Misty just stared, an empty look of shock covering her face. Her eyes followed the man's facial features, as would a small infant just learning to see. She looked down at the electrodes still in each hand.

The man motioned for a guard to undo the straps as he tried to gently pull the duct tape off, finally giving it a quick rip, apologizing with sincerity.

"Tell me your name, please." His voice seemed to echo for a long while—a nice voice, deep and assuring. He peered desperately into Misty's eyes.

As the leather straps fell to each side, she touched her right temple. It stung like a fresh burn, the spot tender. She then looked at the smoking machines, hot lumps of lead having torn through their electronic innards.

The body of Parks lay sprawled on the floor, a leg still clinging to the table. Blood seeped out from beneath his chest, his wide blank eyes staring upward. His mouth hung open as if in shock, yellowed teeth now tainted red.

Misty returned her gaze to the man before her.

"Can you stand?" he asked, that look of urgency still

searching her eyes. He gently lifted her from the metal chair, leading her out into the hallway, away from all the smoke and blood.

When all but Weltz had left the room, the sprinklers burst into a shower of rain, soaking poor Weltz as he lamented the death of his precious machine.

The hallway had filled with alarmed confusion, as men and women in lab coats ran here and there. Misty followed the man leading her by the hand.

When they entered a hall with fresh, clean air, he stopped to rest, huffing as if having run a mile or two.

"You okay?" he asked anxiously. "Please tell me you're okay."

Misty just watched him, studying his eyes, listening to his voice.

"Let's go down to first aid. Get those burns looked at." Like leading a small child, he led her along another hall. "Doggone it," he kept saying, followed by, "Why, Parks, why?"

Nurse Lanna, a young woman with nice eyes and a kind smile, put some ointment and gauze over Misty's burns. She'd been told nothing other than to treat the wounds.

"What's your name?" she asked, working fast yet gracefully. "My name's Lanna."

Misty just watched her, following her movements like a lost child. When nurse Lanna finished, she paused to study Misty's face. "So where are you from?"

But Misty sat trembling, her light-green eyes just staring.

"Want to lie down?" nurse Lanna asked, pointing to a couch beside a wall. Misty continued studying the woman as she brought a glass of water. "Does your head hurt? Any headache?"

Misty shook her head. The James Bond guy had left the room after making a call, his phone chirping with messages.

"You're safe here," Lanna said, gently pushing aside a wild strand caught on Misty's eyelash. She smiled at the young girl's auburn strands bushing out in all directions. "Beautiful, but hard to tame, huh?"

Misty glanced at the clock on the wall. 12:33. She touched her cheeks where the tape had been. For a moment more, she studied the eyes of Lanna, and then, clearing her throat, she asked, "Who was that man… who brought me here?"

At first, Lanna did not reply, her face perplexed. "You don't know?" she asked, then gave a silly grin. "Obviously. That was agent Bellows, head of section twelve."

At that same moment, the man returned, setting his phone down on a small desk. He exhaled a long sigh.

Like a weasel, Misty sprang from the examination table and grabbed the phone. Rushing into the small bathroom, she bolted the door.

"Hey! You can't do that!" The man pounded on the door, commanding Misty to open up or he'd break it down. "There's secure data…" He stopped to look back at nurse Lanna. "Encrypted, of course… the important stuff, I hope." Then he went back to pound on the door, but Misty opened, the phone held out for him.

"Ganny said to speak only with you," she said, looking hard into his eyes, her hand quivering.

"Ganny?"

"Mrs. Quinn, Veronica Tallon."

"Agent Tallon sent you?"

Misty nodded, a gush of tears coming on hard.

"Is she okay?" agent Bellows asked with sudden concern.

Misty fought it as hard as she could, but the sobs came. Convulsing with long, pent-up anguish, she cried. Nurse Lanna held her close, trying to comfort, clueless to what had happened.

When she had cried her last, Bellows suggested they go to his office where Misty could tell him all that happened. Misty shook her head, insisting they stay there with nurse Lanna.

So, sitting with Lanna on the couch, Misty told everything from the day she'd been taken from school until the ordeal with the phony agent Bellows—the now dead, Walter Parks.

He became more and more disturbed after hearing of Ganny's death and the details of Misty's account.

"Midnight, tonight?" Bellows rubbed his chin. "Do you have proof? Any evidence at all?"

Misty slumped. "Supposedly in my locket."

"I can't act without some kind of evidence." The man continued to rub his chin. "We'll go see Coppenheim, but I need... if this is real..."

"Whose Coppenheim?" Misty asked, wiping her nose.

"Deputy director." The man seemed surprised at Misty's ignorance. "You need to tell him all you told me."

"Can we trust him?"

"He's head of CIA."

"So can we trust him?"

Bellows straightened, startled by the idea. "I would sure hope so."

They entered through a frosted-glass door into the assistant's office, a clean, modern room, where an attractive young woman greeted them. Her shapely figure was accentuated by a tight business dress, her blond hair falling freely about her shoulders.

"The director is on his way," she said, smiling at agent Bellows. She led them into the director's office where they both took a seat, the chairs like something straight out of seventeenth-century France.

Misty glanced around the office, concluding it was most certainly designed by someone, probably a woman, who loved classical French décor.

"Baroque," she said to herself, weary eyes following the ornate crown molding that connected the high ceiling to the papered walls. Two large double-hung windows with off-white curtains looked out over the grounds below. Between them sat an elaborately carved wooden desk, like something straight from the Palace of Versailles. Behind it was a worn-out leather office chair, the only item that did not fit the room's décor.

Misty looked up. Behind the director's desk hung a large painting of men on horseback galloping after dogs hot on the scent of a panting fox, its tongue lolling out.

For a moment she could only stare at the fox, feeling its desperation, its frantic effort to escape the clamoring dogs and men on horseback all bent on ending the poor creature's insignificant life.

"Can I get you anything?" the curvaceous assistant asked them, her attention on Bellows.

"Have you seen my friend Roman?" Misty asked.

"Oh, is he here in the building?"

Misty gave the details, and both Bellows and the assistant assured the troubled girl they would find him.

As Coppenheim was home with his family for Halloween, it would take some time, but he would get there as soon as possible. Misty continued to ask about Roman as they waited, but always the reply was the same— 'We're still looking.'

Misty knew Roman wouldn't leave without her, that he would search for her. She tried to keep calm as Bellows suggested but found it hard to sit still.

When Coppenheim finally arrived, he was rather curt, agitated even, for he had planned on spending the day with his family. An average-looking man, he stood Misty's height with blue-gray eyes and near-shaved head. Wrinkles creased his face as stained teeth showed signs of life-long smoking.

Do they all smoke a pack a day? Misty wondered, following the man's movements as he took his seat behind the ornate desk. He took out a leather-bound pad, and with pen in hand, looked up at Misty with an expression of, 'I'm listening.'

"Tell him everything you told me," agent Bellows encouraged.

Misty cleared her throat, giving a little cough. This was the third time within the CIA headquarters that she was to tell her tale, and for Misty, it was more than just recalling events. Every feeling, sensation, emotion, fear and pain came with each description, each account of her ordeal over the past week. As hard as she tried, she could not suppress the tears and sudden outbursts that came with those events of trauma and heartache.

Coppenheim listened, jotting down occasional notes, his eyes fixed hard on the sixteen-year-old. He tapped his pen like some toy machine, hammering steadily at the notepad. It slowed, then stopped when Misty mentioned seeing the open files back at the farmhouse.

"You saw passcodes?" he asked, his gaze intense. "You're saying they have passcodes to our missile systems, our security network, and…"

He looked at Bellows. "Have you verified any of this? Checked with cyber branch?" He glanced back at Misty. "Is she legit?"

"Checking, but thought to bring her straight to you, sir," Bellows replied.

The two talked briefly, then asked Misty to continue. When

she explained the whole plan of using the digital bomb to take down the infrastructure and economy, then government sites, ultimately holding the U. S. hostage in exchange for gold, Coppenheim grew stern. He looked at Misty with a questioning expression, his pen bouncing more than usual.

"You have a detailed memory," he said, his brow thoroughly wrinkled, "or a *vivid* imagination." He looked her over, taking his time, his face tight. His gaze then snapped to Bellows. "So you've talked with cyber?"

Bellows nodded, stating that his team, or rather the only two of his team that were available, were looking into any leads possible.

"Other than Parks," the director shook his head in bewilderment, "what have you found?"

"There is some evidence," he said. "Most of her story checks out." He had been regularly glancing at his phone, sending and receiving messages from his staff. Misty had left out the bit about Parks trying to fry her brain, since the director had already been informed of the ordeal.

It had been over an hour since the shooting, and her body still went into fits of mild trembling whenever she recalled the nightmare with all its terrifying feelings and vivid memories.

Coppenheim stood, taking in a deep, troubled breath. He held it for a time, exhaling slowly, his eyes fixed on Misty Grey.

"I don't believe it!" he finally said, shaking his head. "Simply impossible."

Misty stared up at him, mouth open.

"Well," said Bellows, "we'll know soon enough." He looked at his watch—1:49. He glanced over at the girl, her hair and clothes a mess, speckles of blood on her face. She showed signs of pain yet hid it well. And she stunk like garbage.

"Sometime tonight, huh?" the director mused, now reconsidering. He looked to Bellows. "Anything off? Anyone reporting anomalies, or…?"

Misty watched with pounding heart. "But can't you take

precautions or something?" she asked. "Ganny died getting this stuff." Her voice tightened.

"Ganny?" the director asked, but then nodded, remembering the connection. After another sigh, he consented. "I'll make some calls."

"Call the president," Misty pleaded.

The director shook his head with a dismissive chuckle. "Not how it works. Need solid proof." He went to the door. "Thank you," he said sincerely. "You looked tired, Miss Grey." He paused, waiting for Misty to stand, then addressed Bellows. "Get her some food, Bellows. Find her boyfriend. I'll keep you up to speed."

Misty left with Bellows, her head aching and perplexed. Was she just exaggerating the whole thing… imagining it all? *No way!* She limped along beside Bellows, her head slowly wagging.

"Ganny wouldn't send me if there wasn't something going on, would she?" She looked about the hall. "And Parks, why would he try to… you know… silence me?"

Bellows agreed, his face tight with concern. "He'll look into it, Misty. Old Coppy has been around a long—"

Misty stopped, her wide eyes staring up at him. "What did you say?"

"He'll look into—"

"No. What did you call him?"

Bellows looked around. "Hey, don't mention I said that."

Misty pressed herself against the wall, her eyes looking back the way they had come. "Larkin called him that," she said, keeping her voice low.

Bellows nodded. "Yeah, that's what we—"

"No," Misty said again. "She said, 'Even old Coppy's in on it.' She said that! Larkin said that!" She glanced back down the hall. "Mr. Bellows, your director is… Oh, God!" Her face tightened.

No sooner had the words left her mouth than a squad of an armed men came running around the corner. With weapons drawn, they called for Bellows to put his hands on his head. Within moments, the tall man was cuffed and being led away under armed guard.

"Follow me," a bulky guard said, his deep voice solemn. He led her back the way they had come, seating her inside the director's office, stationing himself to guard the door, as Coppenheim was gone.

At first, Misty sat stunned, her heart thumping loudly in her ears, horrible dread creeping up inside. *Roman!* Her gut filled with painful fear, now knowing the director had obviously lied about the young man's whereabouts. Aware that cameras were watching, she sat as still as she could, her hands clenched tight.

She would not declare what she knew, hoping to yet escape and warn someone, the president himself, if she had to. She thought of all the attempts on her life. Had some of those come from this office?

She sighed, a sudden weariness engulfing her. *He won't let me leave here, not alive.* She fought to keep calm, forcing her mind to think of possible escapes.

Her insides soured, recalling all she'd put Roman through. "I've ruined his life," she said under her breath. "And he's my… how can he be? But everything he said…" She stopped herself, glancing back at the guard.

After a time, Coppenheim stepped in, his eyes watching her carefully as he took his seat. Misty felt small sitting in the gold-gilded chair, her weary, frightened eyes peering over the large wooden desk.

"You have family, don't you?" he said, his face dull and pale. Misty nodded. "It's painful… to think of losing them," he said, then paused. "I made some calls." He took out a cigarette but then put it back. "Looks like Bellows is part of this," he said, slowly wagging his head.

Misty straightened, her eyes searching the man's face.

Coppenheim continued. "He's after my job, you know. Trying to undo me. Using you and agent Tallon, creating this whole mess to bring me down." He shook his head at her. "Putting the whole nation on high alert, shutting down utilities, the internet, businesses losing multiple millions, all because I acted on some crazy girl's delusions."

He took out another cigarette, rolling it between his yellowed fingers. "I've arranged a room for you where you can get some rest. I think it's best you stay here for a while. I'll notify your… well…" He paused, seeing Misty's alarm.

"Where is Roman?" she asked, the words gushing out.

"Yes, I forgot to mention. Security said he left during the fire alarm. Don't worry, we'll find him."

Coppenheim rose to escort Misty from the room. "Trust me," he said with a forced smile. "Everything's going to be fine. Halloween can play some mean tricks on a young girl's mind. Go get some rest."

The guard took her down several floors to a door with a security code lock. Misty faltered, her knees suddenly buckling. The strong guard helped her into the room, then turned and left without a word. Behind him, the lock clanked shut, followed by a single beep.

Misty stood, fighting back the overwhelming urge to collapse and cry. She looked about the tiny room—a bed, a small table with some fruit and bottled water, an open toilet, and four blank walls. A secure room, designed for containment.

For at least ten minutes, she just stood where the guard had left her, wanting nothing to do with anything inside the room, inside the whole building, inside the whole stinking world.

A tear dropped to the smooth concrete floor. With it, fell all hope. Misty touched the small red capsule inside her pocket, recalling the words from the blond. 'They say it's painless… you just fall asleep… and forget everything.'

A message buzzed the black phone on the wooden desk. 'Girl?'

The stained fingers typed a reply. 'Contained.'

* * * * * * * * * *

Misty sat at the small metal table, staring at the basket of fruit. Between her fingers, she gently rolled the capsule, a plastic bottle of water in her left hand. She glanced up at the globe of smoked glass behind which a security camera watched her every move.

For some time she sat, rolling the pill, turning her hand this way and that. After a slow sigh, she glanced up at the camera, then slowly put the pill into her mouth. Raising the bottle to her lips, she drank, throwing her head back to swallow.

For a moment, she sat in silence, waiting, her heart beginning to pound. She slid the chair back a little, her right hand giving a single twitch. She glanced up at the camera, a look of anguish on her face. She rubbed her stomach as if in pain.

Again her hand twitched then jerked, her arm bouncing off the table. As if suddenly struck by some unseen force, she flew backward, falling hard to the floor, her whole body erupting into violent fits of convulsing.

In full seizure, she writhed on the floor, kicking the metal chair, her arms and legs flailing, her body bouncing as if under electrocution.

In half a minute, two guards rushed into the room, scooping

up the twitching body of young Misty Grey. Eyes rolled back and mouth drooling, she quivered and jerked, her breath coming in short, sporadic gasps.

Rushing her down the hall, then up flights of stairs, the two men ran, turning toward the medical room just as nurse Lanna was locking the door. She paused upon seeing the limp body of Misty hanging from the arms of the two guards.

"She took something!" one of the guards called.

Nurse Lanna quickly unlocked the door and directed them to lay her body on the examination bed. Arms and legs hung in twisted, torturous positions as the body of Misty lay still. Her sudden, short gasps came at random intervals, some a dreadful half minute apart. Nurse Lanna flew into a rage.

"What have you done!"

"I told you," the guard answered. "She swallowed a pill or something."

"Or something?" Nurse Lanna eyed them both with suspicion.

"Where's the doc?" the other man asked.

"It's Saturday! Where do you think he is?" She spun about, rummaging through a cabinet of drugs. "She needs her stomach pumped. I can't do that here. Call an ambulance."

They both stood firm. She stared at them, her face reddening.

"Total confinement," one said, his eyes looking past Lanna.

"What! She's just a girl!"

"Do what you can," the man said coldly. "We'll notify the director."

As if dismissed by their superior officer, they both spun on their heels and promptly left the room. Nurse Lanna fought back rage, her mind racing. She again went to search the cabinet, uttering fierce words of angry protest. It wasn't the first time she had treated someone forbidden to leave the premises. But it was the first for a dying young girl.

Cursing the guards, she opened a bottle of ipecac syrup. With Misty in a comatose state, she had no way to force the syrup down. "Need a pump," she snarled through clenched teeth.

She had to blink back tears as she lifted the head of Misty, preparing to pour the ipecac, praying she would still have enough life left to swallow. As she lifted Misty's head, the girl's lips moved.

"Are they gone?" Misty asked in a faint whisper. Lanna jerked back, dropping Misty's head back onto the bed. The young girl lay perfectly still.

Nurse Lanna approached. "Misty?"

"Come close," Misty said, barely moving her lips. As Lanna leaned over, Misty half opened one eye. "Cover me from the camera," she whispered. "I need your help." Her eye searched the face of nurse Lanna. "The director… is… in on it," she said slowly, trying not to move her lips. "Bellows arrested."

Nurse Lanna's heart thumped as she tried to swallow the sudden dryness in her mouth. Being relatively new to this position, which she liked very much, for the most part, she knew only a handful of agents well. Bellows being one of them, the one she liked best. As he was a married man, she found herself needing reluctant restraint, her natural affections drawn to his pleasing appearance and personality. For him to be arrested…

"So you didn't take anything?" Lanna whispered.

"No," Misty muttered.

"Just faking?"

Misty smiled ever so slightly, to which Lanna rolled her eyes.

"It happens tonight," Misty reminded her. "It will destroy everything."

Nurse Lanna set the girl's head down, pretending to have been unable to administer the syrup. She shook her head, walking away from Misty, who quickly caught on and let her mouth hang open, her eyes once more rolled back.

Lanna set the bottle back inside the cabinet, returning to Misty with a sigh.

"I don't know," she said softly. "What can we do?"

"Declare me dead. Will they leave?"

"The guards?"

At that moment, one of the guards returned, his face grim. "Director says…" he paused, staring down at Misty's limp, contorted body, "to… just let things be." He studied the lifeless form. "And call disposal."

"Disposal? She's still—"

The guard spun and left, closing the door firmly behind him.

Nurse Lanna leaned over Misty. "Oh God, oh God, help me, help me, help me," she muttered.

Misty opened one eye. "And I think my friend Roman is locked up too."

"I'm getting you out of here," Lanna said, picking up the phone.

"I have to find Roman," Misty said sternly, her mouth still hanging open.

"I'm calling disposal."

"But I'm not dead yet."

"You will be if we don't get you out of here."

Misty sighed, letting her arms and legs fall limp as if the last of life had passed.

Lanna called disposal, telling herself she was doing nothing wrong, just doing her job as commanded. Determined to get Misty to safety, she asked them to come as soon as possible.

"Another body?" the man asked. "What's going on up there?" He then told her it would be after dinner, to which Lanna firmly protested. "Hey, we'll be there," the man assured her. "Don't fret. It's not going anywhere, is it? They usually stay put, you know."

After frustrating attempts to persuade them otherwise, she relented. Pulling a sheet up over Misty's body, she tucked in the twisted hands and legs, finally drawing the sheet gently over her face.

"Get some rest," she whispered. "You look dead tired." After turning out the lights, she whispered that she would return, promising to see what she could learn of both Bellows and Roman.

"And don't move from this bed. You'll make me look bad."

When the lock turned, Misty exhaled a long, tremoring sigh. Although filled with great angst for Roman, her mother, and the world, she managed a hint of a smile, delighting in her ruse.

In welcomed stillness she lay, her mind flooded with scenes from the last hours. Careful to not think of the car chase, which made her jerk upon recalling the collisions, she tried to formulate some plan of action.

But then tears filled her eyes, rolling down into her ears. "I love you, Mother," she said softly. "I miss you and Max so much." Her thoughts turned to James. Never had she so longed for his embrace, his gentle voice of assurance. Her chest rose with each breath, the tears flowing more and more.

Then thoughts of Roman came. Was he really her brother? It was all too crazy, way too crazy. Where was he? Somehow she knew he hadn't left. How would she find him? Help him escape?

Despite her efforts, sniffles were unavoidable. She was on a bed with a sheet over her face, waiting for the men from disposal, whatever that was. *How morbid is that?* Her mother facing murder charges, her little brother with who knows who. And Ganny... *Oh, Ganny, why?*

She tried to lie still. Who would be watching a dead girl on a bed, lying in the dark? She longed to roll over, to actually sleep. The night in the dumpster, the fight in the jail, the bumps and bruises from the crash... She was sore everywhere and *so* tired.

The dials on the brain-melting machine would not stop bouncing, the humming always in her mind. The yellowed fingers of 'old Coppy' tapping his pen as she told him everything, now joined in with the droning hum. The voice of Larkin swirled by, her jubilant boasting of their evil scheme. Gunshots rang loud and clear, fragments of rock bursting beside Roman's head, blood pooling under the ATM man's leg.

Image after image, scene after scene, poured through her troubled mind. When a thundering train blared its whistle, its mass of iron bearing down, she jerked, arms and legs flying outward.

Breathing heavily, she tucked the sheet back around her body. She had slept. A fitful, troubled sleep, but somehow she had slept.

For a long time Misty lay there, the sheet of death over her face. Heavy doubts and fears pressed down. She had promised Ganny to try and stop this scheme, an evil scheme for which the woman had given her life.

"I can't, Ganny," she mouthed, her heart caving. "He's in on it. They'll…" She shuddered at the thought of dying here, inside this concrete den of secrets. "No one will ever know," she whispered, tears trickling. "They'll destroy all evidence. Oh, James, you'll never know."

Escape. She had to escape. But the thought of running without knowing Roman's fate, deeply troubled her. And what good would it do to save her own skin only to see the whole nation crumble?

No, she had to do something, to tell someone, someone powerful, someone like… *the president!*

A host of troubling fears raced through every nerve. She searched for a plan, her heart thumping crazy. "Must find a way to escape," she mouthed, "to contact the president."

So much fear came with these thoughts, it made her shiver, trembling as if deathly cold.

He's going to kill me, no matter what. And James. She whimpered. "And probably Roman too."

But then a sudden anger rose, a deep twisting hatred. She saw the little man, Vladimir, whipping Ganny. Then saw her father, raising his leather belt.

Trembling, she slipped out from beneath the sheet and crept to the door. Unbolting the lock, she peered down the empty hall. Then walking fast but casual, she went straight for the stairs. For Misty, recalling directions was as simple as playing a movie in reverse.

When she reached the level of Coppenheim's office, she stopped to survey the hall, peering through the door's narrow window. Two armed guards stood outside his door as if the director were expecting trouble. Misty pressed back against the cold concrete of the stairwell, hands quivering.

"Now what?" A harsh wave of woe crashed over, drowning any hope that had flickered within. *What am I doing? I can't do this. He's the director of the CIA!*

For some time, she stood pressed against the cold wall. Tears tried to come, but she clenched her teeth. Taking a deep breath, she peered back through the door's narrow window. *Oh, God, those are big guards. Focus! Think!*

She looked to the steps going down, leading to some possible escape. But like a movie screen, the battered face of Ganny peered up from the basement, her eyes pleading. 'Promise me you'll try.'

Heart thundering, Misty turned and reached for the door's cold lever. But in that instant, the thick metal door swung open, catching Misty's foot and knocking her to the floor.

"What the...?" A security guard with red hair stood over her. "Are you hurt? What are you doing here?"

Misty jumped to her feet, turning to escape. But the guard caught her arm. She spun and kicked, striking him soundly in the groin, something Ganny had taught her well. The poor man buckled, his eyes bulging. Though he still gripped her arm, she shoved him backward, pushing hard with both hands to break herself free.

A clang resounded, his head striking the fire extinguisher that hung beside the door. Groaning, he slid to the floor, head slumped to one side.

For a moment, Misty stood stunned. It had happened so fast. Through the glass, she saw Coppenheim's guards now coming her way, hands on their holsters. Misty turned to run, her lungs winded. The face of Ganny flashed once more. Then she saw her own hands strapped to a metal chair, more machines humming.

'Hold still!' came the grating voice of Dr. Weltz. Then the

angry voice of Parks. 'You've made a mess, ya little snake!'

They'll never let me leave!

She spun, glancing through the narrow window. The guards were drawing their weapons, a heartbeat away.

Kneeling beside the downed guard, she placed her foot against the door. Frantic, she fumbled with the holster. The door latch dropped. Steel pushed against her foot. She pulled on the gun. It didn't budge. The door pushed harder. She yanked the gun, finally jerking it free. A semi-automatic—she knew how these worked.

Pulling back the slide, she then flipped the safety off. Wincing, she jumped to crouch behind the door.

As the body of the downed man partially blocked the door, the two guards had to force it open. With weapons drawn, they glanced down at their fallen comrade, then scanned the stairwell.

"Don't move!" came a tense, teenage girl's voice. Misty stood behind them, arms extended, both hands gripping the gun. "I know how to shoot."

The men stood speechless. *Held at gunpoint by a girl?*

"Drop your guns, now!" Misty's hands were now steady, a fire igniting her veins.

Neither man moved, both weighing their chances, their guns at waist level. The one on her right, standing near the stairs that led down, tensed his gun arm.

Misty's face tightened.

Like bombs within a bell, the stairway rang with painful sounds. Concrete exploded just behind Misty's left leg as the man flew backward, tumbling down the stairs. His gun fired once more, blasting into the concrete overhead.

Misty swung her aim to the man standing over the red-haired guard. She knew they wore body armor, knew she had not killed the man and that he might soon be back. Lifting her aim to center on this man's forehead, she pressed her lips.

His eyes widened. Without a word, he dropped his gun onto the body at his feet.

"Turn around!" she barked. "Lay down!"

The man slowly turned, prostrating himself onto the stairs that led upward. She quickly grabbed the other gun, flinging it behind her. The man she'd shot lay silent, scrunched at the bottom of the stairs. Her stomach suddenly churned, a heave twisting her gut. His first bullet had passed her left leg so close, she'd felt it. The image of both Viktor and Score writhing in the dirt, their precious blood pooling beneath them, flashed in perfect detail.

"Go down and see if he's alright," she ordered.

The man looked at her with surprise, slowly rising up off the concrete steps. Holding his hands overhead, he walked down, checking his partner's pulse, the gun still within the fallen man's hand. Misty stood a few steps back, ushering firm warnings to not touch the gun.

"He's alive," the man finally said.

Giving more orders and stern threats, she soon had all three handcuffed to the metal railing. The redhead was conscious but groggy. The alert guard watched her with keen interest.

"Are you the girl?" he asked. "The one gone missing?"

She gave no reply.

The man she'd shot suddenly jerked awake. "What the...?" He looked about, huffing, mumbling, then cursing. Wincing as he struggled to breathe, he glared at Misty. "You shot me!" he growled with added expletives.

He tried to sit up. "Who are you?" he asked gruffly. "You some crazy freak that's—?"

"Shut up!" Misty leveled the gun at his chest, her aim steady. "Your director's dirty. Colluding with... with Russian hackers."

She yanked the door open and surveyed the empty hall. For several seconds she stood breathing hard, the door's simple threshold a point of no return. Glancing back at the guards sprawled on the steps, she shook her head. "No, I'm not a freak."

50 CONFRONTATION

She hobbled down the hall, both hands tight on the gun. A host of protesting voices shouted in her head. The red-haired guard had wrenched her left arm and she now hissed through her teeth, jaw set in a tight grimace.

Pausing at the director's outer office door, she glanced about. Everything hurt, every bit of her again trembling. She swiped a quick hand over each eye. Finding the frosted door unlocked, Misty nudged it open, peering warily inside.

Seeing no one, she swung the door wide, gun up and ready. The lights were down low, for the assistant had gone, her desk neat and clean. The ornate wooden door to the director's office hung open only a crack, a slender column of warm light glowing through. It fanned out over the floor like a welcome mat, fading as it reached Misty's feet.

Winded and quivering, she approached. Holding the gun in both hands, she slowly shouldered the door. It swung in total silence. Lit by only the desk lamp, the ornate decor seemed to now hide in the shadows, as if ashamed of its extravagance.

To the left of the large wooden desk stood Director Coppenheim, his back to Misty as he stood gazing out the large double-hung window. He seemed fixed on the plaza and walkways three stories below. The lower pane was open a foot or so, allowing a host of sounds to creep through. In his right hand, he held a small framed picture, which Misty recognized as one from his desk.

She stepped forward, the ornate rug beneath her masking all sound.

Suddenly, Coppenheim turned about. Seeing Misty, his face twisted. "You?" he said in complete surprise, his focus then going to the gun. "What are you doing here, and with that?" He looked toward the outer office door, alarm sweeping his face. "Where's security? What have you done?"

Misty shut the inner office door, left hand twisting the lock. Both hands back on the gun, she hobbled forward, her gaze intense. "What have *I* done?"

Coppenheim stepped back toward the window. "Is that loaded?" He glanced again toward the door. "My god, were those shots? Did you shoot them?"

At first, Misty didn't answer, her chest surging as if she'd just run a hard mile. "They're not dead," she finally said, now struggling to hold the gun fully extended.

The director glared, his face darkening as he sized up the frazzled girl. "That's a real gun. Don't point that at me."

Misty just stood breathing hard through flaring nostrils.

Coppenheim studied her a moment more, then glanced over his shoulder at the large double-hung draped with the fine embroidered curtains.

Through the window, Misty could see the plaza and gardens, the huge building across the way. In the distance, she noticed a crowd gathering at the main security gate.

Coppenheim straightened. "So, you going to shoot me or something?" he asked, staring at the gun. "For the crowd out there?" He nodded back toward the window. "Boost your views?"

Misty gave no reply, the gun heavier.

The man looked her up and down, a single vein pulsing in his forehead. "Who do you think you are?" he demanded. "What are you doing in my office? Answer me!"

Rage swelled inside Misty, a burning zeal of righteous anger. "You're working with those hackers," she said. "You're selling us out. Selling our… whole country." Her voice tightened as she spoke.

Coppenheim shook his head. "You know nothing!" he said with disgust. "Don't you realize who I am? Look at this!" He swept his arm across the room. "You don't get here by playing nice." He scowled, his gaze returning to the battered teen. "I have the only windows that open in the whole god..." He paused. "You know what that took? To just get windows that open?" His voice, neck, and jaw all tensed. "They're sound-proof, bullet-proof, heck, probably bomb-proof, but not if I open them!" He shook his head in disgust. "You got your windows, Director, but don't you dare open them."

Misty watched him, her face tensing as she struggled to follow.

His face darkened, his mouth moving as if chewing invisible gum. "I've given my all for this country. And you... you don't have a clue."

His scowl slackened, revealing a dismal face—worn and weary. He set the picture down on the wooden desk—a family portrait of an attractive woman with three teen girls and a young man like Roman. Misty stared, thinking of her mother and Max.

"No choice," Coppenheim continued, now speaking softly toward the picture. "If I don't play ball..." He glanced up. "What would you do, Miss Grey? Sacrifice them for Uncle Sam? Watch them be tortured? Burned alive? Huh?!"

Misty twitched, his voice having risen suddenly to a demanding shout. But she continued staring at the family picture, the gun now very heavy.

The director dropped hard into his seat behind the desk. The room felt dark. Misty tried to swallow, her mouth pasty dry.

"Put your hands... where I can see them!" she ordered, struggling to keep the gun up and aimed. "Now... call the president!"

The man's eyebrows lifted high, then he chuckled. "You're crazy, aren't you?" He once more looked her over. "No... you don't have a clue." He looked long into the girl's eyes, his mouth again chewing gum that wasn't there. "Miss Grey, it's rather simple. Put the gun down… or your boyfriend dies… painfully… very painfully."

For a second, Misty didn't budge. Then, like pulling the center pole from a circus tent, the girl's chest seemed to slowly implode, her arms lowering, her face sagging into an ashen stare.

"James?"

The director nodded, lifting a silver locket from off his desk. He held it by the fine chain, the well-worn metal softly glinting as it slowly twirled.

"We can't stop them, Miss Grey," he said coldly. "We can only do what we must… to protect our own."

Misty slowly shook her head. "James? No…" Her voice had become weak as she stared at the dangling locket, her thoughts far away.

The director sighed. "And your mother, your brother." He spoke sharply, cynically. "You didn't stop to think of them, did you? Galivanting about, meddling here and there, messing where you don't belong." He slowly shook his head. "Give me the gun." He set the locket down, extending his hand toward Misty.

She continued staring, her head slowly wagging. "No," she said weakly. "You have to stop them. Don't let them…" Her face had become ghostly pale, her legs shaky. She had to blink fast, her vision blurring. "Is he here? Is James here?"

Coppenheim nodded, still holding his hand out.

Misty kept shaking her head as twilight slowly spread over the plaza below.

"The world is cruel, young lady," Coppenheim said, his tone softening, like a father gently consoling a daughter. "Always has been. Always will be. We can't stop it. Can't fix it." He looked to the framed picture. "Can't fight it."

Red and blue light flickered through the windows, coming from the distant security gate. The faint squawk of a police siren startled them both. Then voices shouted through bullhorns. Gun still poised, Misty moved warily toward the window. For a moment, she stared in wonder.

"Should start anytime now," Coppenheim said. "Billions of dollars will disappear, snatched up in cyberspace." He seemed drugged, as if in a sullen stupor. "And that's just the teaser." He rose from his large, plush chair. "Give me the gun, Misty. You tried. *We* tried."

A massive crowd had forced its way through the security checkpoints, many of them now running into the plaza, some with posters and signs. Beyond the checkpoints, police cars blocked off the streets, their red and blue lights clashing with the gentle twilight. Officers and security guards fought to keep a line, as a mass of people, mixed with media crews, pushed and shoved, slowly working their way into the CIA compound.

What's going on? Misty wondered. *Someone's going to get killed.*

The director stepped across the room to the other window. Misty only glanced his way, her attention fixed on the crowd flowing into the plaza below.

He stood staring, equally stunned. "What are they doing?" he said angrily. "Where is security?" He cussed, no longer guarding his speech, sounding much like Mr. Grey.

Misty's gun had sunk to her side as she stared out the large window. A grown man with a cardboard sign caught her eye. For a second, she thought she'd misread the bright yellow letters.

'Free Misty Now!' Then she saw another. 'We want Misty!'

"What's going on?" she asked, her voice weak.

Again, a siren squawked. A security guard with a bullhorn ordered the crowd to disperse, while a second ordered them to all lay face down. Through the open window, the two could hear the angry commands. But the people kept pouring into the plaza, running through the gardens, pushing for the front entrance, which now had a line of security with automatic weapons aimed.

The director undid the latches and opened his window up a good foot or more. "Finally," he muttered, his foul language increasing.

"Who are they?" Misty asked. "How do they know…?"

The director lifted the window higher, pulling it up enough

to lean out.

"What the devil is going on?" he exclaimed. "How has this happened?"

Suddenly a host of arms began pointing their way, a rush of shouts surging through the crowd. Several beams from powerful flashlights passed over their faces, forcing them to turn aside. Like a wave, the crowd pressed toward the glass entrance doors, some people nearing the very steps on which Misty had almost died.

"How do they know I'm here?" Misty muttered, stepping away from the window, her face drawn. She tried to keep the gun aimed at Coppenheim, but her thoughts swirled.

The director continued cursing, his hands going to his sides as he stepped to his desk. Behind his back, he slowly slid open his top drawer. While Misty watched the billowing commotion below, old Coppy withdrew a small pistol.

For a moment, Misty stood peering out at the chaos, a numbness tingling her cheeks. She hadn't noticed Coppenheim withdraw his gun. When she turned back to face him, she stared into its short black barrel.

"Drop it," he said sternly, "or I will shoot you!"

Mr. and Mrs. Longmire watched the special report with gapping faces frozen by a cloud of shock. Broadcasting live from Langley, Virginia, the female news reporter spoke with an urgent excitement, her arm continually gesturing toward the crowd and all its signs. Flashing lights spattered the scene as a horde of people surged toward the security gates of the George Bush Center for Intelligence compound.

"What started as rumor has now exploded into full-scale pandemonium," she said, her face glowing with excitement. "Marie Elsa Grey, popularly known as Misty, the girl we've all been searching for, the girl who's been missing since her father's fatal shooting, the girl who, as of this morning's recent findings, is indeed, or rather highly suspected of being, ah, is the daughter of Sterling Whitehall, of Whitehall, Kohen, and Luwik law firm." She paused to catch her breath. "And many on the coast know this name, for Mr. Whitehall is a well-known philanthropist giving generously to many charities."

She glanced about, again gesturing toward the growing crowd, her manner almost giddy.

"So, as you can see, Cal, there are hundreds, no, thousands coming from all directions, as, according to reliable sources, it's been reported that Whitehall's daughter, or rather alleged daughter, ohhh…"

A group bumped her aside as they pushed past. "Ah… so… it's been reported that Marie Grey, the missing girl, is being held hostage… or held here… against her will, within the CIA headquarters."

She then wagged her head, licking her lips with a childish delight. "And that's not all, Cal. She's here because, our sources tell us, she knows something… ah, something about a plot to bring down the global economy. It's… it's Russians planning to destroy the internet, and…" She got bumped again, this time by a young couple shouting to the camera, calling for them to, 'Free Misty now!'

After several deep breaths, she continued. "Spotted this morning at Pappy's Café, Marie, or rather Misty and her traveling companion, who authorities speculate as Roman Whitehall, son of Sterling Whitehall, apparently diverted arrest by speeding off in a stolen police cruiser. It was that trail of wreckage we saw earlier, Cal, created by them, using the stolen vehicle to plow their way into the George Bush Center for Intelligence compound.

The woman shook her head with a beaming smile. "As if that isn't newsworthy enough, a source within CIA, who wished to remain anonymous," the woman continued with even more elation, if that were possible, "reported that our missing girl, Marie or Misty, indeed has inside information regarding this plot, this plot to overthrow the U.S. economy."

She then leaned in close as if telling her camera audience a special secret. "And she claims Director Cole Coppenheim is in on things, working with a Russian syndicate or Mafia, or government, it's not quite clear." She paused to shake her head, taking another deep breath.

Watching from their home, Mr. and Mrs. Longmire did the same. They stared with jaws hanging as the woman continued.

"A digital bomb, our sources say. Cyber terrorism set to strike the World Wide Web this very evening." She again shook her head. "Just moments ago, witnesses said they spotted Misty in a third or fourth-floor window." The camera cut to zoom way in, trying to find the partially opened window of Coppenheim's office. Two blurred silhouettes could be seen through a large double-hung window.

The news reporter went on to say how unprecedented the whole matter had become. "Something like this can only happen on Halloween," she said. "The crowds have... seemed to come from everywhere," she added with bewilderment, "as if they've been called or signaled through some hidden network. I mean, look at their signs." She again flung her arm out over the crowd. "What will come of this? Who can say? We'll keep you up on all the action, Cal. It's indeed exciting." She exhaled, flashing her giddy smile. "For WLJP news, I'm Holli Ferns, reporting live from Langley, Virginia."

Mrs. Longmire sank back into the sofa, completely bewildered, her drawn face pale. "Misty... a wealthy man's daughter?"

Mr. Longmire said nothing, his jaw just hanging.

James had also disappeared, causing great alarm to all who knew him, except the nerds and Bucky.

Mr. Longmire finally moved, leaning forward as the camera zoomed in on the shadows within Coppenheim's window. "Misty?" he asked himself. "What on earth are you doing?"

Mrs. Longmire sighed, her head slowly wagging. "And what have you done with my James?"

As the director held his gun at Misty's chest, he shook his head in disgust. "Drop it! Empty your pockets!" He added a few words of vulgarity, his yellowed teeth snarling. Misty squatted to set the gun on the wooden floor, but her hip cried in protest. She dropped it, the dull thump echoing with finality.

"Now empty them!"

"My pockets?" she asked, her own voice sounding distant.

Coppenheim nodded, glancing down at the locket. "They want that card."

"What card?"

"Just give it to me!" His tone had become fierce.

Misty turned the pockets of agent Larkin's jeans inside out. She offered up the only thing that they contained—the small red capsule and some lint.

"What's this?" Coppenheim asked, snatching the pill from her hand.

"A pain—" Misty was about to say 'a painless killer.' She swallowed hard. "A pain-killer... prescription."

"Where's that SD card?" He set the pill next to the locket.

Misty shrugged. "I don't know anything about that."

Coppenheim muttered some more curses, his face reddening. "They're holding my wife," he said, glancing at the framed picture. "I have a good family... not like your mess," he said with disdain. "When they threatened to kill my wife, I didn't budge. Know why?"

He actually waited for Misty to reply, so she did.

"You... chose to do the right thing?" she said, her voice dry and weak. Coppenheim laughed, wagging his head.

"No. They can have her." He pushed a button under his desk. Misty knew it signaled security. "'Just be the gatekeeper,' they said. 'Stop whatever gets through.'" He glared at the frightened girl. "Like you and Tallon." He straightened, tilting his head in a most haughty manner. "I ordered your silence. Blundering idiots. Why won't you just die?"

Misty struggled to stay upright, the weakness overtaking her. "Why?" she asked. "Why are you helping them?"

He rubbed his thumb and forefinger, a haughty air lighting his face. "Their pension plan is in gold, lots of gold."

Misty shook her head. "They'll just kill you."

Coppenheim smiled. "Yup. To the world, I'll be dead." He glanced at the framed picture. "My dearest will have a breakdown. Conveniently end her life... pills they said... painless." A sigh held him for a moment. Misty glanced at the pill on his desk.

"The world is indeed cruel, Miss Grey," he continued. "But six million in gold..." His thoughts drifted off. Then his eyes narrowed. "But you... you almost ruined everything." His face twisted, his cheeks reddening. "Idiot Parks. Can't believe he didn't just do his job."

Misty glanced toward the open window, the chants rising from three stories below. She inched closer, seeing a host of news media and cell phones aimed her way. The director shook his head, pointing his pistol at her chest, sighting in on her heart.

"No, Miss Grey, your little episode is over."

Suddenly the cell phone on his desk buzzed. He glanced to read the caller. For a moment, he watched it buzzing, drawn lips uttering profanities. Issuing a stern warning to Misty, he answered.

"Hello, Mr. President. What can I—?"

"What the hades you got going on over there?" Misty could hear the president's voice, for he was clearly angry.

"I'm not sure, I think—"

"You're not sure? You're the director of Central Intelligence, confound it! How do you not know what's going on in your own front yard?"

"It's just come to my attention, sir. I—"

"And what's this stuff about that Grey girl, Whitehall's girl? You holding her?"

The director looked down the barrel of his gun. "I think there's some mistake, sir. I don't know anything about—"

"She's been in the news all week, Cole. How can you not know anything? What's going on over there?"

Misty glanced out the window, her nerves tingling. She watched the crowd below, wondering how and why they had assembled. Coppenheim shook his gun with fury, motioning for her to step away.

Misty strained to see through the lights, ignoring his threats. For a brief second, she thought she'd seen a familiar face in the crowd, but that couldn't be, and it was getting dark, and so many people.

She stepped toward the window, shielding her eyes from a host of lights. She scanned the crowd, searching. The mass surged toward the line of security, some yelling and pushing, many with arms pointing toward her.

Who did I see?

Coppenheim stepped her way but then stopped, moving back into the shadows. Face livid, he motioned with his head, telling her to step away. Misty watched him, her thoughts torn. Trembling, she slowly complied.

Staring straight at the girl, Coppenheim spoke to the president. "I promise you, Mr. President, this Grey girl is not on CIA property. It's a media ploy, some Halloween prank."

"Well, what's this talk of a major cyber-attack? Why am I the last to know?"

As Coppenheim stammered, telling him it was all a media ploy, Misty whispered under her breath. "Oh, God, help me. Oh, James… please forgive me."

"What am I watching, Cole? All be hung, is that your office?"

Coppenheim scowled, his eyes burning. He backed away, now beneath the huge painting. He shook the gun furiously.

He's watching the news! Misty realized. Heart in full gallop, she suddenly stepped toward the window and shouted, "I'm here, Mr. President! You have to—"

Boom! The flash from Coppenheim's gun blinded Misty's eyes. Stumbling, she fell backward, her left arm catching the drapes, her right chest on fire.

With the burst of light and resounding gunfire, the crowd below gasped as one, a sudden hush of silence then settling over them.

As in a fog, the president's irate voice faded, his demanding questions drifting into a muffled drone. Misty lay stunned, mouth open, but empty... empty of breath. She stared at Coppenheim, his lips moving without sound.

Gasping loudly, Misty bolted upright, her bleeding lung burning and gurgling.

"We're taking fire, sir," the director shouted into his phone. "I'll try to stop them. Tell my family..." He then held the phone up, and with more deafening booms, fired two rounds into the back of his leather chair. Slamming the phone onto his desk, he then smashed it with the gun, shards peppering the large desk.

Misty jerked with each shot as she lay struggling beneath the window, left arm still clutching the fine drapes. She tried to rise, but her whole body went into spasms.

"Stay down!" Coppenheim shouted, his voice sounding like Mr. Grey. "Don't make me shoot you again!"

But in the chaos, a voice kept coming, Ganny's plea from beneath the farmhouse. 'You must do this. Promise me you'll try.'

They'll kill James, she told the voice. *I tried. What more can I do? He shot me!*

'The world needs your gift.' Never had a voice spoken so loud within her. *But I'm a freak. And the whole world's out there.*

'The world… needs… your gift.'

Gasping, Misty glanced at the pointed gun, its owner still hiding in the shadows. Biting down hard, she pulled on the drapes, dragging herself up to the window's sill.

"Get down!" Coppenheim shouted, shaking his gun in rage.

Kneeling, Misty looked out over the turbulent plaza, her blood-soaked shirt and sweater smearing the clean white sill. A massive crowd had somehow filled the entire central plaza. Signs and banners, flashlights and cameras, all waved about, all aimed in her direction.

"He's watching," she muttered. *They're watching. The world… is watching.* Every breath came at a price, pain screaming, lungs gurgling. More blood soaked her shirt and sweater, *her* blood, warm and sticky. A spotlight from a news chopper shone straight into her eyes, flooding the window and office behind her. As one, the crowd gasped, then burst into outrage.

Coppenheim cursed, commanding her to get back. Growling, he aimed at her head. But the collection of lights now flooded the room.

Panting like a dying animal, Misty pulled on the drape, her numb legs trembling.

"Get down!" Coppenheim shouted, "or I'll shoot!"

"James," she whimpered, "I'm so sorry… but I must… tell them."

Glancing at the gun aimed at her face, she clenched her teeth, her eyes hardening. In a cry of pain, she pulled herself up, squeezing her head and torso out the open window. Coppenheim ranted, as another spotlight joined to highlight the bleeding girl, their white light flooding his office. He kept looking toward the door, his face twisted with frustrated rage.

Sirens, bullhorns, and angry shouts rose from far below. News cameras panned and zoomed as a thousand cell phones recorded every second. Streaming, tweeting, and broadcasting, it all went out live from the CIA compound, an evening of Halloween chaos racing to the towers, fanning out into endless hashtags, channels, and media stations, flowing into homes, pinging computers, bouncing from newsfeed to newsfeed, all as Misty's warm blood reddened the sill, her breath clogging more and more with every painful, desperate gasp.

"They're watching," she mumbled. "I'm not… a freak."

For a moment, Misty just lay folded over the sill, her lungs fighting for every breath. Each heartbeat expected another bullet to tear through her battered flesh, to rip another painful, burning hole.

"Get back here!" Coppenheim shouted, cursing her with absolute rage. He would reach for her, but draw back as soon as any light touched his face.

The crowd surged toward the line of security, the guards still standing with weapons ready. Misty lifted her head, weary eyes blinded by the lights sweeping the building. She worked hard to form the words.

"It's… starting… tonight," she tried to shout, but her gargled voice found only empty space. "Malware… Whisper…"

"Quiet!" a male voice shouted from below. "She's saying something! Everyone, quiet!"

"Malware…" Misty tried again, pushing herself up, putting her face into the full light. "The Whisper… software… has Russian… malware."

But even with a hushed crowd, her cry went out unheard.

A loud bang shook the office door. "Director, are you in there?" Without awaiting his reply, the door burst open, shards from the jamb scattering to Misty's trembling feet. Five armed guards rushed into the room.

Without glancing back, Misty swung her right leg over the sill, eyes blurring.

For a brief second, Coppenheim watched in amazement. The stupid girl was going to jump, or rather, fall to her death.

"Seize her!" Coppenheim shouted. "The crazy nut tried to kill me!"

Misty craned to look back, her bruised body straddling the sill.

"Freeze!" The lead guard aimed his pistol at the bleeding girl.

She inched out further, her left hand smearing the glass of the raised sash with blood.

"I said, freeze!" Reluctant to shoot a young girl, the guard glanced at the director.

"Grab her! Shoot her!" He swore at the guards. "Just shoot her!"

Misty slid her hips and torso all the way through. With a bloodied left hand clutching the window, she looked down with alarm.

"Oh, God…"

Misty drew up her left leg, her weight now teetering over the sill. Three stories up suddenly seemed very high.

An arm grabbed her left wrist. Another caught her about the waist. Two guards pulled at her as the director screamed, commanding them to 'just shoot the stupid girl.'

The crowd below surged toward the building, skirting security to stand directly beneath. Some shouted for her to jump, that they would catch her. Others, to climb back inside.

Misty fought the guard's pull. To go back inside meant death. To stay out here…

She pulled hard on the sash, bringing it down behind her shoulder as her weight fell through. The men tugged on her left leg and arm. She wriggled and writhed, lungs filling with blood. Twisting in desperation, she broke free to flop out over the sill. Hanging upside-down, she dangled by her left leg. Screaming as she swung, her body smeared the wall with a swath of fresh blood.

A newsman far below raised a microphone on a long pole. The men inside struggled to get a grip, yanking her leg. Blood filled her mouth, dripping down her face, trickling into her eyes.

She tried to see the crowd, all so strange, so upside-down. She drew a gargled breath and spit blood. Her lungs filled with air. She drew another, a good breath, her lungs clearing just enough. She glanced at the man with the long boom mic, headphones covering his ears.

"Norad!" she shouted, finding her voice. After taking several coughing breaths, she found she could mostly breathe. "Tonight. Cyber-attack. Using..." She coughed up blood and tried to spit, but it fell into her hair. The men above jerked her leg, pulling her up. "Whisper program," she cried out. "Norad launch code 742-C."

As she slid back up the wall, she rattled off a string of letters, numbers, and symbols. The crowd had gone deathly still.

From inside the director's office came a host of shouts, new voices joining the chaos. Hands grappled for her leg and waist, men struggling with men. A sudden drop. She screamed. A strong hand clutched her ankle.

"Homeland... security code... F21-2G." Her gargled voice felt so weak as she hung upside-down. Knowing at any second she'd either fall or get yanked up, she forced her mind to focus. "Mountain Lake project... A...990... G3B." Like at the pi contest, her lips kept spewing out whatever she had seen in Larkin's little notebook and the data from the papers on the floor.

Shouts filled the room above as several hands pulled her quickly up the smooth cold wall. The sash slid up, and Misty's hips painfully scraped back over the sill. A set of strong hands gripped her right thigh, the pain intense.

Almost inside, she kept spewing out codes and call signals. "They have... your numbers," she tried shouting, hacking out the words, spitting bright red blood. "Everyone's!"

The hands inside jerked. Misty screamed with pain. "Tonight!" she shouted, coughing up more blood. "Mr. President... stop them!" She tried to blink away the blood blurring her eyes, squinting at the lights swirling about her face.

"I'm not… a freak," she cried out in one last desperate plea. "I'm not a—"

One bright flash lit the office as a loud cracking boom rattled the window. Misty cried out, burning metal tearing through her right thigh. The hands gripping her leg went suddenly loose.

Another rattling boom shook the window. The man holding Misty's arm groaned as if punched hard, his hands suddenly gone.

Someone pushed her. A brief, gargled scream echoed out over the crowd as Misty's body fell. Like some discarded doll tossed carelessly aside, she plummeted headlong, arms and legs flailing, her blood-smeared body racing to the cold, hard ground.

Blinking eyes full of wonder and disbelief, Misty stared into the face of James. *So this is death… and we're together?* "I'm so sorry, James." Her lips barely moved. "I made them kill you."

"Shhh, don't speak." Together with the other men who helped catch Misty, James carried her through the bustling mob, which fought to keep anyone in uniform from coming near. As the crowd parted for the wounded girl, she reached her bloodstained arm out for James.

"Don't leave me," she tried to say, her voice fading.

"I'm right here." He took her hand as some paramedics came with a stretcher. Wheeling her through the crowd, she heard some stern commands, someone ordering security to 'stand down.'

A fog drifted over Misty, her lungs panting shallow breaths. Dried blood clogged her lashes, clouding her eyes. Hoisted up into an ambulance, she reached for James, calling his name, her voice a desperate whisper.

He jumped in beside her, taking her hand, squeezing it tight. As the ambulance doors swung shut, her crusted eyes caught a glimpse of an elderly face.

"Ganny?"

She tried to sit up, coughing and grimacing, pain rushing through her chest and thigh. Misty looked up. "James… are we *all* dead?"

"You're not going to die, Misty." He looked up at the two paramedics working fast to stop the bleeding. Neither gave any response.

The gunshot wound in her leg had soaked her jeans, which the medic had already cut open, telling James to apply pressure. The wound in her upper chest bled but not nearly as bad as her leg.

"What's her blood type?" the medic asked.

James shrugged, looking to Misty.

"O positive," she whispered. "You're A positive. Max is…"

"Shhh, lie still."

"Any allergies, medical conditions?"

James shook his head.

"Her full name?"

"Marie Elsa Grey."

Misty suddenly tried to sit up, her head weakly shaking. "No… I am… Misty…"

She lay back, letting her eyes close, a pleasant smile gracing her stained lips. "Misty May…" A long sigh gurgled out as both arms went limp. A brief silence followed, then a bustle of urgent activity. Calm yet quick, the medics worked over Misty's lifeless body.

James stepped back, face ashen, lips uttering desperate prayers. Overhead the sirens blared and squawked, the ambulance making its way through the mass.

"No, Misty… NO!" he shouted, his flesh turning clammy cold. "You can't, Misty! You can't!"

November 1

Two men in dark suits stood over a naked body covered by a single sheet, their faces grim. The taller of the two was a handsome, secret agent-looking guy. They stood in silence as the ashen corpse slid back into its holding chamber. A latch clicked, echoing in the sterile room.

"Why does it always feel cold down here?" the shorter man asked.

"It's the silence," replied the taller.

"Need to see any more?" a middle-aged woman in a lab coat asked. They both shook their heads.

"Life's a riddle," the shorter one said.

"With an odd sense of justice," said the other.

They both left the city morgue, heads slowly wagging. The woman in the lab coat took up a clipboard and ran her pen down the list of names. In the column marked, 'Identity Confirmed' she scribbled her initials. She then glanced at the brief description pertaining to the cause of death. 'Poisoning. Ingested. Potassium Cyanide.'

"Why Cole?" she muttered. "What were you thinking?"

"You need some sleep," Roman said, helping James to his feet. "You can't sit here forever."

James rose from beside the bed, eyes dark. He sighed, reluctant to withdraw his hand. Face distraught, he stared down at the body of Misty, his heart in shreds.

Roman put his hand on the teen's shoulder. He too watched with troubling angst. "She'll pull through," he said quietly, hoping to believe his own words. "She's tough."

James sighed once more, yearning to find hope in Roman's words. "I need to be here when she wakes," he said, his voice dry.

"I'll call you if anything changes. Now go get some rest."

It was late afternoon, November first. All through the night and now the day, it had been touch-and-go with Misty. The bullet fired by Coppenheim into the guard's hand and so into Misty's leg had nicked an artery, causing extensive blood loss, which, coupled with her chest wound, kept the girl hovering for several long and desperate hours. Never had the gate of heaven gotten such urgent pleas, as James cried out with anguish, begging for Misty's life.

Praying and pleading, he had stayed at Misty's side, her hand always held between his. Only now with Roman's insistence, did the haggard boy relinquish his post.

Roman sat beside Misty's bed, his mind whirling with all the recent events. He had been contained at CIA, knowing nothing of Misty's whereabouts. Only afterward did he realize how close he had come to death, for he was the boyfriend referred to by

Coppenheim. Regardless of how that night transpired, he'd been marked for deletion. Sighing, he watched the sleeping girl, her hands and legs occasionally twitching.

Misty pulled her mother's arm, but the woman didn't budge, her eyes staring blankly into the morning sky. A policeman came and helped, his breath smelling of liquor. "Mommy fell," Misty told him. "I think she hit her head." The man nodded, helping the attractive woman to her feet. Placing an arm around her waist, he led her and Misty to his police car.

"What's your name, little girl?"

"I'm Misty. I'm four. Is Mommy hurt?"

"I'll take care of her, little Misty. Don't you worry. Everything's going to be just fine… just fine."

"She… fell…" Misty softly muttered, her lips and mouth tacky dry.

"Misty?" Roman jolted upright, his heart surging, but the girl drifted back into restless sleep.

For another hour he sat watching the news with the volume off, reading the subtitles that continually rehashed the story of the heroic teen girl and the mysterious syndicate behind it all. The details of the 'digital bomb' had gone viral, thanks to Bucky and the nerds, sparking discussion groups like: 'Cybersecurity Jokes,' 'The passing of the password,' and 'Top Secret Cyberterror.'

The soaring price of gold had also become a major focal point, predicting it to double by the end of the day. 'Gold—the age-old standard for a secure future,' proclaimed the gold merchants, as many now felt that digital commerce was too vulnerable. 'Return to hard currency,' some said. Others talked of new measures of security—ID implants, retinal scanners, fingerprint readers, even DNA microdots. Some Christian groups said it would all end in a one-world government, requiring everyone to receive a mark or implant to buy and sell.

Roman watched, occasionally glancing at Misty who would twitch and moan in her sleep. In less than twenty-four hours, her name had become known throughout the world. He winced at the idea.

Gold, he thought, recalling Misty's account of holding the U.S. for ransom, demanding its gold supply. *Crash the U.S. to get its gold reserve, then watch the price soar through the roof?*

"It almost worked," he whispered, a sudden shiver coming over him.

Misty moaned, muttering something. Then her eyes opened wide, her face tense with alarm. "She… lost her memory," Misty croaked, her voice dry.

"Misty?"

Puffy eyes squinting, head groggy and sore, she turned toward the voice. "James?"

The handsome young man took her hand, his face still anxious but smiling. "It's Roman, your brother. James just left." His eyes welled, his face beaming. "I knew you'd pull through," he said, tears now trailing.

"I… saw Mom," Misty said weakly, trying to tell him the memory long forgotten. "She'd fallen… hit her head. That's when… everything changed." Her eyes moistened at the realization. All the evil her mother had endured began that fateful day. "I finally remembered."

Roman gently squeezed her hand. "I know," he said. "Everybody knows." He then smiled wide. "I've talked to her… your mom… my mom… *our* mom." He squeezed her hand again, shaking his head, overwhelmed at all that transpired. "I'm so glad—" He suddenly stopped. "James! I have to tell James." He pulled out his phone.

"He's not dead?" Misty asked.

Roman chuckled. "No, he's been at your side since you came out of surgery." He then told how James had stayed all through the night and into the day, leaving only recently. "He wouldn't leave you. Had to drag him away." Roman smiled, blinking back tears. "He really, well, I think you know."

Misty just stared at him, then slowly looked around at the IV tubes and monitor wires, her body drugged and weak. "You talked to my mom?"

Roman nodded. "She's coming here tomorrow, with Max and Dad." Roman smiled even more. "He's our little brother, Misty." He told her briefly about the final testimony at the trial, confirming her memories before waking.

Police officer Clayton Grey had been on duty that Sunday morning, his alcohol levels higher than usual. When he found Misty and her mother that cool morning, it didn't take him long to capitalize on such a golden opportunity. When he realized the woman had lost all memory and then recognized her as the kidnapped Mrs. Whitehall, a scheme of pure evil entered his heart.

Only two nights previous, his own wife had angered him for the last time, to which he made sure would indeed be the last. He had just disposed of the body when he stumbled upon this new woman, same size and height, same hair color, even eyes of similar kind and shape. Luck was clearly on his side. Nurturing bitter spite for the greedy upper class, he would make Mrs. Whitehall his replacement wife.

Misty listened, following the gentle eyes of Roman, her head and heart a jumbled mess.

He sent a text to James, then continued. "No one knew but his partner. The guy kept apologizing, damning himself to hell, wishing he hadn't been such a coward. Grey had put the fear of death into the man, keeping him silent all these years." He took her hand. "Enough of that. How are you feeling?"

"Terrible… wonderful. Are you really my brother… my big brother?"

"I don't know, let me see your hip."

Her chuckle brought a sharp wince as Misty sucked air

through her teeth. "Don't do that. Ohhh, that hurts."

"Sorry," Roman said, still chuckling. "Yes, I am your brother." He gently squeezed her hand. "I've really missed you… like really, really missed you."

She smiled, warm tears trailing. For a while, they sat in silence, faces glowing as the monitor beeped a steady pulse.

When the door opened, they looked, expecting to see James. But, without a word, there came an elderly man, his small frame hunched and moving rather slowly. Shuffling over the polished tile, he made his way toward Misty's bed. A cane in one hand and a package in the other, the old man wobbled up beside Roman.

"Package for Misty Whitehall," his creaky voice said. Small dark glasses covered his eyes, while a white fuzzy beard covered his face.

Misty and Roman watched with rising alarm. "Who are you?" Roman asked, placing himself between Misty and the old man.

The old man chuckled in short bursts, like a toy running low on batteries. He reached up and took off his glasses, looking straight into Misty's eyes. For a moment, the girl just stared, her expression growing more and more bewildered, the heart monitor signaling a rapidly rising pulse.

"But…" Misty shook her head.

The sporadic chuckle came once again. Then a finger to the wrinkled lips. "Shhh."

Misty squinted, trying to understand the figure standing near her bed. "No…" she said, her voice a breathy whisper, "the whole house…"

Roman glanced at the monitor, the beats still climbing. Fear tore through his chest. He reached to grab the old man, but a firm hand caught his.

"Takes more than a house on fire to kill this old root," the old man said, his voice now sounding like an elderly woman. Removing the hat, the hunched figure leaned over and kissed Misty on the forehead. "You did well, my dear. You did… very well."

The old man chuckled, glancing at Roman with a nod. "An older brother, a fine-looking older brother. Now that doesn't come by every Tuesday, does it?"

"But… but how?" Misty said, her heart rate galloping. "The whole house exploded. I saw it."

The old man nodded, telling Roman all was well, that he was not a he, but rather an old friend called Ganny, the one responsible for getting Misty into this whole mess.

"I am so sorry, Misty. So very sorry."

After numerous tears and questions, Misty lay back to let Ganny tell of her ordeal. Left for dead, the tenacious woman climbed into the moldy freezer, but only after breaking the gas valve on the furnace, thereby flooding the basement with enough propane to launch a rocket. Cracking open the freezer lid, she flicked the lighter taken from her inept guard, who, totally underestimated what an old lady can conspire while faking a heart attack. And so the house erupted into the fragments witnessed by Misty and Roman.

Escaping the inferno was no easy task, which the bandages beneath her disguise could testify. But eventually, she had made her way home, and, having followed James to the home of Stanton T., took the flight secured by Bucky. She and James had arrived in Langley just before noon on Halloween.

"It was James and his friends who brought the crowd," she said. "I went to find Bellows. A chance encounter with nurse Lanna saved my life, and yours as well." She nodded to both Roman and Misty. "James explained everything to the boys back home… that young man, Bucky…" She shook her head in amazement. "He infiltrated every platform, calling people to rally at the compound, to rescue the missing girl, Misty Grey. Called it the *Misty Conspiracy*. Warned everyone of the 'digital bomb,' telling them how to protect themselves. Remarkable! Truly remarkable!" She chuckled. "Where is James?"

"Still sleeping," Roman said. "He's been up all night and all day, waiting for Misty to pull through."

Ganny nodded. "That's our James."

"Did we stop them?" Misty asked.

Ganny nodded. "Yes, you did." She then told how the president went ballistic watching Misty broadcast to the world the security codes to missile programs.

"I didn't give the whole code," Misty said in her defense.

"He had things shut down so fast the world was left in a Halloween fog. All commerce ceased by his direct order, declaring martial law. Most understood and were grateful. Grumblers and ingrates are still complaining."

"Why the disguise?" Misty asked, looking Ganny over.

"They want me to keep on the trail. More than just high-level hackers are behind this. My funeral's tomorrow. Wish you could be there."

Misty stopped the rise of laughter, wincing hard with a painful groan. She then asked about the locket.

"I was afraid they would just burn my house and kill me," Ganny said. "I needed to hide a copy elsewhere. I am very sorry, Misty. I didn't think they would target you."

They sat together in silence for some time, Misty softly smiling at the two of them. When the teen girl became groggy, Ganny rose and shuffled toward the door.

"I'll keep in touch. But remember, you didn't see me today."

Misty smiled. "I'll remember. That's what I do."

November 3

"There's someone to see you," a young nurse announced.

Two men in dark suits stepped into the room, their eyes quickly scanning. "All clear," one said, speaking into his lapel.

A moment later, the tall figure of agent Bellows stood over the bed of Misty May Whitehall. He held a large bouquet in both hands. Beside him stood another man, equally as tall with dark features, slightly gray. This man smiled down, his eyes kind yet commanding. For a moment, he followed the numerous IV lines and leads that ran to hanging bags and blinking monitors.

"You saved a nation, young lady," he said, his voice deep and resonating. "I wish to personally thank you."

Misty smiled, trying to sit up, but winced with a groan. "Good morning, Mr. President. What a… oooh… surprise." Misty paused for a moment, waiting for the pain to subside. "Sad to hear about Mr. Coppenheim. I didn't think he'd take the—"

"No, no." The president waved his hand. "No apologies from you. We're looking into that. Not sure what happened there." He stepped close and took her hand in his. "That was mighty brave," he said solemnly. "Taking on a malicious syndicate *and* the CIA. Not something I'd recommend."

Misty smiled, glancing up at agent Bellows, soon to be the new director of CIA. "Congratulations," she said.

"How are you feeling?" Bellows asked.

Misty bobbed her head. Although sore and still on lots of pain meds, a warm excitement stirred within. The day before had been monumental. She had seen her real father—a wonderful man, whom she immediately recognized, calling him 'Daddy,' which brought back a flood of memories and joyful tears to match. When her mother and Max appeared a few hours later, she thought she would die from sheer joy. Had the nurse not cut the weeping reunion short, Misty very well might have.

To now have the president standing over her bed, she wondered if the happy reunions were just some beautiful drug-induced dreams.

"I see it worked," she said to Bellows and the president. They both nodded. Misty had been watching the news, learning all that had taken place. It was strange how some called her the heroine of the decade, while others twisted the whole affair into something other than what it was, even vilifying Misty as a glory-hound.

After some brief discussion and more words of appreciation, the president invited her to his office. "Whenever you're feeling up to it," he said, shaking her hand gingerly. "I'll make time for you." He studied her face for a moment. "You know, Bellows told me everything." He stood to leave. "I've got a proposal I'd like you to consider, when you're feeling better, of course."

Misty nodded. "Of course, Mr. President. Thank you for coming to see me."

He smiled, shaking his head. "Young lady, you are indeed one of a kind." He paused to give an affirming nod. "We could really use a girl like you. Except, you're the only girl… like you. Look forward to seeing you soon." He smiled, then turned to follow his two dark suits out the door.

Bellows set the flowers beside her bed. "Thank you," he whispered. "You saved my life, you know."

"I saw Ganny," Misty whispered. "She told me everything."

Bellows put a finger to his lips. "We'll sure miss her. One fine agent." He gave a sly smile. "Went out in a blaze of glory."

When Bellows left the room, James and Roman entered.

James handed Misty her locket. "Found this under my bed," he said, gently holding her hand. Misty smiled, knowing he had just gotten it from Bellows.

"Thanks for doing what you did, James."

"Thank the nerds and Bucky."

"I will, but they aren't getting, you know, all they asked." She wagged her head with a smirk. "But I will gladly do the dinner thing, with all of us."

As James took a seat, he noticed an empty pudding cup on Misty's lunch tray, an empty *chocolate* pudding cup. He glanced curiously at Misty but said nothing.

They talked some more, careful not to make Misty laugh. But then Roman switched on the TV just as the face of Nikki Laurens appeared on the screen.

"Do I know Misty? Heck, yeah." Nikki flipped her bangs. "We go way back. Besties for sure. Done lots together."

Misty fought back the painful laughter as James just shook his head. He had told her how the whole town was being interviewed, how Bucky had been approached by NSA, CIA, *and* FBI, how his mother was going nuts with all the reporters and photographers, some sneaking into their house—at night!

"You got first prize," he said, "for the pi contest." He muttered another grieving apology for how that all turned out.

"Have them give it to the runner-up," she said, urging James to let it go.

As they shared stories of their adventures, Misty became very solemn. She described with vivid detail how Parks had planned to wipe her memory clean.

"For as long as I remember being able to remember, I have longed to just forget." Misty looked off into the distance. "When Parks said he could wipe it clean, I felt a strange relief. He could erase it all."

She paused to look at James, then Roman. "Then I thought of you... both of you. There will always be good and bad things.

That's what life is. So there's going to always be good and bad memories. But there's also a future. 'Does not the road ahead reign over that which is behind?'" She smiled. "From an author I like."

Both boys just listened, each following her every move.

"We all do dumb stuff," she continued, "and bad things happen. But there are good things too. Sweet things." She smiled at James, then at her brother.

"It's a package deal, the good and the bad. It's so naïve to think that the world's perfect, that you're perfect, and you'll never do something dumb." She paused. "We should be kind when others make mistakes… even those that hurt us, 'cause we all do it. More than we like to remember."

She sighed, glancing at the empty chocolate pudding cup. "I accept it all, the bad with the good. I'm done grieving the past. There is a future of memories to be made." She smiled at both boys. "'Though the past haunt as a spirit, I do not ask to forget.'" She gave a silly grin. "Felicia Hemans, a poet."

She smiled with a long satisfied sigh. "Unique… but not… you know."

As Roman offered up a righteous 'Amen,' Misty's nurse popped her head in the door.

"Hour's up," she said.

The excitement over the past few days had almost put Misty back into intensive care, so the nurses had limited visits to one hour with no more than two people.

James sighed, and Misty took his hand, holding just his fingers.

"Of all my memories," she said, "know which one I treasure most?"

James shook his head.

Misty bit her lower lip, eyes twinkling, a shy smile lighting her face. James suddenly blushed, to which Misty smiled.

"A wonderful memory, Mr. James," she said coyly, "one I shall *never* forget."

EPILOGUE

A heavyset man sat before several large screens and a dozen monitors, all displaying scenes from around the world. On the central screen before him, a young girl, bleeding from a chest wound, hung upside-down from a window ledge, shouting out numbers and letters, a crowd below watching in stunned silence.

"So it's true," he said, his voice deep like a frog.

"Affirmative."

"How droll." He gave a snort. "I once relieved her father of his gold... and now she of mine." His pockmarked face darkened. "Bring her to me... alive!"

"Yes, sir."

He leaned back, his stern gaze still watching the girl hanging upside-down. "In time they will learn. It cannot be stopped. Some will understand and thank us... but all will obey, owning nothing." He snorted once again, rolling a gold-plated pen between his thick fingers. He continued to watch as the girl now dropped, plummeting into the crowd below. "Yes, night must fall, covering all in its darkness... only then will the new day arise."

His deep-set eyes followed the pandemonium as the crowd ushered the bleeding girl toward a flashing ambulance.

"Yes, night will come," he said, face now hardening, "for the new day is near... very... near."

ABOUT THE AUTHOR

Lew grew up enjoying whatever adventures he found or imagined in the backwoods of his family's farm. Now married with four adult children, he and his family spent six years in Northern Asia helping impoverished schools while teaching English. "Often, I'd be the first 'white man' these mountainous areas had ever seen."

After receiving his M.A. in the Philippines, he returned to pastor a church in his home state of Minnesota, where he still enjoys roaming the woods.

"I have always loved writing, as I believe we were meant to be creative—to then share our talent for others to enjoy. Many underestimate their natural gifts, fearing failure or criticism. I encourage you to explore those riches—to dream big, to work hard, and never give up."

For more about Lew Anderson and his writing, you're welcome to visit *www.lewanderson.com*